A CODEX OF METAL

ALSO BY CL JARVIS

The Edinburgh Doctrines series
The Doctrines of Fire
A Treatise of Air
The Chronicles of Earth
A Codex of Metal

Dark City Rising

A CODEX OF METAL

CLAIRE L JARVIS

PEWTER LYNX PRESS

First published in 2024 by Pewter Lynx Press

ISBN 978-1-7392644-9-9

To the ones who became better.

I

EDINBURGH—FEBRUARY 1787

Elizabeth Fulhame selected her navy linen gown for tonight's outing, on account of any ensuing bloodstains being less visible on it. This wasn't saying much, because she was down to three dresses: one of which was her cheery yellow 'good dress,' and the second was her brown 'chemistry gown,' which currently had a lingering smell of vinegar attached to it. While the colour may be discreet, its signature aroma was anything but.

"Ye ready, love?" A spluttering of the tallow candles and creak of floorboards heralded Thomas' return to their apartment.

Elizabeth raised an eyebrow. "Well?"

"Well, what?"

"Any luck persuading George?"

Her husband waved a hand, as if that had never been in question.

"Of course he's joining us, Elizabeth."

The whole point of Thomas heading out was because George Stephens' involvement in tonight's affair was far from a certainty. Elizabeth turned back to her tarnished mirror, so Thomas wouldn't catch her rolled eyes.

"He wasn't sure he'd commit yesterday, and that was *after* Drs Black and Cullen having a word. Are you positive he wants to do this?" She straightened her shawl and turned around. "I'd rather he stay at home with his wife and bairns if he's still wavering."

"It'll be fine." Thomas kissed his wife's forehead. He had to stand on tiptoes to accomplish this. "We have the professors, and Dr Stephens. I can't imagine what would go wrong."

Well, that was the problem with her charming husband. He wasn't always perceptive with these issues. Her imagination was a lot less constrained.

Elizabeth patted her head, checking her braids hadn't worked loose. They were supposed to meet the professors upon the hour, so she hadn't time to argue with him, nor could they afford to arrive in a distracted, biting mood.

"Where's yer dagger, my dear?"

"Already in my purse. What about yours?"

Thomas patted his coat pocket. Elizabeth touched the thin silver bracelet hanging loose around her wrist. Her sole display of ostentation was on loan from Dr Black for tonight.

"In an emergency, you can tug it off your wrist and wrap around your knuckles," he'd explained.

Thomas helped himself to a glass of wine and glanced at the door.

"We should be off..."

"I'm nearly ready." She would have been ready sooner if Thomas came back earlier, as promised. Still, they weren't late yet.

Thomas caught her staring at the shuttered window next to the bed.

"There's still a draught," Elizabeth said by way of explanation. "I stuffed some dish rags between the windowpane and the shutter, but I can hear the wind whistling through."

"They didn't fix the pane?" Thomas tutted.

"Or else another pane cracked." Elizabeth snuffed out the remaining candles and opened the door. "I don't think Mr Levy has the foresight to break more of our windows to drum up additional business."

Thomas followed her out of their lodgings into the stairwell. "I could well believe he cracked one of the glass panes in the process of fixing the other one."

Despite the chilly air blowing on her back all evening, the Edinburgh night had an extra edge of coldness sharp enough to cut.

Her hopes for a peaceful week bundled up conducting experiments were rudely dashed yesterday, when the pair called upon Joseph Black for afternoon tea.

When stepping into his parlour, Elizabeth almost collided with William Cullen, professor of physic, as he paced around the room, snorting like an agitated horse.

"Apologies, Mr and Mrs Fulhame. I should have cancelled our plans, but, well..." Black glanced apologetically at Cullen. "We got rather distracted."

"Is there a problem, Dr Black?" Thomas asked.

"We can leave..." Elizabeth began, before her husband caught her arm and squeezed a protestation.

The professor of chemistry had risen to greet them. His queue flicked as he moved, which was often a sign of bubbling displeasure. Unlike previous occasions, though, the Fulhames were not the source of today's agitation.

"William told me he saw Kitty Holm back in Edinburgh." Cullen had resumed his pacing on the other side of the room. "This doesn't concern you, fortunately..."

"Is that the woman who stabbed you, Dr Black?" Thomas asked. He must have heard about this from George.

Black sat down on his settee, putting his head in his hands. "As it happens, that's one of her few actions I considered justifiable," he replied.

Oh, Elizabeth had heard this story.

"This attack occurred moments after George killed her husband?"

Black's head nodded between his arms.

If Elizabeth remembered the story right, George's actions were equally justified, because Malcolm Holm had been in the process of attacking Black, George, and their friend Dr James Hutton.

"She's a dangerous woman," Cullen muttered from the other side of the room. "Just as fanatical as her husband, with no concern about how they advance their moral agenda."

The Fulhames were back in Ireland during the spring of 1785 when all this transpired, but as soon as they returned to Edinburgh they learned of Reverend Malcolm Holm's thwarted plans to quash Hutton's new geological theory, which he deemed non-biblical, and slaughter prominent nobles to bend the Town Council and university back towards the control of the kirk.

"I hoped we'd seen the last of that woman," Cullen continued. "She vanished from Edinburgh after her husband's death. We assumed she returned to Paris."

"But she has family in Edinburgh, does she not?" Elizabeth tried to recall George's tavern tales, yelled over accordion players one night years ago.

"She's a MacBride by birth," Cullen said distantly. "But for most of her life, she lived in Paris with Reverend Holm. Call it wishful thinking on Joe's and my part that she'd remain on the Continent."

"Is she causing trouble again?" Thomas asked, unconcealed excitement brimming in his voice.

"Well, that's what Joe and I were discussing." Cullen's orbit brought him in front of the settee. "Her sister Ellen MacBride passed away a few years ago, so we think she's staying with her cousin. I saw her walking down the High Street this morning with a reedy gentleman of a similar age. I'd recognise her a mile off. The lad whose strep throat I was treating—we were looking out of his third-floor apartment window at the time—said he recognised the fellow as living in James Court, and one of his sisters—the lad with the throat's, not the other one—claimed his cook was in the fish market at the same time as her, talking about a party they were throwing in Kitty's honour. Oh, and neither of them remembered the cousin's name."

That was as coherent a summary of the situation as she was going to get.

Elizabeth took in the tableau of the two professors—panicking in their own genteel ways—and wondered how best to help.

"Well," she tried. "The other residents of James Court might know a little more about what's going on with this woman."

Cullen shook his head. "I used to be in and out of James Court all the time, visiting David Hume. God rest his soul. Has it really been ten years since he passed on? Unfortunately, Joe and I were wracking our brains and couldn't think of anybody we knew who lived there anymore. Besides, the sight of Joe or myself poking around outside will immediately alert Mrs Holm."

She had a hard time understanding what the problem was. "Well, don't the venerable professors know of anyone who can conduct enquiries on their behalf, whose face isn't familiar to Kitty Holm?"

Black brightened. "An excellent proposal, Mrs Fulhame. Do you have any pressing engagements this afternoon?"

Which was why Elizabeth found herself sheltering in a turnpike door off James Court with an adolescent pie seller, waiting for the worse of the sleet to pass.

Loughmuir House was a compact, two-storey turreted building surrounded by the tenements making up James Court. Discarded household waste littered the close, nearly tripping Elizabeth as she manoeuvred around semi-frozen puddles of slurry.

Twenty years ago, this house would be the envy of well-heeled Edinburgh nobles. Today, it was tiny compared with the grandiose New Town terraces. This put the owner, Hugh Godfrey, in middling economic circumstances.

Unfortunately, all Elizabeth ascertained through enquiries was that Widow Holm was probably the owner's only living relative. The man kept to himself and lived a modest lifestyle. He was possibly a draper.

"I 'eard the cousin is leaving tomorrow," the pie seller said cheerily.

"Indeed? Where is she going?"

Elizabeth claimed she was a herb-seller, intending to hawk her wares to the man she'd heard was organising a dinner party. But no one answered when she knocked on Godfrey's door, and she baulked at persisting in case it brought her into contact with Kitty.

"Can't say." The youth scratched his fluffy chin, then wiped the resulting meat juice off his jaw. "That's what his cook telt me. Might be a tour of the Highlands?"

"Have you met the lady in question?" Elizabeth thought she detected an edge to the lad's voice.

"Naw, but she 'bout scared my wee brother to death. Him and his pals were playing as she walked past with her cousin—I admit they're wee devils, but so was I at that age. One of them probably shouted something rude, but she pulled a knife out of nowhere and 'bout sliced my brother's nose off with that thing. Maybe the little prick deserved a good fright...but you threaten to tan his backside, not slit his throat." He trailed off, then shrugged.

This was precisely the update Elizabeth *didn't* want to convey to the professors: Kitty carrying a knife and wielding it, and ready to depart Edinburgh immediately after the dinner party.

"Can we not be glad she'll leave Edinburgh almost as soon as she arrived?" she asked the professors that evening.

"I worry she's planning something," Black said. "It doesn't appear she's changed her ways."

"I suppose I can return to James Court after the dinner party and learn if anything transpired," Elizabeth offered limply.

Cullen clicked his tongue. "The situation requires more a more direct intervention than that."

This didn't sound good.

"But you do not have an invitation to the dinner party, or know anyone in attendance?" Elizabeth asked, suspicion rising.

Cullen frowned at this interruption. "Of course not. Why would we need an invitation?"

"Well, if you're attempting to..."

"Nonsense, we just need to convince the servants to let us in; after that, it'll be a lightning operation to find and interrogate the woman. Our purpose is to uncover her intentions: we don't need to waste Mr So-and-so's sherry, or dance a rigadoon."

Cullen spoke as if the words coming out of his mouth made sense. The way Black nodded along made Elizabeth question if the defect lay with her hearing, and that his sensible and measured pronouncements appeared flimsy in her head alone. In the end, she nodded and went along with them.

"Will Mrs Kitty Grenville be separated from her shipwright husband?" Thomas asked, his breath forming a mist in the dark street.

That was the only other piece of information she'd gleamed from the day's investigations: following the death of Malcolm Holm, Kitty had remarried.

"Professor Grenville is deceased, love, and he was never a shipwright."

Thomas' walk slowed. "Hold on, it was Mr *Greene* I was thinking of this whole time, wasn't it? Yer telling me Kitty Holm married the old natural history professor? He's over seventy, and she's still in her early thirties?"

"God rest his soul," Elizabeth commented dryly. "You don't remember Dr Black telling us the widowed Mrs Holm disappeared from Edinburgh at the same time as Grenville?"

Her husband was in the same room as her when Black explained all this. Thomas had nodded along as Black described how the natural history professor was sympathetic towards the biblical creation timeline Holm supported, which led him to shelter the reverend while he orchestrated the kidnapping of James Hutton.

"Aye, but I didn't put two and two together when ye told me the name," Thomas insisted. He grimaced like he'd swallowed a lemon. "For all her piety, the Widow Holm really transformed herself into the bawdy punchline and married a man forty years her senior?"

Elizabeth had a vague recollection of meeting Professor Grenville once while her husband was a medical student—he eyed everyone in the room with an air of smugness, as if he knew more than they did.

However, she also might be confusing with someone else: that same air of smugness surrounded plenty of academics.

"She probably assumed it was improper to go on the run with a gentleman as an unmarried woman," Elizabeth said. She held little sympathy for the woman. "But how could you confuse Edgar Greene with Nathanial Grenville?"

Thomas chuckled to himself at the ridiculousness of his mistake. "Now ye point it out, love…I'm as puzzled as ye to explain it. I think this is one of those occasions where if ye don't question the validity of the fact at the point ye first think ye hear it, ye'll never question it."

"The natural history professor passed away in Southampton before Christmas," Elizabeth said, closing the loop back to the earlier point in their conversation. "That was the only other salient point I uncovered in my enquires."

"I was upset we missed all that excitement," Thomas said, nudging his wife. "Looks like we have an opportunity to revisit it."

'That excitement' involved Hutton being kidnapped by Holm, his rescue from a country manor in the East Lothians, and Holm's attempted mass slaughter of nobles through electrocution shortly thereafter.

"Dr Cullen is quite fond of the novel *Don Quioxte*, is he not?" she asked her husband as they headed down the turnpike stairwell.

"Yup. He's always saying that if a physician is familiar with one story, it should be that one."

"Does the venerable professor consider its titular hero…aspirational?"

Thomas smirked in response.

"I think he's counting on the presence of four accomplices enough to overcome any obstacles Mr Hugh Godfrey and his household will pose. At that point, love, Dr Cullen doesn't need a complex plan."

Still, a realistic one would be a bonus. Elizabeth patted her pockets. She had a dagger stowed in her purse, though she felt confident her phlogiston-wielding abilities would provide adequate protection against anything her target might attempt.

2

EARLIER THAT DAY

"It's funny in a sense," George admitted, surveying the town beyond the university. "But if you asked me at the start of my studies how the city might deal with its awkwardly positioned hills, 'hiding them' wouldn't be one of my answers."

"Nor mine," Black admitted with a slight smile.

They stood at the corner of the college grounds, looking north towards the High Street. But instead of a tight knot of wynds and closes snaking down to the depths of the Cowgate and back out, a frenzied construction site spread from the college to the Tron Kirk. What looked like a low-lying bridge spanned the space, but George had already wandered down the Cowgate, and seen the gleaming edifice towering what felt like miles above him.

"A South Bridge, to match the North one," Black commented.

"Several friends wrote to me with descriptions of it," George said. "I thought they were exaggerating when they said the end of the bridge stretched *past* the college's eastern flank. I supposed they tore down Monro's anatomy theatre because it got in the way of hauling construction supplies. But it really was in the way of the bridge."

The central college buildings remained, but they now abutted the speckless South Bridge road. Monro's octagonal anatomy theatre had already been clipped off. The wintry air smelled of brick dust and flax.

"There are a lot of changes on this side of town," Black said. "In another five years, I wager this entire area will be unrecognisable. Have you seen the plans for our new university buildings?" He raised his right hand to gesture at the space behind them. As he did, George caught a flash of silvery metal under the professor's cuffs, laced around his wrist like a bracelet. When Black lowered his arm, there was a corresponding soft clink.

"I hear they're very grand."

George felt his eyes sting, which was embarrassing and caught him off guard. When he left Edinburgh two years ago to study in London, he told himself not to grieve the departure: his city would still be there when he returned. A foolish part of him hoped time would pause on June 1785, and Edinburgh would remain preserved as it was. Instead, he came back and found the once-familiar college area almost unrecognisable, and his beloved professors visibly older.

Black's laboratory, the one he'd petitioned the Town Council so hard for, was still standing, but the chemistry professor must recognise its days were numbered, too. He could see a wistfulness in Black's eyes as they watched the construction workers swarm the bridge, but asking how Black felt about all this seemed too intrusive a question. He would have time to watch Edinburgh change and accept the cycle of destruction and renewal in a way George could not.

"When are they going to complete the bridge, Dr Black?"

Black shook his head with a rueful smile. He'd expected

George to call him Joseph—he'd allowed that level of informality for a while—but noted the slip, and probably understood why it occurred.

"We should be able to walk across the South Bridge in March, Dr Stephens. You can't quite jump across the gap yet, but they're putting planking down, and in a few weeks it will only be the paving left to take care of."

Hammers, curse words, and the rumbles of carts filled the air. George didn't want to think how disruptive the years of demolition and construction had been for faculty and residents. Nor would he want to be one of the nearby wynd dwellers forced from their home to make way for the monstrous bridge.

Deciding his companion had enough of the sight, Black beckoned George away from the view in the direction of his laboratory.

It was strange walking across the Yards as Black tipped his hat to various clusters of fresh-faced, anxious students. George still looked in the mirror and saw a fretful country bumpkin, but no one else did any more.

"I don't want to imply I dislike seeing Thomas and Elizabeth in Edinburgh," George began. "But I have to ask, um, what are they doing back here? I thought they returned to Ireland for good."

Black hummed in a noncommittal way. "Have you spoken to Dr Fulhame about his decision?"

"Aye. I considered his answer...evasive." George sighed. "He said he was tired of Dublin and missed Edinburgh, and that after a few months, they realised they didn't want to remain in Ireland after all. Yet I got the impression something...happened, because I received a letter from Thomas last summer that everything in Dublin was fine, and his family was doing well, yet barely a month later he writes from Edinburgh.

No warning at all about the move." The deeper George progressed into this conversation, the more he suspected it was unethical to ask Black for potentially sensitive information concerning his friend. But the words were out in the open now, and Black was never immune to the earthly pleasures of gossip—he merely had better self-control than most.

Indeed, the way Black swung his umbrella as he walked signalled the professor's willingness to share what he knew, without upbraiding George for asking.

"I understand Thomas ran into some family trouble, making it difficult to justify remaining in Dublin."

"Do you refer to trouble caused by his brother, Patrick?"

Black unlocked his laboratory door and ushered him into the familiar musty gloom.

Half of the time, Thomas brought up his wayward older brother as the subject of amusing anecdotes: Patrick getting into altercations with innkeepers, or having funny arguments with Navan's other ne'er-do-wells when they all got too drunk to control themselves. The other half of the time, Thomas spoke angrily of his useless older sibling, who agitated his mother, frustrated his other brother John, and caused them all endless worry. That frustration played no small part in Thomas' decision to change the spelling of his name to Fulhame, the extra letter providing satisfactory distance from his embarrassing family. It was also why the couple decided to settle in Dublin instead of twenty miles west in their home village of Navan.

Black, having heard many of Thomas' 'Patrick stories' at the same time George did, nodded.

"Back in May last year, Patrick ran off with a year's worth of rent money belonging to his mother. He came crawling back to his family a few weeks later, but their money was nowhere to be seen." Black glanced at his correspondence folders on his shelves for a brief moment, leading George to believe Thomas wrote about these woes as they occurred. "Their family home—the one his mother lived in since their father died—was put up for auction. Thomas seemed in great distress at the time, for he'd no idea what his mother would do once evicted. Aside from the heartbreak of losing the home, their immediate family would struggle to accommodate her. Their only hope was pooling funds and trying to buy the home back at auction.

"Hearsay claims while orchestrating the purchase of his family farm, Thomas passed on a falsified bank note to a priest and brothel owner involved in the sale. Or at least that's what they claimed after being caught and imprisoned for forgery. Thomas walked free."

"They both claim he gave them falsified bank notes?" George asked.

Black frowned. "Who?"

"The brothel owner and the priest."

"No." Black shook his head. "They're the same person." He looked amused. "Reverend Patrick Fay has quite a reputation in Dublin."

George shook his head, hoping to diffuse his rising blush. "So this Reverend Fay used a forged bank note to complete the purchase of the Fulham house, which he claimed came from Thomas?"

"Apparently, this Fay fellow is a cousin of Thomas' late father. He's not strictly speaking a member of the clergy," Black added. "Just a couple-beggar who marries people for a nominal fee. Apparently his businesses are profitable, because he agreed to buy the Fulham's house at auction and sell it back to the family under favourable terms. Thomas gave him some of his own money as part of this arrangement. That is not disputed."

George would have to tell Phoebe all of this and see her reaction, before he decided if this was information he should or shouldn't have prised out of Black. He hadn't expected to learn anything this exciting about Thomas from the conversation.

"I don't believe Thomas' honest dealings in this situation were ever in doubt," Black noted carefully. "Even though Fay claimed the falsified documents came from him. Forging bank notes was, apparently, in-keeping with this gentleman's character. But as you can imagine, it left the Fulhames on bad terms with many people in Navan, and the couple wished to return to Edinburgh to be done with it."

Black's word choice was very deliberate. This suggested the professor had parsed Thomas' account and noted irregularities, but didn't wish to investigate further.

"They executed the forger?" George asked, feeling a drop of nausea settle in his stomach.

"I understand Fay was shipped off to Nova Scotia in a last-minute piece of clemency," Black said. "Obviously, he'll face the noose if he returns to Ireland."

George scanned his memories. Had things seemed fraught between Thomas and Elizabeth? Not that Thomas' wife would air what she considered private marital grievances, but he knew how little patience Elizabeth held for brother-in-law Patrick, and how excited she was for her husband to begin his physician practice back home. They seemed to be doing decently for themselves in Edinburgh now—Thomas told him they were keeping afloat with a mixture of tutoring and patients—but competition for patients would be stiffer here than in Dublin or Navan.

Oh yes, at the farewell dinner before the couple first departed, Elizabeth reminded Thomas his physician friend in Navan was thinking of retiring soon. No doubt she'd planned out their Irish future, hoping he could take over his mentor's practice in their hometown.

Thomas could be lackadaisical, but his wife was a driven woman. Try as he might, George couldn't imagine Mrs Fulhame's reaction to their abrupt departure from Ireland as being laced with anything except fury.

3

"Dr Stephens!" she exclaimed. "You're looking well."

It had only been a few years, but looking at George was like looking at a different man. The gangly youth was gone, replaced by someone who filled out his clothes and was practically broad-shouldered. He kissed Elizabeth's hand as if she were a dowager countess.

"Well-fed, more like!" Thomas enthused, smacking his friend on the stomach.

George winced behind his smile, and Elizabeth thought the jocular remark had hit a little too deep.

Yes, though it was dark in the street, perhaps there was a bit extra weight on Dr Stephens, beneath the waistcoat and crisp linen jacket, that he wished he didn't have.

"How are Mrs Stephens and the weans?" she asked.

"Doing well." A more assured smile crept back onto George's face. "The twins are teething, and that's wearing us both out, but they're healthy and happy as we could hope."

Twins. Poor Phoebe. Elizabeth wished every strength to her. She shook her head to refocus.

"It's good of you to join us tonight. I'm sure the professors will tell you how much help this is."

George adjusted his hat. Exposed to his former university friends, it seemed some of his old anxieties were creeping back in.

"I'll be guarding the wynd behind the building in question, making sure no one tries to sneak in or out, that sort of thing. I've kept up with my phlogiston-wielding in London and Oxford, but between my practice and the family, it's been hard to keep active." He shuffled on his feet.

"I'm surprised the missus is letting ye rest at all," Thomas commented good-naturedly.

"It must be a relief to have your physician practice up and running in Oxford," Elizabeth added, trying to put her friend at ease. "I know how hard you've worked to get this far."

"Hmm, I suppose." In the dark, George might have blushed. "We're only visiting Scotland for a few weeks, to see Phoebe's family and my own." He was trying to change the subject onto less awkward ground, so Elizabeth nodded encouragingly as he spoke about coach times, lodgings and a laundry list of social appointments ahead.

Maybe George should have stayed out of this. There was an aura of uncertainty about him, and the last thing she wanted was for him to falter or get injured because he was no longer that athletic former soldier of his twenties.

"Doctors and madam..."

Two dark figures approached the group. Thomas and George immediately doffed their hats and froze with an almost guilty expression on their face, as if they'd been caught chatting during a lecture.

Professor Cullen approached slowly, leaning on his physician cane. In his eightieth year, he was finally slowing down physically, even if he battled his limitations. Under his tumbling physick wig was the same drooping face and piercing eyes. He nodded to Elizabeth.

Relations between the pair were mostly civil. It had been years since he said anything dismissive about her practice of chemistry and phlogiston-wielding, but she suspected it was thanks to Cullen holding his tongue, as opposed to the absence of negative thoughts.

Behind him, Dr Joseph Black, similarly garbed in dark robes, inclined the brim of his hat. She glimpsed silver hair, delicately curled and braided into his usual queue. Black raised one of his dark eyebrows in acknowledgement, and a sly smile passed his lips, releasing a spiderweb of lines around his mouth. The professor of chemistry was getting on in years too, but he always glided smoothly through the world, when his former teacher forcibly bustled, so it was hard to notice any changes in his appearance.

When Black shook Thomas and George's hands, there was a faint clink of metal beneath his clothes.

"We are ready?" Black asked.

His thick wool greatcoat was buttoned up to his chin, but Elizabeth knew under his sleeves there would be a network of hair-thin platina wires and chains interlinking from his chest to right-hand fingertips.

"Yes, I was just telling the Fulhames I'd stay round the back," George blurted out, probably afraid if he didn't stake that claim, the professors would change their minds. As it was, Cullen merely nodded.

"The host, Mr Godfrey, is not familiar to Joe and I. I confess most of the guests are of scant acquaintance, too."

For a moment Cullen looked mentally worn. He'd often bragged that when he first moved to Edinburgh, it was possible to be know the names of everyone who lived in the town. An exaggeration, perhaps. But now there were too many people, and the city itself had burst beyond the confines of its medieval walls. The most famous physician in Britain might not be recognised within his own city.

Still, the presence of two uninvited, famous physicians in a private gathering was going to raise eyebrows.

"Shall we make our approach?" Elizabeth asked brightly.

The party split up: George melting swiftly into the shadows, the rest heading into the close. As agreed, Elizabeth and Thomas approached the building first while the physicians hung back.

Thomas squeezed her hand. Elizabeth squeezed back. She should be annoyed that Cullen was tossing them into a deadly situation without a plan...but she couldn't deny the thrill in her chest.

They were back at their games, playing with sharpened wits.

In Godfrey's doorway stood a stout, balding manservant. He glowered at the approaching couple, daring them to try his patience.

"Excuse me, sir..." Elizabeth raised a gloved hand and smiled apologetically. The manservant didn't yield. "We were looking for Nairn's Oyster Cellar and I worry we took a wrong turn..."

"That ye did," the manservant grunted. Elizabeth doubted a misplaced limb or crying newborn could elicit sympathy from a man like this. He'd know exactly where Nairn's Oyster Cellar was located—you could practically see it if you looked down the close and across the High Street—but he didn't volunteer this information.

She sensed a pulse of excitement in her husband. Inspiration of some sort had struck him.

"Ah..." Thomas rubbed his hands in a show of sheepishness. He took a couple of steps towards the manservant and lowered his voice. "To tell ye the truth..."

Where smiling feminine charm failed, a furtive appeal

from the husband succeeded. Instinctively, the manservant stepped closer to Thomas and lowered his head, listening to whatever embarrassing excuse this stranger was about to admit.

Instead, Thomas' hand shot out. A yellow-white light burst from where his fingers touched the manservant's neck, and the man folded to the ground.

"Nicely done, Dr Fulhame," noted Black, hurrying out of the shadows to help Thomas catch the falling body. "Perhaps Mrs Fulhame can open the door?"

She could only see two steps ahead with their plan, but that was better than nothing. Elizabeth opened Mr Godfrey's door and looked around.

"Goodness," she breathed to the startled crowd in the side room. "Is the gentleman outside in your employ?"

"Who, Watkins?" A wiry forty-year-old man with daring side burns strode towards her. From his irritated reaction to her intrusion, she suspected he must be Mr Hugh Godfrey himself.

"He must be…"

Elizabeth didn't have time to finish that sentence, because Black and Thomas crashed into the entrance, carrying the unconscious Watkins.

"Good Lord!"

"It's nothing grave, fortunately," Elizabeth interrupted. She could see Black and Thomas hesitate, trying to get their bearings as fast as possible. "My husband and I were passing your door when we saw the poor fellow swoon. It gave me quite a fright! But Dr Black says it's just a temporary fit with no lasting ill-effects."

Godfrey frowned, as if undecided whether the temporary nature of Watkins' incapacity was a good thing or not.

"Perhaps there is a quiet room he can rest in to recover his senses," Black said, trying to straighten as much as he could while still holding up a hefty body. "Dr Cullen here..." and Cullen came through the door, clearing his throat. "Has some efficacious smelling salts on his person that will speed his recovery."

A few of the dinner guests had risen and were craning towards the tableau, some still clutching napkins and cutlery.

Elizabeth watched them, heart pounding. She saw two women in attendance, but both watched the scene impassively. Likewise, Black looked at them without reaction. Whoever they were, they weren't Kitty Grenville.

"A temporary swoon, you say?" Godfrey stared at the four intruders. He was on the defensive and suspicious, but the party of august physicians didn't fit his conception of a threat.

"I wager the chill night air got to him," Black continued. "It can affect even the heartiest constitution when you're not careful. It would be professionally remiss of Dr Cullen and myself if we didn't at least observe his recovery and establish nothing serious underlies the swoon."

The smell of roasted pheasant and sea bass wafted from the dining room. Godfrey still held a full wineglass. His ten or so guests remained awkwardly fixed in their places; not curious enough to draw closer to the ailing servant.

"We can see ourselves out," Cullen said, bowing to the guests. Several inclined their heads in return. "I would hate to disturb your evening more than it currently is." He too scanned the faces behind Godfrey.

Godfrey waved a hand. "His bedchambers are through the kitchens, second door on the left. I'll be with you shortly."

"She wasn't with the dinner guests, was she, Joe?" The four switched to proculopathic communication as they manhandled the prone Watkins through the narrow servants' passageway.

"No," Black responded, his tone even.

"The whole point of the party was to show her off. Are ye sure she wasn't one of the woman in the room?" Thomas huffed and grumbled as he led the way to Watkins' chamber. *"Maybe she dyed her hair or donned a wig?"*

Black shook his head.

"George has also seen this woman before?" Elizabeth asked. Like the others, she assumed identifying Mrs Grenville a simple task. Now, instructing George to hide around the back seemed foolish.

"He just told me no one has come through the back lane," Cullen said, loudly bringing up the rear.

"Can he see the building? Could he tell us if there are any rooms upstairs occupied?" Elizabeth asked.

Thomas fiddled with the door handle, and they stumbled into the manservant's private quarters. It was a typical servants' abode: simple furniture, sparse decoration. The man's second coat draped over the back of a chair. Godfrey did not run an ostentatious house: the manservant and a cook might be the only servants he employed.

They dropped Watkins on the bed. Cullen shooed them out and slammed the door behind them.

"George says there are two rooms upstairs with lit candles. One on the leftmost side, the other overlooking the front door."

It took a couple of moments for everyone to orient themselves.

"So up there…" Thomas pointed. *"And there?"*

Both he and Black were breathing hard. Watkins was a sizeable object to transport. Neither were especially strong.

"There will be a back stair," Elizabeth said. *"Probably at the end of the corridor."* There were no candles, so she couldn't see what was at the end, but assumed one door led to the servants' stairwell.

"We better move quickly." Cullen glanced around,

checking no one was near. "Thomas, return and speak with Mr Godfrey. Distract him for a couple of minutes. Mrs Grenville may already know we're in her dwelling."

Thomas nodded and took off, smoothing his hair and adjusting his cuffs.

Black regarded Elizabeth. In the dim light, it was impossible to see his expression. "Perhaps you want to accompany your husband, Elizabeth?"

Elizabeth took that as her cue to head for the back stairwell. Few things would encourage her towards a knife-wielding fanatic faster than insinuation from a lauded physician she best rely on her husband for protection.

She suspected the professors would try to restrain her if they caught up, so she took the stairs as fast as her cumbersome skirts could allow. Besides, Cullen was old and Black was winded.

Upstairs, it was quiet. She could hear a dog barking, some drunken singing and a horse cart rumble along the High Street, but no dinner party noises filtered up.

She emerged into a tiny wash room and crept out onto the landing. The main stair was at the other end of the floor, and three doors led off this corridor. If George and Cullen were correct in relaying their information, there were signs of occupancy in the room on her left, and the room two doors on the right next to the main stairs.

Clattering, the professors emerged behind her.

Elizabeth drew the dagger from her purse. Her other hand gripped the silver chain.

"I'll take the far right room," she instructed the professors before they had time to form an opinion. "You can check the one on the left."

The downstairs dining-room door must be closed. No sounds carried up, not even her garrulous husband.

Elizabeth's hands grew damp. She tried to hold her breath to quell all noises.

As Black stepped onto the landing, a floorboard creaked. She heard an intake of breath from Cullen.

So much for discretion. Maybe their quarry hadn't heard yet.

She brushed against the door handle, trying not to lose her grip on the metal chain.

Come to think of it, she didn't know what would happen when she wielded phlogiston using a conductive metal to boost it. How much would it enhance her natural power? This was the wrong time to experiment with a new tool.

While she was debating whether to drop the chain or keep hold of it, the door swung inwards.

Elizabeth almost fell into the room.

There are subtle ways a lady recognises another room belonging to the fairer sex: the fragrant perfume and pomade, a greater attention to the aesthetics of the space, the use of charming quilts. This is all before one spots the giveaway identifiers such as women's clothes and toiletries. Or in this case, as Elizabeth's gaze dropped to the floor, a woman lying on the ground, vivid blood pooling below her walnut gown.

"Providence have mercy..." Elizabeth dropped to her knees. As she reached out, it occurred to her this might be an elaborate ruse—the prone 'body' might leap up with a cry and slash at her with a dagger. But the woman's skin was an ashen grey no cosmetics could replicate. The room itself was barely large enough for a bed, armoire and stool.

Elizabeth grabbed the shoulders and rolled the body from its side onto its back. She expected the woman to groan...but there was silence.

Brown hair, fashioned into tight glossy curls. A doll-like face, albeit one looking lined and worn. A Bible carelessly tossed onto the bed. She was looking at Kitty Holm Grenville, and the woman was dead.

4

EDINBURGH—AUGUST 1784

"What are all the old leaves for?" Thomas asked, chuckling slightly. "Trying to recreate the outdoors *very slowly?*"

Of course, he knew it was part of a science experiment—this was her husband's typical light teasing.

"A strange thing happened with one of my experiments last week. Remember how I showed you the silver nitrate salt solution didn't reduce back to silver while I kept it in the dark?"

"I couldn't exactly miss the fact we were out of closet space, and that ye kept yelling at me when I tried to open the door."

"Well, last Tuesday when I took the handkerchief-sized piece of silk out of the closet and put it on the windowsill, I was standing over it for a second. And I could have sworn the area of silk under my shadow was slower to reduce than the bits in direct sunlight. In fact, it left a silver silhouette of me on the napkin."

Thomas looked intrigued. "Can I see it?"

Elizabeth twirled a dried leaf through her fingers. "Well, shortly after I moved to get a better look, the silhouette I left behind disappeared...so I created more silhouettes, just to see if I was imagining things." She held up the leaf to the window. It glowed emerald, the tiny network of veins visible within.

"That could be really pretty, love." Thomas tucked a second leaf behind his ear. "Shame there's no way to fix the silhouette in silver once ye captured it."

"I'm thinking of rushing the fabric back into the closet as soon as I've generated the ghost leaf." Elizabeth set down her leaf and looked out the window. It was an overcast day—she'd have to wait until this afternoon in the hope the clouds broke. "Maybe they'll last long enough for Drs Black and Hutton to take a look."

She long ago gave up on informing Cullen of her scientific progress, even though she assumed everyone else told him what she was up to. James Hutton had been very encouraging of her scientific experiments applying metallic dyes to fabrics. However, his attention was a little too intense, though well-meaning, and Elizabeth could only handle it in moderation.

The whole reason for her going down this rabbit hole with light sensitive reactions was because the art of dyeing proved a cruel mistress. Her experiments worked well with small quantities of silk dipped in her metallic solutions, usually the size of her palm, but so far scaling up the reactions proved ineffective: the metallic colouring was applied inconsistently, leaving splotches of silver or gold interspersed with browns. She'd worked on these experiments for years now, and it felt she was no further towards her goals than when she started. Side questions seemed to point her towards new solutions or alternate discoveries, but a month later she'd conclude they were nothing more than a distraction which had just stolen a month from her she could have spent on something else.

At least money was a little freer these days. Thomas was managing with a combination of private tutoring and assisting faculty members with their patients. Sadly, he was stuck with the poorest patients, who could barely scrape the coins necessary to have their ailments treated. Thomas had enough of a conscience to accept lower or delayed payments from the worst of his practice, but it meant they stayed ahead without ever getting comfortable.

It will get easier, she promised herself. Soon, your hard work will be recognised.

5

"Mrs Fulhame?" Cullen took one step into the room. It sounded like he hadn't expected Elizabeth to find anyone and was about to warn her to leave. Instead, she heard the professor stutter to a stop and stifle a gasp.

"She must have perished minutes ago," Elizabeth whispered, hands still on the body. "She's still warm."

Usually in moments like these, Cullen would rush into action, barking commands and disrupting everyone else's attempts to manage the situation. That he paused should have raised alarm bells for Elizabeth. Instead, she stared at the deceased Mrs Grenville in confusion, dagger resting on the carpet by her knee.

She'd no idea what they were supposed to do now, so looked back at the professors for guidance.

If Cullen was in shock, she at least expected Black to hurry forward, but both professors appeared frozen in place: Cullen with one hand on the doorframe, Black his customary one step behind.

Before Elizabeth could speak—to plead with them to do

something, for pity's sake—Black took an uneasy step backwards.

"Doctor...?"

Black took two more steps, as if he was about to topple over. Then he turned and ran.

Elizabeth was initially too confused and alarmed by the sight to utter the obvious admonishments. It made no sense that the deadly, proficient Joseph Black would turn tail and flee from the sight of a murder.

Then she looked at Cullen, her next hope for rescue. His arm was still braced against the door, but she saw his hand bunch into a fist.

"Silver Protocol," Cullen whispered, almost to himself. "Don't move, madam."

"But..."

"I said, don't move!" Cullen barked, making her flinch. His eyes had a slightly unfocussed quality, which told her he was conducting a proculopathic message.

This was the point Elizabeth finally registered how much trouble they were all in, and that her short-term future would be filled with much unpleasantness.

* * *

Black almost broke his neck pelting down the stairs then tripping over the atrium carpet. Another servant dived to one side, probably assuming he was rushing outside to vomit.

All Black could do was hope Cullen and George had caught his rushed proculopathic message, so he concentrated on getting outside as fast as he could. Had he actually communicated his intention to run the Silver Protocol? Cullen probably would have guessed, but he had to hope George heard his message and remembered what that meant.

Outside the house, Black turned to face it, heart racing.

He raised his right hand. There was the faintest clink of metal under his coat.

"George and William. Commencing Silver Protocol in two...one..."

A blast of aether shot through his body, the platina wires running down his arm magnifying his power. The glowing white force that came out of his hand visibly rippled through the chilly night air. Lamps in the building flailed, and he thought he heard gasps from indoors, either in response to the distortion of flames, or the momentary downward spike in temperature as the aether rippled past. The blast wasn't intense enough to injure living beings, but it would be felt as a tingling sensation.

What felt like an eternity later, but was barely a second, two blasts of aether struck Black simultaneously.

Cullen, George and himself had practiced this before, but never on a situation this complex. He half feared absorbing a garbled mess of energy.

But the two blasts of aether—discharged at the same moment with the same quantity of force from two triangulating points—washed over him with different strengths.

Rushing back through his body, the platina wire focussed the signals, pressing into his body and veins. Then they washed out of him again, and Black was left staggering to the cast-iron railings. Now, the retching was unfeigned. A grey blur swallowed his vision. When it receded, he was surprised to find himself still vertical.

"Dr Black!" Someone was scurrying down the steps towards him. Black tried to take a steadying breath, but swallowing a mouthful of oxygen made him nauseous. He gritted his teeth and focussed on small inhalations.

"Thirteen," he murmured, willing it deep into his memory. "Four, one, eight..."

"Dr Black?" The voice was now next to him. Black grit his

teeth and tried to regain focus. His whole nervous system was twanging. If he spoke, he was sure he'd vomit.

"Pardon me. I felt a little lightheaded inside, but I'm better now," Black lied, trying not to open his mouth too wide.

One of Godfrey's party guests had followed him outside. Or rather, a married couple: both pale and delicate. The man had half-dragged the woman behind him, wide-eyed in terror. As Black's vision returned and he refocussed, the man tugged his wife's arm, pulling her towards him. She gasped faintly, swaying on her feet. Her husband didn't appear to notice her distress. "That Irish wench stabbed Mrs Kitty Grenville, and the cook caught in the act. We just sent for the Town Guards."

"Ah." This was an unfortunate development. "Is Dr Cullen upstairs?"

It hadn't occurred to these guests that Black had been upstairs with him minutes ago. "I believe he was the first to stumble upon the murderer. It's lucky that he did, before the villain made her escape. He seemed too shocked to react."

Black willed his body to behave, and cast away from the support of the railings. His companions barely noticed the state he was in—he supposed the murder of a party guest was too much of a distraction.

"It's entirely possible the Irish girl merely discovered the body," Black said, keeping his voice calm. He had to focus on every step back into the house: too fast a movement and dizziness would crash back over him. "Like Dr Cullen did."

"Hmm," the man allowed. "No one knows who the girl is. You just happened upon her outside as you and Dr Cullen entered the close?"

He heard a fragment of Thomas' voice carrying from inside. He must be still inside the dining room, talking to the guests.

Not all the guests had pieced together the fact the Irish

woman caught upstairs and the Irish man in the dining room arrived together.

"Actually..." Black began.

Then he paused.

He'd made it over the threshold. Ten or so people huddled in the dining room, cooling platters of stew, dumplings and soup forgotten. One of those individuals had stabbed Kitty minutes ago, and was now content to let guilt fall on Elizabeth. Right now, everyone's memories were fresh.

He needed to act fast before the actual murderer had a chance to get away or hide crucial evidence. They needed to question everyone in that room before they colluded or came up with watertight lies. Every wasted minute increased the odds of the culprit slipping away.

"Pardon, Dr Black?"

"No." Black swallowed. "Nothing."

6

"Elizabeth?" A proculopathic message bearing her husband's tone roused her from a stupor. *"Where are ye?"*

The voice was already fading.

"Yes!" Elizabeth gasped, scrambling to her feet. Her thin shoes slipped on the wet flagstones. *"I'm here."*

Identifying the proculopathy as emanating from below and to the left, she rushed to the cell window, hoping to see Thomas.

No such luck. The window was too small, set into the deep Tolbooth prison walls, for her to see down to the High Street. The iron bars scratched against her palms. She'd probably have rust stains on them, if she had any illumination.

"Where?"

She tried to wiggle her hand through the bars, but gave up before her elbow wedged. Frigid blasts of air blew into the cell, making the prison insides barely warmer than lying on the cobblestones outside.

"I'm on the fourth floor...I think." She'd been hauled up several flights of stairs, past the open communal cells to the fetid private ones. She glanced at the even rectangular stones

that made up the walls. *"I have a window, but I can't see much out of it. I'm in the eastern wing."*

"They didn't put ye with the debtors?" Thomas sounded outraged.

"No." The two halves of the prison were essentially two buildings knocked together, the western half built hundreds of years after its original counterpart. The stonework was a clear demarcation of those halves. *"I'm locked up with the murderers."*

"Yer alone?"

She checked the room again on reflex. It was only slightly longer than she was tall, with a mouldy lump of straw and rags in the corner. If the rags shuddered and revealed themselves to be another inmate, she wouldn't have been surprised.

"Correct."

"Right. We're all down here. I mean, the professors and myself," Thomas continued.

The main entrance was located on the rear side of the building, in the corner next to St Giles. She hoped whenever they were congregating wasn't visible to any guards.

"Good." Elizabeth drew her shawl tighter across her shoulders. It provided no warmth. *"The eminent professors can use this opportunity to explain why I was carted off to Tolbooth gaol on suspicion of murdering Mrs Grenville, due to the conspicuous absence of anyone speaking in my defence."*

Silence. Her teeth were chattering, and Elizabeth hoped they couldn't be heard in her proculopathic signals.

"Are you injured, Mrs Fulhame?" That was Black's voice, measured in proculopathy as it was in spoken form. *"Have the guards treated you properly?"*

"Oh, I imagine they'll be taking their time with any planned discourtesies. It's barely gone eleven o'clock, after all."

There was a long pause.

"To answer your question..."

"Accusation, more like." That was Cullen. *"And quite unjust in light of what actually transpired..."*

Elizabeth's sigh must have carried down to street level.

"We had to conduct an aetherial sweep of the surrounding area," Black interrupted. *"Before the murderer had time to escape. It's the Silver Protocol that William and I practised with George on Monday."*

A bark of laughter escaped Elizabeth. It itched her parched throat.

"You haven't even tried to conceal its provenance! You took my imaging experiments with silver nitrates to capture shadows and light, and used aether as the light and Man as the shadows. Did you intend to tell me about this application of my idea?"

She remembered telling Black about those experiments a few months before Thomas defended his dissertation. The chemistry professor was intrigued, but Elizabeth feared she was selling her discovery short without images of her captured shadows to hand. Black promised to call for tea one afternoon with Dr Hutton to see the images, but that was right before the first medical students submitted their dissertations, and of course he never had time.

"We're telling you now," retorted Cullen. *"Once the sweep was concluded, we could either get distracted by you and the Town Guards, allowing the real murderer to slip further from our grasp, or quickly ascertain the location and identities of as many people in the building as we could while memories were fresh and people remained where our sweep caught them."*

What really hurt her, the thought that caused a few self-pitying tears to fall when she was thrown into this cell, was how little time the professors seemed to spend debating this. It took them seconds to decide her fate. *"Oh, so I should be thanking you?"*

"We can get this misunderstanding cleared up in the morning, Elizabeth." Black continued to speak in mollifying tones,

not concealing his awkwardness. *"I will say you were with our party and got caught up in the confusion before we realised what was going on. Blame it on the foolishness of old age and shock, or what have you."*

Elizabeth didn't need to glance round her cell again.

"I can't spend the night here."

Black spoke first. *"We tried to reason with the guards on duty, but they told us to come back in the morning to sort it out with their captain. I don't believe there is a risk upon your life, Mrs Fulhame. Or a serious suspicion of murder."*

She wasn't sure how long had passed between the guards locking her in and the professors finding her. It could have been hours, or minutes. But the silent duration was long enough to work through her knotty memories of what transpired. *"Well, I believe differently. I don't know if the quick-thinking Dr Cullen noticed a letter in Mrs Grenville's hand when we discovered her body..."*

"I did, as it happens. But I couldn't grab it before Joe needed us to run the Silver Protocol."

"Well, by the time I was rudely dragged from the room by three Town Guards, visibly excited at the notion of apprehending a lady..."

"Madam!"

"The letter was nowhere to be seen. Do I need to spell out the obvious to the present company?"

"One of the guards took it?" asked Thomas, who did need these things spelled out sometimes.

"None of the servants or guests got close enough." Elizabeth rubbed her gooseflesh arms. *"Aside from me, the guards were the only ones who handled the body. If a member of the Town Guard is involved in this murder and attempting to clean up incriminating evidence, I'm the only other person who would even have noticed the letter to begin with, or its subsequent disappearance."*

She heard Thomas swear from four storeys down.

"We have to get her out of there," he said, a note of panic entering his voice.

"*If the guards won't let us in, then how?*" Cullen sounded as if he was pacing below her window. "*The Tolbooth isn't known for its permeability, especially not on her half.*"

The shared proculopathic conversation tailed off. Elizabeth pictured Black and Cullen on the street, arguing silently amongst themselves.

"*Fine. Well, what do you have on you, Joe?*" Cullen's voice returned after a few minutes.

"*There's a nail on the cobblestones,*" Thomas piped up. "*Look. Maybe it came from a loosened window bar up there?*"

That would be unlikely. Half the town's detritus ended up on the High Street.

"*I've got Adam's silver corkscrew in my coat pocket,*" Cullen said. "*He left it at mine and I intended to hand it back yesterday at the Oyster Club, but it completely slipped my mind.*"

"*I beg your pardon? How did Adam Smith leave* his *corkscrew at* your *house?*"

"*It arrived in his pocket, I imagine. Then he took it out and forgot about it.*" She could hear Cullen shrug.

Oh well. There was no time to get distracted trying to understand the vagaries of Adam Smith.

"*So, that's the extent of your tools for breaking in to the heavily fortified Tolbooth gaol? A rusty nail and corkscrew?*" Despite her best efforts, her voice shook.

Another pause. "*Don't worry, Elizabeth,*" Black said. "*We'll think of something.*"

"*Say...*" Cullen again. "*It occurs to me Dr Fulhame here is rather, err, diminutive in stature...*"

. . .

His plan was the stupidest combination of ideas and words she'd ever heard. And they had no other choice but to make it work.

"Once we send this plan exploding into motion," Black said. *"There won't be an opportunity to hesitate or request clarification. Can you assure me, Mrs Fulhame, that you have no questions or concerns?"*

"You'd be better off asking my husband that," Elizabeth replied testily. *"I know what I'm doing."*

There was a minuscule pause down below, where Black probably turned to Thomas.

"I'm fine, gents." She detected an undercurrent of nerves in her husband's voice and imagined him rubbing his hands together repeatedly.

"Good." Cullen sounded impatient. "Shall we get in position?"

"Can I have the...?"

"Oh, yes, yes."

"Thanks, Dr Cullen."

"Ready?"

Thomas cleared his throat. *"I'm ready."*

"Are you ready, Elizabeth?"

She took a half-step away from the window, extending one hand to touch the bars, and the other to point towards the door.

"Ready."

* * *

Looking up at the tiny window, Black feared misjudging the distances. Or that the energy required for this was far more than they calculated.

Slipping the corkscrew and nail into his pockets, Thomas took a hop and grabbed on to the drainpipe on their right.

They assumed it was also serving as a lightning conductor for the Tolbooth.

Not for the first time, Black doubted Cullen's ability to form a plan. His colleague's ideas came together so quickly, yet fully formed, it was easy to doubt their solidity. And yet vexingly, since Black felt he was slow and cautious when forming his own ideas, Cullen's always proved successful.

Black's brain was like a bucket, collecting a steady drip of ideas. Cullen's was the lightning rod.

"Ready, Joe?" Cullen squeezed his shoulder.

Thomas managed a few scrambles up the pipe. It was an awkward ascension; they all feared the rickety pipe tearing loose from the wall, even though Thomas seemed light as a feather. But he needed a little bit of clearance from the ground for this to work.

"Yes..." Black dragged the syllable out, so Cullen wouldn't mistake it for the signal. He stretched his palm out under Thomas' flailing feet. Last time, he had the benefit of Mrs Fulhame for this exercise. *"Now!"*

The collected phlogistic force from Cullen and Black flew through the chemistry professor's fingers, blasting under Thomas' feet. Their former student must have let go of the pipe as Black shouted, because Black thought something kicked his palm, but a second later Thomas flew upwards by several metres.

Were Elizabeth or Thomas the ones assisting, Black would have preferred asynchronous blasts of force. But Cullen wasn't fast enough on his feet, and there wasn't enough room for the two of them to stand underneath Thomas. Black gritted his teeth and let the force continue to flow through him, bringing another wave of dizziness. It helped that he still had the metal conduit on his arm. Its heat pinched his skin.

"Stop!" It was Cullen who cried out, since he had a better

angle to witness Thomas' ascension. Black snatched his hand away.

* * *

Her husband splayed like a monkey: one hand gripping an iron bar, one foot on the ledge, the other hand and foot presumably clinging on to the drainpipe for dear life. Elizabeth fought against grabbing his shirt—that could tug him off balance.

"My...fuck..." Every word of Thomas' was strained, perhaps from fear of the drop, or the exertion of holding on to rusty metal. "Left coat pocket."

"*Are you ready, madam?*"

"*I've not got the tools free.*" Elizabeth almost screamed, a mix of panic and frustration at the speed of operation this required. Her shaking hand squeezed through the bar and tried to wiggle in to her husband's coat pocket. The action was made difficult because Thomas was doing his hardest to press his body into the jagged wall.

"Other..."

"Fuck! Fuck-fuck-fuck..."

She was expecting to drop whatever objects were in there, but after what felt like an eternity of frenzied fumbling, Elizabeth pulled out the corkscrew and nail.

"Hold on to me."

Now trembling as much of her, Thomas let go of the drainpipe and grabbed the bars with both hands. Once Elizabeth had shoved the nail between his palm and the bar, Thomas readjusted himself. Now he extended his free arm so the nail scraped against the drainpipe and he leant more towards the window. He got his knee on the ledge.

There wasn't the mental time or space for him to ask if she was alright, or for Thomas to meet her eye. She could only hope Black and Cullen were below him and ready in case her husband slipped.

She grabbed his wrist. *"We're ready."* Their hands were so slick she feared they'd slip apart. Her other hand aimed the tip of the corkscrew at the door hinges.

* * *

Platina wasn't supposed to overheat, but Black felt a groove of raw welts forming along his forearm. With enough phlogiston forced through it, of course the metal would warm. He'd not pushed its limits so far before. The worst thing would be if it disintegrated under the next blast, with Thomas still clinging on for dear life to the pipe and window bars.

Cullen hadn't let go of his shoulder, though he felt his colleague and mentor inhale several times to rejuvenate his nervous system. The Fulhames claimed they were ready. He didn't have time to ask if they were certain.

"Now!"

Where the first blast was pure phlogiston, Black melded the second with an undercurrent of aether. A pure aether strike would disable the nervous system, but probably fizzle out before it travelled two metres into the air. This aetherial-phlogiston blend was electricity, glowing white-blue in the shadows.

As soon as Black felt Cullen discharge his energy through his body, he flung their combined ball of electricity at the pipe as hard as he could.

White-hot electricity shot up the lightning rod, barely losing its brightness or concentration.

* * *

The electricity travelled as fast as the eye could blink, but Elizabeth was sure she had a second warning that the professor's aether blast was coming. Maybe she saw its glow behind her husband's head. Or perhaps she felt the build-up of phlogiston and aether on the ground.

In either case, when the electricity leapt from the pipe to the nail, and ran through Thomas, she was poised to draw it out.

With tensed muscles, she directed the energy through her arms and down to her other hand, letting her own phlogiston rush in and meld with it. What came out of her hand and whirled down the corkscrew was hot and fiery.

Sparks exploded against the door. Instinctively, she flinched and tried to shield her face.

Suddenly, her husband was no longer holding her hand.

The last of the energy passed through her body and Elizabeth was rooted in place: not knowing whether to turn to where her husband had been balanced, or the mangled cell door.

She coughed. A metallic smoke hung in the room, the nasty scent of burnt metal finally quashing the rotten organic odours.

Behind her came a series of crashing noises.

"We caught him!" Cullen panted.

"Alive?" One had to be specific when obtaining answers from academics.

"Unconscious. May have banged his head on the way down."

"I think the aether knocked him out." The corkscrew was still in one piece, though it looked slightly deformed. Elizabeth wiped her palms.

"Can you open the door, madam?"

She worried—briefly—that the exercise would only warp

the door shut. Instead, it hung slackly open, the hinges barely holding it up.

The blast of energy seemed loud enough to rupture her eardrums, but the limited commotion below told Elizabeth it made little noise. At least, not enough to excite alarm or make the guards suspect an attack. If the other cells were occupied, the inhabitants weren't ones for moaning or yells. Elizabeth slipped through the door into a corridor barely wider than her.

Tightening her grip on the corkscrew, she edged into the shadows. Sharp footsteps clicked up the stairway on her left.

"Aye, I'll sort the bitch out alright," a man called, turning onto the landing. Elizabeth recoiled at the ferocity of his words.

The guardsman looked young—cheeks still soft, despite their under-shaven coarseness. His bright red uniform was meticulously buffed and cleaned. She hadn't got a good look at him when he was dragging her down the High Street, but she recognised him all the same

Elizabeth didn't like this one bit. The guard had the appearance of a poseur, and she'd no doubt in her mind that part of his reason for coming up here alone pertained to the letter snatched from Kitty Grenville's hand.

She hadn't seen him take it. But all three Town Guards were stamping around the body while Godfrey berated them.

The guard's attention focused on the swinging door, his hand trailing to the butt of his pistol. He paused in mid-step.

"Damned whore..."

Elizabeth lunged forward. She didn't like this: she'd hoped the guard would get closer to her hiding spot, so she didn't have to rush towards him. But in a second his shock would abate and he'd start casting round to see if she was in the corridor, or calling for help.

"Urgh."

The grunt came more from Elizabeth, who jammed the tip of the corkscrew under his chin.

"Uh uh uh." The guard had instinctively tried to swipe her away, or wrestle back. She pushed into the space, driving the tip in.

If he pulled out his flintlock she'd knock him unconscious with a jolt of aether. But her plan revolved on him remaining conscious.

"If you just stay quiet..." Elizabeth's voice took on a sibilant hiss. "I won't slit your throat." She grabbed an armful of his coat sleeve.

Her heart raged in her chest. The guardsman could fling her down the corridor, while she would struggle to lift him with both hands. But right now, he believed she held a knife to his throat.

The guard's breaths were coming out in ragged spits. Was keeping him awake the wrong option? His eyes pulsated with rage, and she could see him wordlessly muttering curses at her.

A dark patch of blood already stained his neckerchief.

"There has been a misunderstanding. And you will quietly, kindly, escort me to the front gate."

"You won't get far, bitch." The guardsman's face twisted with spite.

"I'll get further than you at this rate." Elizabeth gave the corkscrew a warning jab. The guardsman gasped. She hoped she'd judged this right and missed the femoral artery.

Terror made her sound mad. She forced as much conviction into her words as she could. The guardsman had to believe his life was in danger, that she would slit his throat if he didn't cooperate. As soon as the illusion broke, it would be a brief fight.

"Fine. Let me go and I'll take you downstairs."

"I don't..." Another jab. "Think so."

She half shoved, half dragged the guard towards the stairs.

It was an awkward shuffle down the narrow stairs. Elizabeth kept behind the guard, the corkscrew never moving an inch. She tossed the pistol onto the floor near her cell.

They were too deep in the building for the professor's proculopathy to reach her. She hoped some fluke of positioning would allow their voices to reach her, convincing her everything would be alright. The adrenalin still surged through her body, not giving her the opportunity to worry about anything else.

They had one last turn of the stairwell.

"H…" She'd been about to ask how many guards were down here and where…before realising that her hostage would lie. Anyone would half a wit would lie.

Curse this.

She let go of his arm, and before he had time to lash out, placed two fingers under his jaw. A tiny burst of light flashed in the darkness and the guard fell forwards.

He only had a couple of stairs to tumble down before landing on the flagstones at the bottom.

Peering out, the lower corridor also looked empty. Past the great hall were the hefty gaol doors, with a sentry's office to the side. A door on the right would lead to the general prisoner area, where debtors and aggravating drunks were held.

"*Thomas?*" She pivoted, casting her message out aimlessly. "*Dr Black? Can you hear me?*"

Nothing. It was too much to hope for.

The inner gaol door was secured with heavy bars that one man would struggle to lift. There would also be a key, either in the office or hanging on the belt of the guard.

She jogged as lightly on her feet as she could towards the door. Murmurs and gurgling laughter carried from elsewhere in the Tolbooth—she assumed it was the prisoners, rather than a large unit of guards.

"What in…?"

All intentions of discretion discarded, a bolt of light erupted from Elizabeth's hands. It made her uncomfortable using her powers in such a blatant way, but she had no choice.

The guardsman she struck hadn't time to rise from his chair. Several keys the size of her hand were looped onto his trousers. There was no one else in the pokey office, but that increased rather than diminished her alarm. Perhaps his colleagues were patrolling the Tolbooth, stretching their legs during a long night? How many minutes would that take?

"I'm at the door!" Elizabeth bellowed inside her head. *"Please..."*

Would she be able to unbolt the door by herself? The bolts groaned, then shrieked as she tugged at them.

"Hamish?"

Shit, she'd forgotten about the guard between the inner and outer doors.

Would responding to him ease his alarm or feed it? Could she mimic the voice of the guard she'd just knocked out?

With a final squeal, the bolt rose and slid back. She practically jumped on the handle before it shifted.

"Everything under control?"

The guard sounded more puzzled than alarmed, but for all Elizabeth knew, he was drawing his pistol or sword.

"Hold on a moment..."

Elizabeth's nostrils caught a metallic scent, as pale light flickered through the door gap.

"Careful..." Black's voice. Elizabeth almost collapsed to the floor in relief.

They'd heard her. They were there.

Squeezing through the door, she saw the port in the outer gate was cracked open, and the second sentry sprawled between the two. Black must have knocked on the outer door as she was unlocking the inner one.

"You're uninjured, Elizabeth?"

"Yes, just let me..." The guard she left bleeding at the bottom of the stairwell would awaken any minute, as would the sentry in the office. This sentry had left the key in the lock. These bolts were lighter and better-oiled.

"Danger! Escaped prisoner! All men!" Shouts filled the corridor behind her. "The bitch stabbed me."

"Can you unlock it, Elizabeth?" A note of urgency filled Black's voice.

She'd drawn the outer door closed behind her. Hadn't she? Was she standing there in full view of the armed guards running down the corridor?

"Argh!" The door yielded and Elizabeth stumbled out. Thomas caught her, flinging his arms around her waist.

"Elizabeth!"

"Move! Haste!" Cullen's voice from across the street.

Part of Elizabeth's heart sank. The presence of Cullen implied the opposite of haste.

"Head back to mine," Black said, steering Thomas by the shoulder. "William and I will delay them if necessary."

She couldn't argue. Still clutching her husband, Elizabeth took off at a run, her skirts biting at her legs, and useless shoes threatening to rip from her feet.

"Take the wynd..." Thomas spun them right. "We're better off splitting—I'll find Thomas, ye go to the professors."

They plunged deeper into the shadows. Behind Elizabeth, it felt like the whole of Edinburgh was baying for their blood.

7

"Regrettably, you made the situation more difficult for yourself, Mrs Fulhame." Cullen sank into the chair closest to the fire with the air of a disappointed parent. "Had you stayed in the gaol until the morning, we could have appealed to the captain and explained away the misunderstanding."

Several fraying nerves snapped within Elizabeth.

"Oh really, Dr Cullen? Yes, how weak-willed and foolish of me. I'd just need to push on through minor discomfort and some light rapery, and it would have all been wrapped up neatly within a couple of hours."

Cullen winced. Black nearly dropped his wine class in the corner, so fast did he rush across the room.

"With all respect, madam, I don't think..."

"You weren't there." Her fingernails dug so deep into her palm she knew they'd uncurl bloody. "You, with respect, did not see the way that guard looked at me, or the way he spoke when he didn't think I was listening. You are correct: I could not reach into his mind and determine every one of his intentions towards me, but I can say with full conviction that they would not be pleasant."

Black had physically worked his forearm between Elizabeth and Cullen. She was on her feet, half screaming at the professor.

Half a day's worth of pent-up fury surged through her. Her skin was boiling. The scent of chalk was her only reminder someone else—Black—was in the room with her.

She wished she'd insisted Thomas come with her. She had no way of knowing he'd found refuge with the Stephens.

Against all expectations, perhaps against her wishes, Cullen dropped his head.

"You're right, Mrs Fulhame. We made the wrong call tonight. Several wrong calls. We should have protected you."

Elizabeth backed away, throwing up her hands. "It doesn't matter."

It didn't matter, because women like her were always at the end of a 'wrong call.' There was always a limit to how much men like Dr William Cullen and Dr Joseph Black could be persuaded to care about a young Irish woman of modest circumstances. For all the times Black supported her, tried to stand up for her under pressure from his peers, he would do what he did tonight because it was easier. She was angry at herself for forgetting this.

Seated by the fire, Cullen looked a decade older than he had earlier, too old to move from the chair. She was not so blinded with rage to recognise some of his brusqueness following the discovery of Mrs Grenville's murder stemmed from guilt about what he'd done.

"You are a formidable woman, Mrs Fulhame," Cullen said, avoiding her eye. "Most would not manage what you did tonight."

Elizabeth was suddenly so tired she feared she'd drop to the floor. She no longer cared to argue, or point out that Cullen's mollifications did not make it better. Because of oblivious men like him, she was forced to act strong. Then the same men who drove her to self-reliance and rigid self-control would then throw up their hands and declare, 'see, she doesn't need our help.'

"I very much doubt anyone will seek you here," Black said, glancing at Cullen. Cullen raised a hand, an indication he was withdrawing from further argument. "We can keep a low profile until the situation calms down."

"How many weeks will that take, Dr Black?" Elizabeth retorted. "Kitty was slain, and the suspected murderer— myself—just escaped from justice under everyone's noses."

Black sighed. "If it behooves us to adopt discretion, I can say you are my niece, Miss Isabel Burnett. She is staying with me this spring, and I can tell people she arrived from Ulster early."

She appreciated the offer, but Elizabeth wasn't sure how much help such a pretence would provide. Her and Thomas' faces were familiar enough around Edinburgh, even after a few year's hiatus.

"I don't want to be locked up here while Mrs Grenville's killer walks free," Elizabeth said testily, annoyed she had to make these protestations. "Since there's nothing else for me to do, I can at least assist your enquiries."

Black and Cullen exchanged a dubious glance.

"While we're on the subject, and if it's not too great an inconvenience," Elizabeth snapped. "Perhaps the gentlemen can take a minute to share with me the results of their little Protocol experiment, given its execution was more important than safeguarding this lady?"

Black sighed and perched on the edge of the chair. "We counted thirteen people in the house, one of which was the deceased."

That would also include herself, Thomas, and Cullen. Elizabeth nodded.

Black continued, sounding relieved to return to the facts

of the matter. "Thomas said he didn't see anyone when he walked back down the corridor, and it took a minute for the host, Mr Godfrey, to open the dining-room door."

"Was there a way for the people in the dining room to get to the first floor?"

"Yes, there was a landing on the main staircase, with a door leading to the balcony area overlooking the dining room, and a spiral staircase connecting the balcony and dining room." Elizabeth had glimpsed it before she entered Kitty's room.

Elizabeth scrambled through her memories from earlier that evening. Could she have heard someone fleeing down the main stairs as she crept along the corridor? No such aural memory came to mind. From her estimation, Mrs Grenville must have breathed her last while Elizabeth was ascending to the first floor.

It was a terrifying prospect.

"And every other guest was in the dining room when Thomas was let inside?" It was too much to hope someone was standing there obviously out of breath, and or perhaps hastily wiping a bloodstained knife on the tablecloth.

"At that precise point in time, he had no reason to suspect a murder had just occurred, but Thomas said everyone was milling around the room, and the lighting was inadequate. He barely started speaking when the alarm was raised."

That would either by the cook yelling, or Black rushing down the stairs. She'd have to question her husband about what he saw in the dining room, if they were ever reunited. Right now, it seemed more sensible for them to stay apart.

"And did my valiant sacrifice at least allow you to identify everyone present?"

In the corner, Cullen snorted.

"Committed to paper, madam." He withdrew a folded sheet and waved it. "If the reading material would help you sleep..."

Elizabeth wanted to be left alone, though she doubted sleep would come easily. She plucked the folded note from his hands.

"Leaving aside Hugh Godfrey, who were the other party guests?" She studied Cullen's handwriting. "I admit these names mean nothing to me."

"There's Mr Jeremiah Berry and his wife. Susan, I think her name was. He's a joiner. A Mr Ralph Delancey, who had come up from London to see his family. Clarence Young and Silas Lowell are both from Edinburgh, also merchants of some stripe. Mr and Mrs Weston...no, sorry, it was only Mrs Weston who attended. Her husband was expected to be there but sent his apologies."

This was a strange list indeed. Elizabeth counted on her fingers. "So there's us...and two servants?"

"Molly and Norman. He was the chap we laid out in his chambers, and Molly came up the stairs after us. She moved with a bit of a limp—might have been clubfoot—so the notion of her rushing down the stairs at the other end of the corridor, then running around to catch us from behind, seems improbable."

"Unless she was affecting a lame leg," Elizabeth pointed out.

"Perhaps not the first suspect we should devote time and attention to," Cullen said.

"You spoke with them, Dr Cullen. And Dr Black."

"Everyone seemed shaken and confused. We tried to look for the murder weapon in the dining room, but couldn't find it. People were getting suspicious of Thomas, so we had to shepherd him to safety, too."

Not that her husband rushed to her defence either, she thought sourly. The most charitable excuse was it took a while for people to piece together they were married, and it didn't occur to Thomas his wife would be arrested.

"Everyone invited was a friend of Hugh Godfrey?"

"It appears so." Black shrugged a shoulder. "Not a particularly exciting group of people, nor the most riveting company to introduce to Mrs Grenville."

A pounding at the door caused all three of them to jump. It was an aggressive pounding, by someone with no pretence at discretion.

Almost immediately, the blood drained from Elizabeth's head, leaving her dizzy. Black's eyes narrowed to sharpened slits.

They could hear the professor's manservant Morris in the entranceway, stammering that he'd bring the master downstairs, and gruff Scottish voices mumbling in response.

"Town Guards?" Cullen muttered. "They can't have seen us at the jail."

"Well, it makes sense that they'd call upon me, given I was entreating them to release the Irish lass less than an hour before she escaped." Black ran a hand through his hair. The flicker of his tongue and rapid glances around the room told Elizabeth he was thinking fast.

Morris had reached the landing and cleared his throat outside the door.

She didn't know if she was going to burst into tears or vomit. Of course, this would be the first place the Town Guards checked.

Black hesitated in the door. Cullen struggled to his feet, but Black thrust out his hand.

"If and when they come upstairs, I don't want to see a trace of either of you."

There was an unusual vehemence in Black's voice. Even Cullen looked startled.

"But Joe..."

Black had already stalked from the room, closing the door

with almost malicious gentleness. They heard the genteel patter of feet on the stairwell.

Elizabeth's ears promptly turned off, because the impossibility of the task ahead put her to fright.

"Where are we supposed to hide?" she asked, voice rising like a frightened child.

"Damned if I know," Cullen retorted.

Like most rooms in his house, Black's guest bedchamber was tastefully furnished. Peach velvet curtains...that hung to ankle height. A slender mahogany dresser with the modern curved legs. Only one door, which led to the landing...right in front of the wide staircase leading to the entrance hall. There was only one item of furniture large enough to offer concealment.

"Under the bed?" Elizabeth dropped to her knees, almost at the point of hyperventilating. Tugging back the heavy drapery revealed enough space to crawl under.

"There's no chamberpot under there, madam?"

"No, it's under the nightstand," Elizabeth panted, crawling for her life.

"Good...oh, Christ..."

Cullen almost fell against the bed, groaning like he'd been punched in the face.

"Dr Cullen?" Elizabeth almost shrieked with alarm, before remembering the Town Guards interrogating Black downstairs could probably hear any first floor disturbances. "What are you doing?"

"Joining you." The drapes had fallen back, so all Elizabeth could make out were a series of thumps and ragged breaths from the professor of physic.

"I...um...don't think Dr Black..."

"No, Joe's right." Another thump and curse. "It looks mighty suspicious if I'm sitting here twiddling my thumbs...Ack!"

"They'll hear you downstairs." Elizabeth's heart couldn't take much more strain. Another curse as Cullen's cane clattered onto the floor.

"...Ugh...unf..." An oversized hand poked through the draping.

"I'm offering to walk them through the house." A sharp proculopathic warning from Black shot through the localised cacophony.

"Hurry!"

"When...you...get to my age, madam...kneeling on the floor...requires...several days'...forewarning."

Elizabeth squeezed as far under the bed as she could, before she backed out the other side.

With glacial creakiness, Cullen pushed himself backwards under the bed.

"Careful!" His heel grazed her elbow.

"Ah. Mission accomplished." Cullen tugged his physician cane under, catching Elizabeth's arm. Then, to her blissful relief, he stopped moving.

She could near voices in the entranceway. While they didn't sound belligerent, Elizabeth recognised the serious tone remained. She heard Black's voice: sonorous, modulated, reasonable.

"Um, Dr Cullen? Can you, perhaps, breathe a little...quieter?"

She heard the physician roll onto his back. About an armsbreadth separated them, but she remained fixated on the corner runner nearest the door.

"Can you hold this?" The physician cane was thrust into her palm. Cullen began rifling through his pockets.

"Kindly stop moving, Dr Cullen," Elizabeth begged. Heavy footsteps thumped up the stairs.

"Sorry, I couldn't remember if I picked up Adam's

corkscrew. Does Thomas still have it? No, never mind...left-hand waistcoat pocket. Mustn't forget that."

The door opened.

No one entered.

"Ah, this is the guest chamber I set up for my niece," Black said helpfully.

The pause and murmuring seemed to last an eternity. But then the presence receded, and the door was eased shut.

Cullen released an exaggerated sigh.

"*Well, I won't be doing that again in a hurry.*"

"*No, it seems hurrying is not an attainable state for you in your venerable years, Dr Cullen.*"

Cullen didn't take offence at the barb. "*If you are fortunate enough to reach years as senior as mine, Mrs Fulhame, you'll realise that nothing important is worth hurrying or being hurried towards.*"

The last terrifying minutes seemed to disprove that belief quite dramatically, but Elizabeth kept her mouth shut.

She should probably crawl out and recompose herself before Black returned, but the muted dark of the space under Black's bed, the warmth of the room, and the soft Oriental rug under her were more soothing than claustrophobic.

A gnarly finger prodded her shoulder.

"It will be alright, madam." Cullen still sounded a little winded. "If those Town Guards had uncovered you, Joseph and I would have dealt with them."

Elizabeth started to say that having the murder or incapacitation of more Town Guards to her name would have been a torment, not a relief, but she could hear Black hurrying upstairs once more.

"William? Elizabeth?"

"Give us a minute, Joe...or ten..."

Black stepped onto the landing, making a point of staring

over the bannister. He'd thrown a brown bandua over his clothes, giving the impression he was turning in for the night.

Having got back onto her feet and heard Cullen crashing back into motion, she cleared her throat.

"They weren't here in an accusatory mood," Black explained, ignoring Cullen struggling to right himself in the opposite corner. "Their main purpose was to appraise me of your absconding, to which I promised I would alert them if you reappeared seeking my aid."

Here, Black's disavowal of her as little more than a woman he'd met in the street worked in their favour. The Town Guards were unlikely to suspect he was sheltering her. At least, not immediately.

She set Cullen's crumpled note on the bedside cabinet. Further investigations could wait until morning.

Sensing she was almost done for the night, Black left the room, but Cullen hung in the doorway for a moment.

"I dislike this bleeding mess as much as you do, madam," he said eventually. "I had little time for Mrs Grenville, but even Joe wouldn't consider her sins worth a knife to the ribs."

"Her sins that we know of," Elizabeth pointed out. She wondered if she could get away with collapsing in bed without undressing.

"That may be the case. For those kinds of grievances, the probable cause will likely be aired in every tavern and coffee-house tomorrow morning." Cullen tapped on the door frame, a signal he was preparing to depart. "If that's not the case, Joe and I might have to call for assistance."

She hoped it wouldn't come to that. As Elizabeth blew out the candles, tossed her hairpieces on the chair and crawled under the blanket, she hoped her paranoia about the missing letter was a silly misunderstanding. When it came to criminal matters, there was only one individual the professors were likely to call upon, and it was a man whose mere appearance was enough to break her out in hives.

Dr Andrew Duncan.

8

NIGHT OF THE MURDER REDUX

"It's just myself."

Thomas jogged down the close to meet George, standing on his tiptoes watching Godfrey's house.

George almost sagged to the ground in relief, seeing an unharmed, unbothered Thomas approach.

"What happened? Was Kitty not inside the house after all?"

"Ye heard nothing?" Thomas' expression changed.

"The only thing I heard was Dr Black telling me to ready myself for our Silver Protocol, then doing that. They've not said a word to me since." He'd heard a woman's wails, which he wasn't sure if they came from the house. It wasn't Elizabeth screaming, at least.

"That peculiar wave of aether came from yerself?" Thomas frowned, but dismissed his puzzlement before George could explain. "Kitty's dead. Stabbed, possibly. The Town Guards are on their way."

"Who killed her?" George's first thought was that it must have been Elizabeth, because it struck him as too rash for Black or Cullen to do.

"I think the professors believe it was someone already in the house."

The last time George saw Kitty she was lunging at Black in the shadow of Salisbury Crags, knife raised, face twisted with fury. A thousand times since that day, he'd conjured up the image of Kitty running away, skirts whipping around her feet and tugging on the heather. He remembered lowering his arm. Holm wasn't the first life he'd taken, but it was the first time he'd used an aether strike, and the queer power surged through him, even as he fought with the realisation Black had been wounded.

The emotions he felt in that moment were no longer accessible—washed away by time, leaving only the imprint of his actions. He'd chosen not to kill Kitty. Killing a fleeing woman felt wrong.

There were so many other things he could have done instead of turning round to help his mentor. Chased Kitty. Struck her with a weaker aether blast and knocked her unconscious. At the time, he doubted he had the self-control to discern between killing and non-killing strikes. Who knows whether that was correct?

"Where's Elizabeth?" George assumed she would remain with Thomas, and worried as she hadn't appeared.

"I expect she'll be out in a moment," Thomas said. His calm response assured George no harm had befallen his friend. "The professors are questioning all the guests and dealing with the body."

Two years ago, Kitty stabbed Black because she believed he'd killed her husband. She barely noticed George next to him. That was the other question that kept George up at night: Black survived Kitty's attack. Would the same have held true if she turned on George instead? George, who might have stood an inch closer to Kitty than Black, if his threadbare memory was still reliable.

He shuddered.

She was dead now.

"...Do the professors want us to wait for them?" George didn't know how thorough a questioning to expect, or what Black and Cullen hoped to achieve.

Someone else murdered Kitty. Did she fight back?

Thomas shrugged.

Lacking confirmation one way or the other, they fell into silence.

"The professors don't know who killed her?" George chewed over everything Thomas had said so far.

His friend shook his head.

"I was knocking on the dining-room door as the murder was taking place upstairs. There was a back stair in the dining room, ye see. But Mr Godfrey opened the door and everyone was back in the room."

"None of them seemed out of breath?" George asked.

"Well, I didn't know there'd just been a murder, so I wasn't looking for those sorts of things." Thomas sounded apologetic. "But nothing struck me as amiss."

"Who were the guests?" he asked, still trying to wrap his head around events.

"I'm not sure," Thomas admitted. "There were about eight of them—I don't think I caught any of their names, and none of them looked familiar."

"Well, what did the all look like?" In George's experience, if his more outgoing friend didn't know someone, it was highly unlikely George would. But maybe this time...

"I spoke to a skinny chap with silver buttons on his waistcoat, he thought he recognised me from the Canongate Lodge, and I had to point out I'd never been a freemason." At one point Thomas associated with the Brunonians, whose leader John Brown also played at freemasonry, so that might be where the case of mistaken identity came from. Thomas continued. "His poor wife couldn't stop shaking, and our conversation tailed off because he was trying to calm her down. The pair followed Dr Black outside then came back in with him. Then there were two other gentleman: one surprisingly handsome fellow with very bright eyes, the other looking like someone poured oil on a weasel. They were both standing at the far end of the room near the back stair, which made me suspicious, but Dr Black intercepted them before I could."

"Ah, so the dinner guests nearest the stair were most likely to have murdered Kitty? Because they'd barely have time to get downstairs?"

"That's what I assumed," Thomas' arms reached out, as if he were feeling an invisible chess board. "I *think* they were at the back of the dining room when I first entered, before the cook started screaming murder. There was only one woman—an older one, built like a barrel—still seated at the dining table by that point. The host was talking to a blond man nearly..." Another hand movement on the invisible board. "In the left corner, I knew they'd been in conversation because he was tailing the host when he opened the door to let me in. The blond fella shot me a look of pure contempt that I interrupted their conversation, nearly dropped to the floor and polished his shoes then and there."

George performed the mental arithmetic. "That makes six guests at the dinner party, and the host."

Thomas performed a calculation of his own. "Correct."

"What did the host say when you knocked on the door?"

"He said, 'Well? Is there a problem with Watkins?' That's the servant we carried inside. He sounded annoyed at the interruption—I think he assumed the physicians were going to demand payment for treating him. I had to assure him I was just trying to ascertain the general state of the man's health and the service was *gratis*. I admit I didn't pay much attention to what everyone else in the room was doing before the screaming began; partly because the blond fella was stood too close, trying to intimidate me. He smelled quite strongly of port."

None of this sounded particularly helpful. He hoped Elizabeth and the professors were having better luck. "What are they intending to do with the body?"

"I imagine old Monro or Duncan will examine her prior to burial. Not sure how readily her cousin will agree to that, though."

George wished Black or Cullen would appear—in his head or in the close—to spell out what was going on, because the more Thomas spoke, the more confusing this was. He thought Kitty had been killed in self-defence, but a stranger got to her first? Who then feigned ignorance a scant few seconds after committing the act?

"Who would commit such a dark deed?" George wondered aloud. "I would expect a crime of passion, not premeditated concealment."

It angered him for a long time. Only the two professors and himself knew the evil nature of the Holms. Well, a few of the other college professors and Black's friends knew, of course. But the wider Edinburgh citizenry never found out what Malcolm and Kitty Holm plotted, nor how many people they'd kill in their crusade. The dark chymistry families might have deserved their fate, but the Holms seemed unconcerned if innocents were caught in their traps. He assumed that after she escaped Edinburgh, Kitty would go back to a quiet life of obscurity, her crimes unpunished.

Noises rose in the adjacent court. An overlay of shouting men, probably Town Guards. George shuddered.

[illegible] by gun part [illegible] the blond follows me in too [illegible] introduce me [illegible] I smell I quite a deeply of [illegible] pass.

[illegible] this scientist president [illegible] Light! (Ethiopa) He [illegible] and my professors were on the outside. E. [illegible] my introduction do with the body?

[illegible] Moreover, Duncan will examine her prior to burial. [illegible] how odd, let me sure will give to one [illegible] thought.

Once again, Black or Oil would a part—in his head [illegible] in the dark—m spell out white's a [illegible] consequence a the [illegible]. Thomas, role [illegible] the men-scratching draws plc, both he [illegible] that beauties o me tell [illegible] a long a strange power but leg?! the than legend foot nice a seat s low second after [illegible], though.

[illegible] would somewhere [illegible] a dark steel. George [illegible] loud. I would expect a crime of passion they [illegible] procedure collect during.

Imagine, I'm told, key alive. Only the two professors and [illegible] knew then the picture of the Homes W.L. a few of W.L. other called professors and phot. Hands, James, or course, but the only Edinburgh [illegible] any new [illegible] found out [illegible] Malcolm and King Edinburgh [illegible] front [illegible] new people [illegible] character [illegible] chapter [illegible] night here [illegible] their pin, but the Flam [illegible] amid mount such it [illegible] called to their [illegible] the people they all [illegible] the secret [illegible] we [illegible] pretension of [illegible], W.L.'s [illegible] gases [illegible] quantified.

At least one the direct on copy [illegible] Amoureux of sketching [illegible] probably Texas sketch. George [illegible] stored.

9

The worst thing about Andrew Duncan, professor of Medical Theory and longstanding libertine, was his son, also christened Andrew. Elizabeth saw the boy on her way to their pre-dawn meeting in Black's chemistry laboratory, and winced.

Andrew Duncan junior was just shy of fifteen years of age, though he looked older. He was tall, sandy blond with sparkling blue eyes and a disarming smile. Such effortless handsomeness and charm would presage—in any other youth —conceit, vanity, arrogance, boorishness and complacency. Yet by all accounts, Duncan junior was diligent, conscientious, emotionally mature and perceptive. He tipped the brim of his hat as they passed.

It drove Elizabeth to vexation, because for the boy to inherit such traits, they must have lain latent in his father. Duncan senior took pride in his crudeness of speech, saucy asides and general disregard for societal norms. Yet in another world, he could have turned out like his son.

Unfortunately, she wasn't able to avoid Duncan this time. Black wanted her present in case her recollections of the murder scene were needed.

Black smiled and waved at the departing Duncan junior. "He's taking chemistry classes with me this year," he said by way of explanation. "He's a little young, but is proving an apt scholar..."

Inside the laboratory, Elizabeth was unsurprised to see the dark bulk of Alexander Monro secundus hovering over the makeshift dissecting table, jowls quivering. Duncan was leaning over the grey body of Mrs Grenville, whispering in his colleague's ear. Instead of moving Black's chemical apparatus from the central demonstration table, the physicians had shoved five student desks together in front of it.

Elizabeth concentrated on inhaling the acrid chemicals—nitric acids and acetates—and blocking out the faintly sweet, sour smell underneath them.

She couldn't hear what the physicians were discussing, but Duncan's animated gestures and Monro's hums of agreement suggested they were deep into the medical weeds already.

"Ah, Mrs Fulhame." A cloth was whipped over the body on the table, and the two professors straightened. "We are almost finished our first inspection. Perhaps you can wait in the side room?"

When faced with anything other than a day-old corpse, Elizabeth would have bristled at the dismissal. Instead, she allowed Black to lead her to the side room, which carried an acrid stench.

"This isn't really suitable for ladies," Black said apologetically. "But I convinced them it was better, given the circumstances, you did not linger in too public a space." Given his face was a shade paler than when they'd entered the room, the dissection probably wasn't for Black, either.

"Dr Monro expects me to sprout wings like a harpy," Elizabeth said. "I'm sure Dr Duncan wishes I was *more* of a fallen woman."

In the background, Duncan and Monro continued their back-and-forth. Monro chuckled.

After a few minutes, there was a discrete tap on their door.

The two physicians stood on either side of the re-covered body of Mrs Holm, ready to commence a lecture.

Black nodded.

Monro cleared his throat.

"The cause of Mrs Grenville's unfortunate demise is self-evident. She was stabbed in the lower abdomen. In my experience, such abdominal injuries will not cause the victim to perish instantly, but they often expire within minutes."

Elizabeth nodded. That would fit their hypothesis the murderer was someone in the house.

"It's a painful way to expire," Monro added.

"Would the murderer not be covered in blood?" Black asked, a frown appearing.

His colleague shook his head. "It was a single wound, quickly done. The murderer might have known what he was doing, though abdominal wounds are hard to do precisely. They certainly weren't overcome by frenzy which might accompany a crime of passion."

That was an unwelcome thought.

"Was the lady's bedchamber in much disarray when you entered?" Duncan asked, looking thoughtful.

"No," Elizabeth said, after a moment.

"Hmm, so there was no sign of a struggle?"

Another unwelcome thought.

"She must have known her killer," Elizabeth concluded.

"Or been completely caught unaware," Duncan said. He rubbed his hands together. "Some people freeze when in danger. I have no reference for Mrs Grenville's temperament, so cannot speculate too heavily."

Elizabeth looked at Black. He was the one who knew the

most about Kitty. At this juncture, the chemistry professor kept quiet.

"My dissection only revealed one other thing of note..." Monro said. He grimaced slightly. "The widow was suffering from a cancer of the breast. It was quite pronounced."

One of Elizabeth's aunts had died a few years ago from such a cancer. She bit her lip.

"The main tumour was in her right breast, but palpating the left breast revealed one, or possibly two, smaller lesions." Monro's tone was forthright, as if he was talking about minor imperfections on a painting. "Usually when tumours of the breast are that large and spreading, the patient has but months to live."

The room grew chilly.

"Would she have known that?" Elizabeth asked, the words sticking on her tongue.

"I cannot speak for the quality of the physician care the woman received preceding her demise," Monro said, with just the faintest sniff. "But a reasonably competent physician would have come to the came conclusion as me."

"This is my opinion, too," Duncan added.

The last thing Elizabeth wanted to think of was those two physicians fiddling with anyone's breasts, even after they'd expired. But, fortunately, Duncan seemed to be in a serious mood today. More to the point, she didn't doubt their combined medical acumen.

"Not to mention, Mrs Grenville would certainly be aware of her illness. Such tumours are often painful at that stage."

That may or not may not change things. Kitty knew—or suspected—she was dying. Could that have influenced her decision to return to Edinburgh? Probably. But why? She had scant familial connections remaining here.

"Thank you, professors," Elizabeth said, before Black could open his mouth. "We appreciate your assistance."

* * *

Black motioned for Elizabeth to step outside ahead of him and wait for him in the Yards. Duncan turned back to the dissecting table, leaving Monro hovering over him.

Monro leaned in and delicately cleared his throat.

"How does your aetherial balance feel?"

Black shrugged and refolded his legs. "It feels close to normal, though these days perhaps I've simply become accustomed to a new normal. The aether and phlogiston don't quite feel like my own."

"And the platina wires?" Monro hesitated. "Are those helping you, Joseph?"

"A little. They make both easier to control, even as they take me further from whatever normalcy once was."

Monro continued to hover, evidently wanting to ask more, but questioning the appropriateness of each question. Finally, he clapped his hands and stepped back.

"Good. I suppose 'close to normal' is the goal for men our age, is it not?"

"Yes," Black agreed, a smile playing on his lips. "I suppose it is."

IO

EDINBURGH—MAY 1785

For the first time in over twenty years' professional acquaintance, an expression close to relief formed on Sandy Monro's face at the sight of Cullen striding into the basement anatomy theatre.

"Sandy! Is Joe...?"

"Still alive," Monro replied curtly. "For now."

The warning note in Monro's voice was enough to slow Cullen down, and he didn't immediately push past the younger anatomy professor to go towards the ghost-grey, prone form on the operating table.

Cullen squeezed Monro once on the upper bicep. It was a deceptively simple gesture, communicating a lot.

"Where's Dr Hutton?" Monro asked, glancing over Cullen's shoulder to the open door.

"Consoling George," Cullen replied, following Monro's gaze. "I advised them to wait at my house—get a bowl of broth from Anna, that sort of thing."

Monro nodded.

"James told me a bit of what transpired; George is still badly shaken." Cullen lowered his voice. "I'm told James, Joe and George were up on Salisbury Crags this morning and Malcolm Holm attacked them. He was trying to kill Dr Hutton."

"That is what I understood, too." Monro spoke carefully, every word neutral.

"George landed a killing strike on Holm—they left the body there. But then Mrs Kitty Holm appeared and stabbed Joe. She realised her husband was dead, and fled before she could be restrained."

At that last mention of Black's name, Monro turned, allowing Cullen to approach the man in question.

Black lay as if asleep. Only the presence of bloody bandages around his exposed torso and sickly pallor made it clear this was no gentle slumber.

Cullen took Black's wrist and felt for a pulse.

"The wound was relatively superficial," Monro continued. "More of a graze than puncture. It missed the lungs and heart. I stemmed the bleeding quickly."

Cullen's hand hadn't left Black's wrist. "Then why...?"

"Her blade was poisoned, William." A perceptible crack formed in Monro's voice. "At least, that's what Joe warned me. He was carried here in a sedan chair, but managed to walk downstairs unaided." Monro moved around the table, so he stood opposite Cullen. "It seems like a small quantity entered the wound, and I cleaned the area as best I could."

"So the effects are reversible?" Cullen's expression could have pierced flesh.

"He needs a functioning heart to flush out the poisons, William." Monro looked away. "I'm sorry, William. I've done everything I can."

"But there's a chance Joe could overcome the poison?"

"He's dying, William." Monro pressed a hand to his mouth. "His pulse is fading too fast, and his body is still in shock from the injury. He hasn't the strength or time to recover."

Cullen carefully let go of Black's wrist, as if deciding he no longer wanted to feel it slowing.

"I'm sorry," Monro said again, weakly.

Cullen hesitated. He looked like he was about to brush a loose thread of hair from Black's forehead, then decided against it.

"There have been experiments...have there not...where a stopped heart was revived through electrical stimulus?"

"On animals, William. Dogs, in most cases." Where a second ago Monro's tone was breaking into despair, it sharpened. "There have been no recorded instances where..."

"You know as well as I do, Sandy, how aetherial strikes can fatally disrupt the nervous system. Surely that means the opposite, rejuvenating process can also occur? It's something I've wondered about." Cullen's voice tumbled out low and fast.

"I know he's your friend, and this grieves me as much as you, William, I swear." The last words came out almost as a hiss. "But there's no guarantee this would work, fully or partially. Those dogs didn't live long after the experiments ended, William. They perished within minutes."

"That's why we need more aether than electricity."

"Is this even what Joseph would want?" Monro moved round the table until he was almost nose-to-nose with Cullen. "While he was still conscious, he seemed accepting of his fate, telling me it was alright..." Here Monro's voice faltered. "If trying to bring Joseph back means more pain and suffering for him, whose benefit would it be for?"

Cullen turned away. His fist curled and uncurled. He looked like he wanted to reach for Black's wrist again, and was fighting the urge.

"Did Joe know I was coming?" He spoke so quietly, Monro barely heard.

"Yes." Monro's voice was even quieter. "I promised him you were on your way to the anatomy theatre before he lost conscious."

Left unsaid was that Monro would have no way of knowing when Cullen would arrive, or if he'd received the message hastily dispatched from the anatomy theatre.

"Good." Cullen's quiet voice hardened, like a small pebble. "If Joe knew I was coming, he'd know I'd do everything in my power to save his life."

Monro heaved a sigh. It might have sounded like exasperation—anger that a man minutes away from death had a new chance at life—but of course, nature was more complicated than that. He took a few paces this way, then that, then drew back to the table.

Cullen looked at Black's face. This time, there was no point checking for a pulse. His hand moved to Black's sternum.

"'Everything in your power' means letting *me* do this." Monro spoke so fast Cullen stood blinking for a few seconds, trying to decipher the garbled string of words. "You haven't even read the papers in question, William."

"I did, actually."

"Perused, I'll wager." Whatever vulnerable emotions Monro was experiencing was being stomped under his usual business-like persona.

"So be it." Cullen snatched his hand away.

"I know I'm a poor wielder of phlogiston compared to you and Joseph. Most of your students, in fact. But in this instance, I know enough." Monro dug an elbow sideways until Cullen stepped back, then started measuring fingers from Black's sternum. "Two points of contact on either side of the heart will be more efficacious..."

"This could kill you too, Sandy," Cullen said with a defensive snap. "If you're not careful."

"Well then, resurrect whichever one of us you think is most likely to survive. Or just save Joseph. I don't care." Without waiting for a reply, Monro jabbed his palms into Black's chest. Flashes of white light burst from his hands. Black's body jerked, then sagged.

"Too much power."

"No, not enough. But you need to wait a minute to assess for a response."

Cullen picked up Black's wrist again.

"Nothing."

"Let go."

Cullen barely had time to let go before a second jolt sent Black's body half an inch off the table.

A noise escaped Black's lips.

This time, Cullen let Monro feel for Black's pulse.

"Hmmm..." A deep frown formed on Monro's face. "Pulse is erratic, but it's there."

"His aether and phlogiston is unbalanced." Cullen rolled up his sleeves. "It's not moving how you would expect it to."

"How would one expect it to?" Sarcasm showed a limit to Monro's anatomical knowledge had been reached.

"Everyone has a signature pattern. I know Joe's." Cullen spoke matter-of-factly. "It's flowing erratically."

"To be expected, given it's a function of life. I suppose it may recover normality on its own." Monro was too proud to frame the last statement as a question, but Cullen inclined his head.

The anatomy professor reached towards his desk and picked up a cloth. There was a slight sway to his posture. He dabbed his face and neck as he spoke. "We may just be delaying the inevitable. I'm still uncertain Joseph's heart can sustain itself."

"It seems to be…"

"The next few hours will be critical."

"If it doesn't work, we don't need to keep trying, Sandy." Cullen's voice eased away from its earlier bluster. "If it doesn't work, it doesn't work."

"I think…" Monro looked at Cullen with the ghost of a smile on his lips. "If our first attempt doesn't work, two or three more tries will indicate if the fault lies with our incomplete mastery of the technique, or a fundamental flaw in the premise. No reason to throw up our hands in despair just yet."

"Acceptable by me." Cullen tapped Black on his clammy sternum. "Hang in there, Joe. We've got you."

II

Positioning herself so her back was to the mirror, Elizabeth seated herself in Black's dining room.

"The blonde suits you," Black said quickly.

"It's certainly a change." Elizabeth focussed on stuffing the last strands into her bonnet. She worried if she glimpsed her appearance she'd cry.

She'd always liked her hair. She liked its dark brown hue. Bleaching it felt like cutting off part of her body.

But even the short walk between Black's home on Nicholson Street and the college grounds plunged her into a paranoid terror that she's be recognised as the escaped murderer. She needed a level of protection to make the mere act of existence tolerable for duration.

If Cullen noticed her mortification, he didn't comment upon it.

"While the tragic events are fresh in everyone's mind," he said. "It makes sense to concentrate on the most important questions."

"Well, trying to work out why Kitty's letter ended up with

an enraged Town Guardsman is as good a start as any," Elizabeth said.

As soon as the words left her mouth, she knew Cullen would take a contrary position.

"To me, that letter seems spurious to the matter in hand. None of the Town Guards summoned last night had any connection to the dinner guests, and they clearly played no role in the murder."

"Excuse me? I beg your pardon, Dr Cullen, but it's too early to say that. That Mrs Holm, sorry Grenville, would make writing that letter a priority that evening, tells us of its importance to whatever she was involved with."

Cullen's cane ground into the floorboards. "While not an incorrect sentiment, the private and sensitive matters between the Town Guardsman and Mrs Grenville are a fruit hanging quite high in the branches of the metaphorical tree of enquiry."

"Also noted that you declined to press the good men on the subject. Very gentlemanly." Elizabeth knew her own mind: there was no missing the veneer of viciousness in the guardsman's eyes when he approached her cell. She could well believe its contents were inflammatory enough to drive murder.

Black cleared his throat. "The advantage of a third party assisting with our enquiries is that we can split our attentions. I would recommend returning to the scene of the crime to speak privately with Mr Godfrey. But we can also use this morning to speak with the Town Guards."

"The gentleman you need to speak with is hard to miss," Elizabeth said curtly. "Or should I say, the hole I left in his neck should be self-evident."

Cullen shifted in his chair. "That sounds like a task for Joe."

"Dr Black spoke with the guards last night, did he not?" Elizabeth looked at Black for confirmation.

"I might be more of a liability than a help," Black conceded. "My late-night enquiries annoyed them. Not to mention they may harbour lingering suspicions about my culpability in Mrs Fulhame's escape that I couldn't defuse through last night's conversation. They shouldn't yet be aware of Dr Cullen's involvement in all this, though."

"I'll take George," Cullen declared. "He managed to keep out of trouble last night—good for him—and won't be a familiar face."

This felt less like three geniuses pooling resources to solve a baffling murder, and more like two professors horse-trading unwelcome teaching assignments.

Still, their cooperation was a pleasant change.

"It may be too much to hope for that the killer left a knife embossed with their initials on Godfrey's mantelpiece," Elizabeth said. "But returning to the house and looking for clues would be useful."

"Correct, but turning up at Godfrey's door and declaring you have come to inspect his rooms for blood stains is considered poor form," Cullen pointed out.

"If anybody knows why Kitty was killed, it would be her cousin," Black said, before the exchange became too sarcastic.

"A physician stopping by to check on the unfortunate servant they tended to last night would be within the bounds of propriety." Cullen said, turning to Black.

Elizabeth silently cursed. She hadn't wanted *them* to agree to it.

"I..."

"I worry your return will inflame the situation," Black said before she could finish her protest. "Especially since you and Dr Fulhame were the last thing the manservant saw before he was laid out cold. I'm also unsure whether Godfrey himself believes you killed his cousin."

That was an annoyingly fair point. Elizabeth tried not to pout.

"It is worth speaking to his servants, though," she said. "I imagine they might be more observant than their master."

"Well, we'll engage them in conversation if the situation seems befitting." Cullen stretched his legs. "Knowing yourself, Mrs Fulhame, I'm sure if you put your mind to conversing with Godfrey's servants, there won't be much Dr Black and I can do to stop you..."

12

Guilt mingled with reluctance inside George as he trailed his former professor up the High Street to the Tolbooth Gaol. By all rights he shouldn't complain about getting dragged into this: poor Elizabeth was trapped in this miserable place, implicated in the murder of Kitty while he slipped home to his family. It was only right he should help clear her name.

But he couldn't help the trickle of resentment that Cullen dragged him into this as a supporting player. The Professor of Physic was more than capable of taking care of himself in a non-threatening situation like this. No one would dare attack Cullen! Now he had to make excuses to Phoebe about why he couldn't spend the morning with her mother and relatives.

The walk from Cullen's house in South Gray's Close took five minutes. On the way uphill, Cullen made enquiries at the Guard House—a squat, shambling building in the middle of the High Street. After a whispered conversation with a man leaning against the wall gulping down a bottle, Cullen muttered thanks and continued on his way.

Turning left at the Luckenbooths, a protruding five storey

shamble of tenements growing out of the High Street like a wart, the pair headed towards the main Tolbooth entrance.

"I hear the wig-maker on the first floor is going out of business," Cullen commented with a backward jab at the Luckenbooths. "Such a shame."

George barely had time to think of a suitable response to this tidbit of information about a shop he'd never frequented, before they were ushered in through the front door of the prison, with the jailers mumbling apologies about the condition of the place after a disturbance last night. George resolved to be as viciously cooperative as possible, in the hope he could be in Stockbridge before noon and ride out the family obligations.

"Good day, sir!" Cullen bellowed into the murk. "Who am I speaking to?"

"Um, Corporal Elijah Daniels..." The guardsman squinted at Cullen, no doubt recognising the professor from his goings-on about town, but momentarily forgetting his name.

Seizing upon his discomforted hesitation, Cullen ploughed forwards. "I must say, Corporal Daniels, I'm glad to have caught you. I heard about the business last night in the prison, and was worried you wouldn't be on duty..."

Daniels raised his hand to his neck instinctively. His throat was concealed by a cravat, but scraps of linen bandage poked through the neckline.

"It's best we waste no time," Cullen continued, putting a reassuring hand on the man's arm and steering him to the side. "But first, I must assure you...you have no need to panic or be afraid."

The guard's mouth opened and closed, before 'afraid of what?' came out in the dingy entrance.

"Since I came to you as soon as I heard, it's more than likely I reached you in time to make a difference." Cullen moved heavily to the side room, where the unfortunate corporal had been standing guard at the door. He focussed all his attention on crossing the uneven flagstones, made slippery by the morning's rain.

"Err, Dr Cullen?" The guardsman finally put a name to the familiar face. "What is this about?"

It was clear from his posture he didn't want to be dragged about the gaol by Cullen, and for any individual of less renown he would have shaken free of the old man's grip already. Cullen's knuckles were white, but he wouldn't be a match in force for a guardsman in the prime of his life.

"I heard about what transpired last night from Dr Black," Cullen said. He eased Daniels into a chair and set his case of vials on the sideboard. He made sure the labels for laudanum, opium and other potent mixtures were visible. "And my memory was instantly brought back to a lad from Shropshire in similar circumstances. Only...he passed away. It was tragic; maybe if I'd arrived a few hours earlier I could have saved his life. As it was, I could only do a little to take the edge off his final suffering."

"My...my neck wound?" In the dim light, Daniels had lost his colour, and a thick sheen of sweat coated his forehead.

Cullen blinked, as if taken aback Corporal Daniels was only now making the connection.

"Of course, lad. The potential for neck wounds to get infected is very high. This isn't common knowledge—I can see by how you've dressed the wound that you weren't aware of the danger."

Daniels looked on the verge of whimpering.

Anybody with cursory physic understanding would know neck wounds carried no outsized threat of infection, but Cullen spoke with such gravelly voiced conviction even George momentarily doubted his training.

"Fortunately..." Cullen leant over and placed a reassuring

hand on his trembling shoulder. "If you follow my instructions, the likelihood of your survival increases dramatically."

He could not have spun a greater weave of terror to cast over the boy. It took several minutes for him to unspool his cravat and bandages, flecked with rust stains, because of his shaky his movements seemed. Cullen simply frowned and pursed his lips.

When eventually revealed, the wound was a dark scab under Daniels' jaw, with the surrounding redness more from the tight binding of the bandage than a nascent infection. Had Elizabeth threatened the man with the rusty nail instead of the corkscrew, the outcome might be closer to the scenario Cullen painted.

George felt a flicker of pride at his friend's handiwork. Elizabeth hadn't been afraid to cause damage.

"Hmmm, let's see what we can do." Cullen made a show of cleaning the area, dabbing multiple ointments on it, and rearranging clean bandages in a complex folding pattern. Daniels sat rock-still all the while, too afraid to tremor for fear it would interrupt the physician's work.

George thought the professor might call upon him to assist with the administrations, but in Cullen's eyes he was no longer an assistant, but an equal. All he need do was stand in the corner looking thoughtful.

"Well, that's all I can do. Sit here a minute before we retie your cravat. We need to give the poultice time to settle."

Daniels nodded meekly.

Cullen continued his show of checking his vials, as if concerned he might have missed a life-saving component of his sham treatment.

"As an old man, I should counsel—without judgement— on the wisdom of approaching an imprisoned, isolated woman in her cell. I am sure your intentions were honourable, but you did the equivalent of cornering a tiger. Given those circumstances, escaping with your life was a fortuitous outcome."

"Those weren't my intentions at all," protested Daniels. With the biggest spike in fear wearing off, he seemed to enter the shaky comedown. "I just needed to ask her a few questions about the woman who died."

"That's not your job, is it? Surely, that is the task of the bailiffs and trained advocates?"

Daniels shook his head, then winced when he remembered about the dangers of disturbing the poultice. "Not about her part in the murder, Dr Cullen. I just needed to know if she said anything before she died."

"About what?"

"Oh...nothing, Dr Cullen."

George eased further back into the shadows, hoping his expression remained opaque. While he could no doubt make short work of this Corporal Daniels—even though he was hopelessly out of practice at such things—a petite woman like Elizabeth was no match pound-for-pound in strength. She was lucky to have the advantage of surprise.

"Come on now, lad. I'm a physician; I treat my patients in utmost confidence. I worry that burdening yourself with such stress will have a deleterious effect on your hopeful recovery."

Throughout this charade, Cullen had never let up his solemn expression. The slightest wobbling of his jowls was how he emphasised his sincere concern. It was like the world and George fell away, leaving the two of them in the room together.

Daniels wasn't prepared for any of this. He broke like damp straw.

"It's a rather personal thing, Dr Cullen. But the woman who died...Mrs Grenville?...well, she left a letter on her floor addressed to my cousin."

"In the room where she died?"

"Yes."

"Who is your cousin, lad?"

"Maybelle. I saw her name and street on the outside of the letter, and it gave me quite a fright, Dr Cullen."

"So you took the letter?"

"I know it was a rash act, but it chilled me to think my cousin might be connected to this horrible affair. She is the sweetest girl, Dr Cullen. You must believe me. She would never commit a wicked deed, nor hurt a fly."

Cullen's face was a mask.

"But what has this got to do with the poor Irish girl who discovered Mrs Grenville?"

Daniels swallowed—careful not to move his throat muscles too much. "Well…"

"If this is a delicate matter, I can assure you of my utmost discretion."

"I'm sorry, Dr Cullen. I was frightened and so read the contents of the letter. Its contents turned more ugly than I feared…" Daniels was trembling again, but this time, the primary cause wasn't fear. "A few years ago, sweet Maybelle fell into trouble. A drunken villain at the oyster cellar where she worked took advantage of her. I found her outside my door the next morning. God knows how long she stood there waiting for me to appear, trembling so hard her teeth clattered. It was hours before she could speak. She only told her mother and mine what occurred, but I was able to piece it together. Was near ready to kill every man in the city when I found out."

"That grieves me terribly." Cullen spoke calmly, but with feeling. "And the late Mrs Grenville alluded to that attack in her letter?"

Now Daniels' rage was impossible to miss. "Or more accurately, that bitch somehow found out about what came after. Not even her fiancé knew about that—we thought we'd done everything to keep Maybelle's secret safe. The little boy was blameless, but he needed to go to the foundlings. Maybelle didn't deserve to have her life ruined by that despicable beast. No one would have bought her lace; no one respectable would have married her if they found out her shame."

"So you wanted to know if Mrs Grenville said anything to the Irish girl in her dying moments about Maybelle? Or perhaps you worried that she'd gleaned the contents of Mrs Greville's threatening letter?"

"Threatening is putting it nicely, Dr Cullen." Daniels must have forgotten how he'd feared for his life minutes ago. Or maybe he figured his hour of mortality was almost nigh, and better to unburden himself. "That woman deserved to die for the poison she penned. It horrifies me to think how Maybelle would have suffered if Mrs Grenville lived. She had another child recently, a girl this time, and she was trying *so* hard to make it work with her husband. You couldn't find a girl in Edinburgh less deserving of blackmail, Dr Cullen. I had to make sure her secret didn't get out. I didn't have a chance to explain myself before that crazed hellcat attacked me."

George had come across plenty of men like Daniels when he served in the Americas. They were capable of despicable acts and extreme viciousness...unless you apprehended them before the deed, at which point they'd swear on their nana's Bible that they intended no harm. The flow of excuses replaced the flow of malice.

Before he knew any better, George had tried arguing with those men. Didn't they recognise how awful their intentions were towards the milkmaid who refused their advances? How could they lie and claim they weren't intending to hit the woman if she refused them again? It was pointless. Even if you interrupted them a second before the act, hand raised over the cowering girl, by the time you lowered their hand, they'd have convinced *themselves* they meant no harm.

"So, Mrs Grenville demanded money from your cousin?"

It was impossible to tell if Cullen battled the same disgust. The physician concealed his feelings, but at the very least must wonder why the relative of a lowly Town Guard would be the target of financial extortion from a woman in better circumstances than her.

"Only the Almighty knows. The language was too vague to make sense of what she wanted, and I admit I tossed it in the fire as soon as the words sank in. I imagine she wanted to meet with Maybelle to discuss demands."

"How awful for your cousin to get mixed up in this. How would Mrs Grenville have known of her and her secret?"

Daniels stiffened. "I don't know, and I don't want to know, Dr Cullen. Poor Maybelle has suffered enough. Even alluding to what she went through brings her into great distress. I refuse to inflict more anguish upon her."

"Even if her connection to Mrs Grenville and her death might endanger her?"

Daniels glowered. "It can't endanger her if no ones knows where she is, Dr Cullen. I'll make sure of that."

They regarded each other in hot silence for a moment. Then Cullen nodded, pretending it was not that big of a concern to him anyway.

"Your poultice is probably set now, Corporal Daniels. Let me help you re-tie your cravat. I wish the best for your cousin, and pray she avoids any unpleasantness. She is fortunate to have such a caring family."

There wasn't more Cullen could do without Daniels growing suspicious. To George's relief, he didn't push further.

"I've seen what happens when word of a scandal like Maybelle's gets out," Daniels said, relaxing a fraction. "Clarence Young is a pertinent example of that."

Was that a name on Godfrey's party guest list? He recalled scanning the list and seeing a Clarence, Clark or Claude who worked as a tyre smith.

If Cullen also recognised the name, he neither looked surprised nor confused. Instead, he tilted his head and blinked slowly.

"When he was exposed as Lord Nicholson's bastard offspring, it led to quite a furore," Daniels continued, not realising he was telling Cullen and George something they didn't already know. "Did his business no small bit of damage. Lady Nicholson was quite vindictive in driving away clients, and her husband did little to stop her."

High society gossip was more of Cullen's forte. George might or might not be able to point out a Nicholson in the crowd: he couldn't recall dealing with any of the family.

"Lord Nicholson passed away last year, did he not?" Cullen asked vaguely.

That said, bastard children were a shilling a dozen in Edinburgh. George had plenty of the run-ins with them.

"Possibly two years hence. Mr Young was entirely left out of the will. It's said relations between the Nicholson family and Mr Young have soured so badly the ladies cross the street to avoid him. Their treatment of Mr Young's mother—God rest her soul—was even worse."

13

Trailing Molly proved a greater test of Elizabeth's skills than she expected.

Not that the servant was difficult to keep up with—quite the opposite, in fact. Molly moved painfully slow. Her limping gait was not an affectation at the murder scene.

Elizabeth was a woman who took pride in striding through the world, so slowing her pace to stay behind Molly was agonising. To make matters worse, her quarry was in no rush to reach the Grassmarket. It seemed every person she passed was an acquaintance of some sort, worthy of conversation.

Elizabeth hung back and tried to think patient thoughts. At least this exercise gave her time to study the woman. Molly was a naturally talkative soul, though solemn in her manner. Elizabeth wasn't close enough to catch all the exchanges as they journeyed down the West Bow, but she doubted they were discussing the death of Kitty. She caught a few shadows passing across Molly's face as they began circulating through the market stalls.

If she were in Molly's shoes, would she be talking about

the death of her employer's cousin? Elizabeth would, but that didn't mean Molly was acting odd.

"Excuse me..." Seeing a lull in the crowd, Elizabeth made her move. "Ye're Mr Godfrey's cook, are ye no?"

Her fake Scots accent and hair colour change was concealment enough. Molly stared at her in surprise, mouth popped open.

"I dinnae mean tae bother ye, hen, it's just..."

"The murder last night? Oh, it was dreadful!" Molly almost sank to the ground in relief. "I couldn't sleep a wink last night."

She *had* been waiting for someone to ask her about Kitty's death. Elizabeth let herself feel a small flush of pride that her assessment of Molly's character proved correct.

"I live opposite ye in James Court, hen." Elizabeth laid a hand lightly on Molly's arm, the universal signal she wished to gossip. "The commotion last night woke me and the man up. Carting away some lass' body? Town Guards everywhere? Gave me quite a fright. I said to my man, 'that poor wifey who works for Mr Godfrey—I see her going to and fro all the time, how horrible for her.'"

"Yer right, poppet. Oh, bless you dear." Molly appeared quite overcome by her concern.

"I prayed for Mr Godfrey's soul last night, shed a wee tear 'cause he's always so polite when passing us in the street. Only I heard it was his cousin who was slain?"

"Such a horrendous act," conceded Molly. "That poor woman. Very kind, couldn't imagine her hurting a fly. What a horrible way to die."

"The ladies downstairs said it was a burglary that happened while everyone was having dinner."

At this, a measure of caution appeared on Molly's face.

"Too soon to say, dear. I know I shut and locked all the

windows that evening—the rooms get awful chilly when I don't. And nothing valuable was missing."

Elizabeth recognised the reason for Molly's defensiveness: thieves getting in could be blamed on her lax attention to detail. Even were this the truth, she may not want to admit it to gossip-greedy strangers.

Elizabeth waved her hand, as if she'd already dismissed this rumour as unfounded. "It was an Irish lass that stabbed her?"

"I heard she escaped the Tolbooth," Molly said darkly. "I hope she gets what's coming to her."

"Did she sneak in to yer house of her own accord? How brazen."

Molly half-nodded, a sign she disagreed with Elizabeth's portrayal of events, but didn't want to contradict her and stem the flow of sympathy.

"How terrifying for ye, though!" Elizabeth changed tack, returning to the subject she suspected Molly wanted most to talk about it. "And the guests. Were they close tae...the poor soul?" She'd almost called Kitty by her name.

Molly didn't notice the slip. She nodded eagerly. "Not as close as me—most of them were strangers to Mrs Grenville, God rest her soul. To tell you the truth...it was more Mr Godfrey's wish to introduce her to them than the other way around, I think. He's a good man, just a little headstrong about what he thinks is right, often at the expense of what's in front of his nose."

Elizabeth knew one or two men like that. She cooed sympathetically.

Molly shot Elizabeth a shrewd look, recognising she had similar tales of misfortunate handling the menfolk in her life.

"I tried to tell him not to push her. Not when Mrs Grenville and Mr Young already had a history."

"Oh, really?" Elizabeth couldn't hide her surprise.

"Yes. He was the only one who stopped by before the

party. Just a few days ago, though it now seems like a lifetime. He called while Mr Godfrey and Mrs Greville were upstairs talking so I set him in the dining room. Mrs Greville came downstairs and headed out, said to him as she passed: 'Man cannot serve two masters.'"

"Heavens!" Elizabeth had no idea how to respond. "She argued with him?"

"No, just stormed out. Wasn't my place to ask Mr Young what all that was about, barely thought of it afterwards. He acted like nothing had happened, never mentioned it."

"Did Mr Godfrey ken how she felt about the gentleman?"

Molly shrugged. "Tried gently telling him, but don't think he got the hint. He was getting all flustered about the dinner arrangements—that's my cue to stay in the kitchen." She flashed Elizabeth a rueful look. "The missus, God rest her soul, didn't seem to want to speak about it. Put her in a sour mood all afternoon, so it did."

14

After a light breakfast, Black donned his hat and set out across town. It was slow going down Infirmary Street, since half the city was using it to either enter or escape the Cowgate.

James Court looked dejected in the early morning light, with slick paving from the drizzle. Black carried his umbrella, though he didn't think the heavens would open far enough to warrant its deployment.

He found Hugh Godfrey grieved, though far from inconsolable.

"She told me she wasn't feeling well around four o'clock, but would come downstairs once her headache cleared. I can't believe that was the last conversation I had with Kitty; over such a trivial topic. What a frightful tableau to find in one's own house. I'm arranging to stay with friends in Dundee. I find myself on edge with every floorboard creak." The dark circles under his eyes testified to that.

"Yours is a very understandable response to violence within one's home," Black said with sympathy. "We all want to believe the place where we sleep, where we enjoy our private, intimate moments, is safe."

Godfrey nodded. "I appreciate your concern for Watkins, but the old boy is right as rain. He and Molly are out running errands in town right now. They shouldn't be away more than an hour...but I admit I'm glad of your company."

"Were you close with Kitty?" Black asked, before the man slid too far into self-pity.

Godfrey shook his head. "Some cousins grow up thick as thieves, closer than siblings. That wasn't the case with Kitty and me. I lived in Dundee for most of my childhood, and when both sides of the family met, I admit I found Kitty a little too quiet and cool. We reconnected as adults on more favourable terms."

"Did you recently invite her to stay with you?"

"Yes. Her husband passed this winter, and I thought it charitable to invite her to stay with me for a bit, rather than be alone. She was close to her older sister who stayed in the Lawnmarket, but she sadly passed a few years ago. They say family's the most important thing, don't they?"

"I suppose they do. It was kind of you to arrange this dinner gathering on her behalf, to introduce her to your friends," Black said. "Was she acquainted with them?"

"No, she told me she'd met none of them before. Kitty lived in Edinburgh before moving to be with her husband. But I told her about everyone I'd invited. She was looking forward to meeting them all."

"Stabbing a defenceless woman to death seems particularly terrible," Black mused. "I don't understand who could do such a thing."

"Me neither." A jolt of pain flashed across Godfrey's face. "I can only assume a robber snuck in, believing all the building inhabitants occupied with the dinner. He stumbled upon Kitty and then made his escape, silencing her so she couldn't identify him."

"Were any valuables stolen?" Black asked. He knew from

George that no one snuck into Godfrey's house or fled the scene in the aftermath. But it made sense to follow the pretence.

"Not that I'm aware. I'm a bachelor of regrettably modest means." Godfrey looked at his knees. "I'm not sure what there is of value to steal, beyond some nice silverware in the dining room."

"Did any of your guests see this robber, or anything suspicious?"

Again, Godfrey indicated the negative. "We were all in the dining room. None of the guests excused themselves from the room once they arrived. You saw that, Dr Black." He looked at the physician. "I can understand why you might think suspicion surely lies with one of them...but I know all those people, and can assure you of their character."

"How long have you been friends with them?" Black changed the subject. He didn't want Godfrey to realise he was being interrogated, because then he might clam up.

"I've known them all for years, at least informally."

To Black, Godfrey was the kind of shy creature who found genuine friendship difficult. While he didn't doubt cordiality between him and his dinner guests existed, their interactions with each other in the murder's aftermath made them all seem like casual acquaintances rather than warm friends. Probably associates from Godfrey's everyday dealings.

"Would you like me to inspect the upper floor to look for signs of forced entry?" Black asked. "I have a little incidental experience of breaking and entering that might be put to good use."

"Really?" Comprehension bloomed on Godfrey's face. "Ah, experience gained in the course of your medical work, consulting legal minds on jurisprudence?"

"Indeed," Black agreed blithely. "Much like that."

. . .

Kitty's room was boxier than Black recalled from his brief glimpse of it last night. Someone—the cook most likely—had attempted to tidy the place. He saw the faint glisten of water where the floor had been scrubbed. It would need a second afternoon's work, because a red tint remained in the wood grains.

The predominant smell was of lavender soap and musty curtains.

Godfrey remained downstairs, puttering about his dining room. He seemed disinterested in Black's investigations. Not that it was easy for two people to move around up here—the corridors and individual rooms were only big enough for one at a time.

His recollections of Kitty were of an austere woman, and the room where she died led credence to that in her final years. The only adornment to her space appeared to be the King James Bible, so well-used Black feared it crumbling in his hands.

He searched through her armoire and trunk, but there were no hidden personal artefacts. Black expected to find a memento of Malcolm Holm among her belongings, but there was nothing.

The absence of letters was vexing. Kitty's quill and vellum roll were set neatly on the dresser, and the quantity of vellum implied a lot of correspondence. Black prodded the hearth ashes. He spotted some charred paper scraps amidst the coal.

She must have been planning something in secret, if she thought to burn her letters. Another confounding hint.

The only piece of decoration was a seashell on Kitty's armoire containing grubby scraps of jewellery and ribbons, as well as a calling card.

Black picked it up. Its corner was crooked, suggesting it

had been in the owners' possession for some time.

'Ralph K Delancey, Esq — Golden Square, London'

That was a guest he met last night, wasn't it? Black set it on the armoire, unsure if it was worth holding on to.

Come to think of it, he'd seen decorative seashells in the other rooms on this floor. This morsel of decoration probably wasn't even hers.

Black felt a pang of something close to sorrow. What trace of Kitty was left in the world? Had she done anything to make the world a better place? A child playing on the beach, rearranging pebbles into a more pleasing cluster, made the world she left behind prettier than Kitty.

He made a cursory show of checking the windows, which were securing fastened. He then opened them—they were stiff and required a shove—but couldn't see any dropped items directly below. Nor was there an obvious way to ascend or descend without ropes.

Next, Black checked the door was shut before dropping onto his hands and knees and examining the legs of furniture. Any charcoal smudges or symbols scratched would be a sign Kitty retained the knowledge of dark chymistry sigils that made her first husband so deadly, and would put a boot through Black's carefully laid hypotheses about what happened in this room. But there was no trace of such markings.

Besides, from where Kitty lay when they stumbled upon her, it appeared she'd been stabbed by someone positioned in the doorway. The murder was depressingly mundane, though no less baffling for that.

A conversation caught the edge of Black's hearing as he left the bedroom. Godfrey was speaking with his cook in the atrium. But as Black pulled the door closed and heard more of the exchange, the voice didn't match the gravelly Scots of the cook. It belonged to a younger woman. The voice provoked a scratch of recognition, but he was too far away to make out individual words exchanged.

The voices rose as he reached the stairs, but before he could slip downstairs to hear what was going on, the front door slammed.

He found Godfrey still in the atrium, massaging his temples.

"Is something the matter?" Black asked. The close was near-empty, the woman already vanished. "Did a visitor call?"

"No, that was just a friend of Molly's, warning me she's delayed at the market." Godfrey's hand came to rest on the door handle. "A minor inconvenience, but nothing more. Now, if you don't mind, Dr Black..."

15

As she approached the Weston's storefront, Elizabeth reflected she was re-learning her way around Edinburgh. Where once she would have strolled up the dark valley of the Cowgate, now she had to detour to avoid the South Bridge construction. She'd ventured as close to the stone pillars as she dared the other week, craning her neck to a bridge arch that seemed impossibly high. The shadows it cast plunged the Cowgate even further into the gloom.

Marion Weston was standing outside the shop, resting her arm on a broom, in the universal stance of a proprietor hoping to distract themselves from a necessary chore. She was sharing a laugh with a pair of caddies, though Elizabeth imagined the broom would whip around to shoo them off if they got frothy with her.

"Yer alright, love?" The boys ran off as she approached, sensing Weston's attention turn towards a potential customer, or mark.

"Quite chilly the day, aye?" Elizabeth had to raise her voice above the hammer blows and shrieks of metals. They weren't quite close enough to the bridge to risk being struck by falling debris, but they weren't far off.

Any concern Marion might recognise her from the night before seemed unfounded. It was enough Elizabeth was affecting a Scottish accent and bore a different hair colour.

"Is the man himself about?"

Her motivation to speak with Mrs Weston was more than a plain belief in womanly connections, as Cullen might assume. Mrs Weston turned up to the dinner unaccompanied by her husband, who apparently suffered an upset stomach. That was a little bold, even for a woman as matronly and respectable as Mrs Weston.

For a moment, annoyance flashed across the woman's face, before she recomposed her face into a smile.

"He's not worth presenting to the world today, love. His stomach ulcer is flaring up, and he's taking another day of bed rest."

Elizabeth could respect her irritation at being passed over for the expertise of her husband, so she mumbled an apology and protestation that it wasn't urgent, or important at all, really.

Mrs Weston must have had several score-years over her at repressing those feelings, because her cheery demeanour barely faltered after.

"Was there something you sought, love? We had a delivery just this morning, everything is fresh. Much fresher than Ardley and Sons." Weston's voice dropped to a conspiratorial whisper. "Lovely man, I have nothing against him, but he only takes one delivery per week, and chooses the day after the market to keep his prices down."

Elizabeth made a show of politely disavowing Ardley, a man she'd never clapped eyes upon before.

"Perhaps you have lemons in stock?" Elizabeth asked. The citrus fruits were more than she could afford—strawberries were a rare treat in the Fulhame household, and they were dirt cheap in the summer—but she wagered a show of affluence would earn her more attention from her suspect.

Weston looked her up and down for a moment, then leaned closer.

"Not only do we have lemons, love, but we received a new citrus fruit you might be interested in."

Whatever could that be?

Sensing intrigue, Mrs Weston immediately launched into her hawker speech.

"These came direct from Barbados this week: an entirely new breed of citrus, quite popular among the beau monde this season." Elizabeth allowed herself to be ushered inside. Mrs Weston kept talking as she bustled into the back room and began heaving around boxes. "Very arresting flavour. I believe one must crossbreed an orange with a pomelo to create them."

She returned with a platter bearing what looked like an oversized orange. Next to it was a slice that Mrs Weston must have stored in an icebox. It resembled an orange in fleshy texture, but was almost white.

This wasn't the most appealing offering, but Elizabeth supposed she didn't resemble that affluent of a customer. If she did, she'd probably be offered more than day-old frozen scraps.

Still, you weren't offered exotic new citrus fruits every day, so she picked up the slice and bit in.

"Oh!" Her face wrinkled like a crumpled tablecloth.

Mrs Weston laughed good-naturedly. "Quite arresting, isn't it?"

"I confess I expected something more akin to the orange..." Elizabeth's face was trying to roll in on itself. "But this is sour and bitter, not sweet."

"About half the patrons have declared instant loathing for it. The other half also declared their loathing...but came back and bought a grapefruit the next day, telling me they couldn't stop thinking about its taste."

She liked Mrs Weston, in spite of herself. Elizabeth had to remember somebody stabbed Kitty Grenville and left her dying while they rejoined the party downstairs and pretended nothing was amiss. Mrs Weston wore an apron: it would be easy for her to slip one on to protect her clothing from bloodstains. Not to mention, she looked strong and hale. This was a woman accustomed to moving heavy boxes—her arms were beefy.

"How have these..." Mrs Weston just told her the name of the fruit, and it had slipped Elizabeth's mind almost immediately. "...Fruits been received at parties?"

Mrs Weston set down the platter and shrugged. "I haven't seen the reactions for myself. But the customers who purchased a grapefruit certainly haven't complained."

She wouldn't admit to attending the party Elizabeth wanted her to talk about. Or she didn't think the gathering was worthy of a grapefruit.

"Perhaps this isn't the best time to purchase one. I planned to host a wee gathering, but then I heard some Irish lass murdered a woman on the Lawnmarket while a party took place. It feels in poor taste to host a gathering so soon after that."

"Hmm, who told you that?" Elizabeth expected a rush of defensiveness, but the older woman merely looked thoughtful and a little disapproving.

"I know it is poor form to spread gossip. I imagine the tale is quite exaggerated. Murder at a dinner party!"

"Naw, I meant the part about the Irish wench is wrong. Girl was a servant who tried to comfort the dying woman— the Town Guard let their unkind prejudices take over."

For a moment, this flustered Elizabeth. She wasn't sure how to react.

"Not that the prejudice is entirely unwarranted," Weston added, mistaking Elizabeth's confusion for contrition. "Just in this case, the Irish girl didn't do anything wrong."

"Then the woman wasn't murdered?"

"Oh, I suspect she was. It's not a conversation I entire into lightly...but it's clear this was a slaying, and I'd wager a warranted one."

The shop bell tinkled.

"Morning, Hughie!"

"Good morning to ye, Mrs Weston."

"It's just on the counter." Weston pointed to a thickly sealed letter. The man, dressed in rough tradesman garb, picked it up, barely breaking the tune he whistled.

"'Scuse me, madam. Kindly gracious." Elizabeth stepped aside to let him pass. The man swapped the letter from his right hand to his left, to allow him to push open the shop door. As he did so, Elizabeth noticed the elegantly looping handwriting on the back.

'For Silas Lowell, Candlemaker Row.'

The other dinner party guest? Elizabeth didn't know whether to disregard her own eyes or run out into the street yelling.

Mrs Weston's smile looked ever-so-slightly fixed.

"So it'll just be the lemons then, love?"

16

Her husband caught up with her a hundred yards up the Cowgate.

"Have you heard of any of these people?" she asked once she'd appraised him of all their suspects.

"I wish I could tell ye something," Thomas said, squeezing her hand. "None of Godfrey's guests sparked any recognition in me upon sight, nor do their names."

"Well, I just learned that Silas Lowell resides on Candle-maker Row."

"Really? That's good," Thomas remarked. "We're halfway there already."

They reached the edge of Greyfriars Kirkyard and began their enquires.

"Naw, yer gonnae find him down the bowling green," a man sitting on his front step wheezed. His tricorne hat had the texture and colour of cobwebs. He pointed, but the bowling green entrance was only half a dozen paces back the way they came.

"Doubt we'll be interrupting the distinguished gentlemen at bowling," Thomas muttered. He mimed the casting of dice.

Sure enough, their target occupied a crowded table at the edge of the green, where no one was paying attention to the bedraggled, frost-covered lawn.

Thomas affected his usual nonchalance, but Elizabeth sensed him tensing up. Gambling tended to remind him of Patrick, and every miserable occasion he needed to stride into a dingy gaming den and prise his wayward older brother off a faro table. This wasn't something her husband liked to talk about, especially not in the aftermath of their family home business, so Elizabeth didn't bother remarking upon it.

"Do ye remember what Silas looked like?" Thomas asked, lowering his voice.

She really hoped he'd be the one who remembered. "I'm not sure I caught more than a glimpse of him."

There was a man who looked vaguely familiar sitting at the edge of the tables. He would be hard to overlook in any situation: the man appeared undersized, like half the size of a normal man. He had numerous pox scars on both cheeks, and a staccato laugh. Despite his position on the outskirts of the gathering, he looked at home in the merriment.

"Would sir and his lady like a spot at the table?" A voice enquired next to them. "My spot is running rather lukewarm, but obligations tear me away."

"With such a compelling case made..." Thomas laughed, slipping his hand into the man's. "How could I refuse, mister...?"

"Lowell. Silas Lowell."

Elizabeth nearly swore out loud. How could they have missed him?

While his face prompted scant recognition, Elizabeth recalled a compact, slender man loitering among Godfrey's dinner guests, his dark features impossible to read. Lowell was about Thomas' height, with impossibly black hair. Unlike the other gamblers, he could be mistaken for a fashionable bowler.

Elizabeth noticed that his clothing wasn't well-tailored, suggesting it may have been handed down from someone else, or purchased from a pawnbroker.

"We live close to Society," Thomas explained. "Though this is the first time we've ventured to the bowling green."

"Not players, by nature?" Lowell's remark could have alluded to the gambling or the bowling.

"I'm a physician, not long in the profession."

"Ah, busy with studying and burning the midnight candles." Lowell spoke with a greasy charm. Elizabeth wouldn't have been surprised if he picked a pebble off the ground and started hawking it to them. Men like that always seemed to be selling something, even when they weren't.

Thomas wasn't bothered, he was happy to keep talking.

"Ye must live nearby, too?"

Elizabeth wished they had a better plan. Why was Weston sending Lowell messages? And what did it have to do—if anything—with the murder they witnessed?

Despite claiming he had business to attend to, Lowell showed no sign of wishing to terminate his conversation with Thomas.

"...I served in the 82nd Regiment," he explained. "As part of its light artillery. Then after my mother died, I took over her lodgings in Brown Square."

"Were ye shipped over to the Americas?" Thomas asked.

"For a while." Silas' response was cagey. They'd have to ask George where the 82nd Regiment was stationed, and if it was involved in any embarrassing defeats at the hands of the Continentals.

It didn't appear that Silas had recognised the Fulhames from their encounter the previous night. Thomas was dressed in physician garb; bewigged and looking the part of a respectable gentleman about town. He'd looked Elizabeth over briefly, then dismissed her. She probably wasn't attractive enough to hold his attention.

After a few minutes of chatter, with no mention of anything useful, Lowell rose and shook Thomas' hand in farewell.

But instead of departing the bowling green, he circled the table and drew aside another fellow. He was almost hidden on the opposite side of the gamblers. Elizabeth had to rise on her toes to see who he was talking to.

"That's Jeremiah Berry," Thomas exclaimed, so loud within the confines of her head she feared she jumped.

"Who?"

"The dinner guest from the party." Berry frowned at the Fulhames, then blanched. *"And, um, the only one who engaged me in any sort of conversation."*

Elizabeth stole one last glance at Berry before turning away, hurrying from the green. He had to be even shorter than her husband, which was an impressive accomplishment.

"He doesn't look like he has the strength to pick up a twig, let alone a knife."

"Nor the heart," Thomas conceded. "Just the thought of a dead body upstairs turned him queasy."

From the looks of it, Berry was a similar age to the Fulhames, though his pale and spindly form made him appear several decades older at first sight.

"A consumptive?"

Thomas chewed his lower lip thoughtfully. "No, probably not. Just an unfortunate constitution."

If she'd caught him speaking, Berry's voice was quavering and high-pitched.

While she tried to not let first impressions sway her, Elizabeth's immediate reaction towards Berry was pity.

"His wife wasn't much heartier," Thomas said, guessing her thoughts. "She acted like she was raised by mice."

Perhaps an unkind assessment. Elizabeth remembered spying a pinched-face woman in the dining room, chewing the inside of her lips. She could see where Thomas was coming from, at least.

"For all the minutes I was in the room, it seemed as un-jovial a gathering as one could muster," Thomas said, cracking a smile. "I was the only one talking."

"Sometimes spirits of similar temperament are better separated, or diluted by someone less melancholic. It seems balancing humours wasn't the goal of Mr Godfrey's soiree."

"But they all know each other?" A frown appeared on Thomas' forehead. "Mrs Weston is sending letters to Mr Lowell, and Mr Berry is meeting with Mr Lowell..."

"The letter!" Elizabeth spun around. "Lowell will hand the letter over to Jeremiah Berry."

"Do ye think?" Thomas asked, but he followed her back towards the green.

Except the bench where the two had sat was empty. She thought she saw Silas Lowell back among the gamblers, but Berry was nowhere to be seen.

"We can't go back. Berry recognised us—it will be too suspicious," Thomas hissed.

"Which way did he go?"

They tried to cut around the green to reach the Cowgate, but it was too late. Berry had vanished into the bustle of the city.

17

"Sorry I'm back so early, Morris." Elizabeth breathily squeezed into Black's entrance hall. Her husband had departed in pursuit of Berry—who might have wandered towards the Grassmarket—but she doubted Thomas would find him.

She noted Black's manservant mildly agitated by her sudden return earlier than promised, but since she didn't know what caused this reaction, her brain was slow to register its importance. Her attention was focussed on the dining room, where voices murmured behind the closed door. "If Dr Black is in, I'll briefly..."

Morris gave a strangled warning, but Elizabeth was halfway inside before she registered it.

"Oh."

The sight that greeted her was perplexing in the extreme. There was no sign of Black. Instead, a handful of servants were seated at the dining table staring back at her, dice and cards scattered across the gleaming cherry wood surface.

During the busier winter season, Black's household staff included a cook, several kitchen maids, and a second valet. All were still dressed in their work clothes, which made the tableau of them sitting at their master's table even more incongruous.

"Dr Black requested use of the kitchens," Morris whispered urgently. "Since he said not to admit guests, we…"

"No, it's quite alright," Elizabeth took in the frozen card game and retreated. "I can call upon the doctor myself."

The smell that hit Elizabeth on her descent into the basement kitchen was a combination of hot alcohol and rubber. Yet her nostrils seemed adamant that she was inhaling a single smell, rather than multiple overlapping aromas.

The smell had an undertow of rotten vegetables.

Sure enough, upon edging into the kitchen, she encountered two thin figures bent over the stove, talking excitedly.

"Um? Dr Black? Dr Hutton?"

"Mrs Fulhame!" James Hutton did a double-take so violent she thought he'd fall over, before rushing over, beaming. "Blonde hair dye? You look extraordinary. How are the light-sensitive experiments going? Did you try zinc?"

Hutton—balding, intrinsically scruffy, elastic in temperament and movement—proved to Elizabeth that the opposite of scorn and indifference to her scientific endeavours could be just as tiring. Hutton had been an enthusiastic follower of her chemistry and phlogistic experiments since the day he learned about them, and conversations with him on the topic felt like being mauled by an oversized, friendly dog.

"I've been a little preoccupied of late, I'm afraid, Dr Hutton…"

"Right, right," Hutton backed off. "You nearly got accused of murder and locked up in the Tolbooth. Inexcusable of me to forget."

"I admit my humdrum concerns are eclipsed by my curiosity about what's going on here," Elizabeth admitted, edging into the room. Still standing next to the stove, Black's expression crept into bashfulness. "Or why your servants are all banished from their working area?"

Hutton's playful exuberance tended to rub off on people, which was why she didn't mind his clumsy enthusiasm. She could see his glamour wearing off Black from the moment she walked into the room: the usually poised chemistry professor was looking like a child caught raiding his mother's biscuit tray.

"We're evaluating another Board of Trades proposal," Black explained with haste, trying to regain control of the situation. "Concerning a novel fermentation and distillation process for the *Daucus Carota*..."

"You're brewing alcohol from carrots?" Elizabeth recognised Latin obfuscation when she heard it. "...Gentlemen, are you attempting to prove or disprove this concept?"

"It's working really well, Mrs Fulhame." Hutton looked ready to burst with pride. "I'm so glad you're excited about the concept, too."

Black looked like he wanted to intervene, but was stuck stirring a massive copper pot on the stove. He stretched out his fingers far enough to catch Hutton's elbow.

"James...James..."

"Apologies." Hutton allowed Black to pull him away from Elizabeth, un-offended by the behavioural correction. "I'm forgetting myself. Sorry. No servants are barred from their working area: it's just that our experimentation puts them on edge, especially after that business with the pressure cooker. Today we're making several batches of the carrot liquor to test the robustness of the proposal, and make sure the submitted claim is accurate. Obviously, there's a bit of chemical knowledge required to optimise the distillation, which is why Joseph and I are investigating."

"So, in that case..." Elizabeth pointed to the far corner of the kitchen. "Why is noted moral philosopher Adam Smith sitting on your stool next to the washtub, eyeing your pile of carrot peels?"

"Good morning, madam." Smith coughed politely. "I trust you are keeping well?"

"He's waiting to sample the final product," Black explained. "Adam was a little upset he missed James, George's and my last experiment tasting stewed snails."

Elizabeth studied the older philosopher, looking grey and creaky in the corner, but set as calmly as if he were sitting through a sermon in church. "Is that so? Forgive me, I thought *le incident escargot* led to a night of diarrhoea and upset stomachs?"

"Oh, it was awful," agreed Hutton, still restrained by Black's forefinger to the crook of his elbow. "Worst stomach ache of my life."

One would be forgiven for thinking the infamous 'snail incident' had a more scarring effect on Hutton's psyche than getting kidnapped a few weeks' later.

"This folly may yet proved as doomed, madam..." Smith nudged a glass of cloudy-brown liquid across the central work-bench. "But I admit a certain morbid curiosity to partake. Call it our foolish desire for connection to our fellow man, even at the expense of personal comfort. Would you care to sample the first batch, Mrs Fulhame? It seems ungracious not to offer."

"Of course!" Hutton broke free of Black's restraint and bounded across the kitchen. "We said, didn't we, that an alcoholic beverage from carrots might prove popular with the fairer sex? Carrots have a refreshing crispness to them after all, which elevates the beverage from tavern fare, does it not?"

"Between ladies and rabbits, who can resist carrots?" Elizabeth commented dryly. She studied the murky liquid. It bubbled gently.

On the one hand, the smell greeting her in the kitchen

made it apparent that 'refreshing' and 'crispiness' were unlikely to be components of the drink before her. And that the effect of carrot alcohol was likely to product identical outcomes to the natural philosophers' last attempt at culinary innovation, with added drunkenness to bear.

But it was also entirely possible she could save untold women from the misfortune of encountering this same drink, in which case her martyrdom would not be in vain.

"If you'll allow me..." She picked up the glass and, before she had time to reflect on her stupidity, took a mouthful.

For a moment, the only sound in the kitchen was the stove pan bubbling, and Black's incessant pan stirring.

"I'm afraid, gentlemen, 'drinkable' does this concoction a terrible disservice." She set the glass down, trying to swallow all traces of the carrot alcohol, lest it linger on her tongue a moment longer.

"Oh." Hutton visibly deflated. "Well, maybe some spices would improve the experience..."

Elizabeth suspected the concept was irredeemable, but smiled politely so as not to disappoint Hutton further.

Black carefully manoeuvred the copper pan off the stove.

Once Hutton and Smith were shooed upstairs, she briskly informed Black of her morning's enquiries.

"Which led to..." she concluded, limply holding up a basket of lemons.

"My purse is in the study," Black said, without blinking. "We can consider the sum a fair transaction for investigative services rendered."

She was glad Cullen wasn't around to hear this exchange: he'd roll his eyes so dramatically they'd risk popping out his head.

"I'm sure your dinner guests will be more appreciative of lemons than any visitors to the Fulhame household could be,

Dr Black." Not that Elizabeth foresaw any dinner guests in their immediate future. "Thank you."

In return, Black summarised the findings of himself, Cullen and George.

"I suppose looking for Maybelle Daniels could keep Thomas occupied," Elizabeth said. She thought of the strained looks Berry gave them. Thomas wanted their name cleared as much as she did, but their presence together was going to raise suspicions faster than if they worked alone.

She hoped Cullen felt a little bit of guilt at dismissing the letter. What role it played in Kitty's murder was still unclear, but there was obviously *some* connection.

Upstairs, the clock in Black's dining room chimed midday. Cullen was busy with lectures and clinical rounds until four o'clock.

Elizabeth's initial plan had been to speak with Susan Berry. But Mr Berry's reaction to the Fulhames made her wary. He recognised her, and didn't seem too pleased about it. There was no telling how his wife would react.

She wasn't sure Black would go out of his way to make further enquiries today, especially with Cullen busy, but he surprised her.

"The individual who is giving me pause," Black said, motioning for her to follow him back upstairs. "Is Mr Delancey."

Elizabeth wracked her brains. "Which gentleman was he?"

"Well, exactly." Black worked a finger into his temple. "You might recall he was the somewhat corpulent, younger fellow…"

Elizabeth had an image of a blond, slightly sweaty man in his late twenties, seated in the middle of the table and looking more annoyed than aghast by the events disrupting the dinner party. But she couldn't say her memory was accurate—it was more of a shadowy impression at this stage.

Seeing something close to recollection cross her face, Black continued. "Last night, he explained he was visiting his father in Edinburgh. I came away with the impression he usually resides in London."

"Who would his father be?" She looked at him.

"Precisely my question. I know of no Delanceys in Edinburgh, certainly not a man of similar standing to this gentleman called Ralph."

They returned to the dining room, now cleared of servants, where Adam Smith sat, jotting furiously into his notebook. He nodded at Elizabeth, as if it were the first time seeing her today.

"Did you have time to look at your records, Adam?" Black asked his friend.

"It was as I supposed," Smith replied, not looking up. "No Delanceys on the Edinburgh tax rolls. There was a family called Lancey, who lived in Bailey Fife's Close in recent years."

The insight was almost too good to be true, but Elizabeth didn't doubt that if there was a Delancey in the tax records, Smith would have caught it.

"However," Smith added. "They don't appear to be at that address in the most recent tax roll. I couldn't deduce where they moved to."

"Your help is much appreciated, Adam, as always."

Smith nodded, slipped his pocketbook into his coat pocket, tapped the brim of his hat and strolled towards the door. He raised a hand to signal farewell, but that was probably for Elizabeth's benefit, because Black wasn't even looking in his friend's direction.

"This so-called Delancey looked more like he was pretending to wealth than in possession of it." She might be forming an opinion too fast, based upon a fleeting glimpse. But her years spent around Edinburgh scholars gave her more insights than she wanted into the distinctions between wealthy and pretenders.

Given her husband amended his name from Fulham to Fulhame, she could hardly fault a stranger for imbuing his humdrum family name with a more sophisticated air. But it gave an insight into his character all the same.

Black nodded. "Even with that caveat, if his father was known in Edinburgh, he could only affect to be so much higher in stature than he actually is."

"Did he say what his connection to Mr Godfrey was?"

"Vexingly, no." Black trailed off. He paused for a moment. "Mr Godfrey implied they were business acquaintances."

That was another annoying development. No one at the dinner party was forthright with their intentions. They claimed to be strangers to everyone but Mr Godfrey, yet their actions suggested alarming familiarity. If all the guests were concealing the same secret—such as who murdered Kitty—it might make the process of deduction easier, but Elizabeth sensed all their secrets were discrete entities existing apart from one another.

This Ralph Delancey or Lancey—assuming either was his real name—had come to Edinburgh for some purpose, and was lying about what that was. And bizarrely, that part of that purpose involved an awkward dinner party with people who seemed to be his social inferiors.

"You gleamed nothing about his address?"

Black shook his head. "Nothing that I believe. "

They sat in silence for a moment.

"If he is as pretentious as he seemed, I imagine he will make an appearance at the new Assembly Rooms."

Black brightened. "Quite right, Mrs Fulhame. Failing that, it is likely a member of that sect will be familiar with him."

18

The new Assembly Rooms on George Street had only been open a few months, and was attracting a sizeable day time crowd. The grand hall was laid out with circular tables for card games and tea, with ample space along the sides for ladies to promenade. A balcony ran along three sides of the room, giving more society members the chance to see and be seen.

Black tapped the brim of his hat to numerous people as they strolled into the hall. Elizabeth was shot a few glances, but the upcoming visit from his niece was well-known about town.

Her memory from Godfrey's house was close enough. Ralph Delancey was a little on the stout side and looked younger than she recalled. He was dressed in a double-breasted ruby coat with a high collar. Unlike most people in the Rooms, he was seated alone at a modest table, which suggested he wasn't expecting company. A porcelain tea set painted with tiny pink roses was laid out in front of him.

Seeing Black approach, he blinked, then scrambled to his feet. Elizabeth was immediately ignored. She noted Delancey did not move like a rich man, since the wealthy she came across had an ease to their movements, even around a man as celebrated as Dr Joseph Black.

"Dr Black? Meeting you again is truly an honour."

Delancey must have been the youngest of Godfrey's guests. She estimated his age at two-score years and change.

"Pleased to meet you, Mr Delancey. This is my niece, Isabel Burnett."

Delancey nodded a brisk acknowledgment, then went back to ignoring her. "I did not know you frequented the Rooms. You are taking tea?"

"We would be delighted to," Black replied, sinking gracefully into the vacant chair.

Delancey obviously remembered their previous encounter, and held a favourable impression of the professor. Or—given his glances around the room—he wanted to be seen conversing with the famous natural philosopher as if they were old friends.

"They are certainly an improvement on the old halls, aren't they? They were dreadfully stuffy and cramped. I said it's about time Edinburgh had Assembly Rooms that could compete with Bath."

Elizabeth knew by this point in the conversation that she didn't like Delancey. He was the type of insecure bore who could constantly worm references into the discussion, hoping to impress his audience—in this instance bragging about his familiarity with the Bath social scene. She suspected he had not actually visited those Assembly Rooms, and thus his insights on the subject would be boring and superficial.

It had never been in Black's nature to show boredom or irritation, so he kept up his polite attention.

"Did you say you hailed from London?"

Unlike Elizabeth, Black didn't need to pretend he knew nothing about the murder of Mrs Grenville, or that he was already acquainted with the suspects.

"Yes, I have rooms in Golden Square."

"What brings you to Edinburgh?" Elizabeth asked. She could have waited until Black asked about his probably fictitious father, but she wanted to see if, given the opportunity and belief Black had forgotten what he initially said, he'd repeat the same lie.

"Nothing exciting. I'm calling upon a few contacts of my father's." Delancey barely glanced at her, but his gaze towards Black turned thoughtful. "If it's not too presumptuous of me to ask, Dr Black, are you acquainted with Archibald McGovern?"

"The glassblower? Indeed, I fill a lot of equipment orders with him."

"I heard a rumour he is looking to redevelop his North Berwick estate. Are you aware of this?"

Black and McGovern were fairly good friends, and Elizabeth already heard this through the chemistry professor. But she'd also heard that the redevelopments were beginning in two months, and all the contracts were settled.

Black did not immediately disclose this, though. He gave a confirmatory smile. "You're quite right, Mr Delancey. Are you seeking new business opportunities?"

Palpable excitement emanated from their new acquaintance, though he coughed it down. "I am looking to expand my client base, that is true. I took the liberty of drawing up blueprints for Mr McGovern to inspect—just as a starting point in our discussions, I might add."

"You're an architect?" Elizabeth asked.

While it was clear Delancey heard her, his other senses had decided there was only one individual seated of note at the table with him, and he devoted his attention to them.

"Quite right. I studied under the brilliant Robert Adam. My clients include Roger Willes-Stock of Golden Square and Viscount Edward Sinclair of Mayfair..." He rattled off a list of names, none of whom Elizabeth recognised. She doubted Black recognised any of them either, but he raised his eyebrows in an affection of being impressed.

"Quite a formidable portfolio for one so young."

Delancey beamed.

"I will pass on my compliments to Robert when he is next in Edinburgh. You do him great credit."

Delancey's smile faltered.

"You are acquainted with Mr Adam?"

Black pretended to ignore Delancey's mounting unease. "A brief acquaintance, alas. He may or may not remember me at our next meeting. I met him when he was proposing new designs for the university and other patrons."

Delancey nodded, swallowing. "He's not expected to return to Edinburgh for some time, is he?"

"I imagine not," Black said. "I understand affairs in London consume most of his time."

That would be where an architect stood to make the most money: the Scottish nobility were tight-fisted in comparison. Plenty of Elizabeth's friends laughed over reports of the petty, frenzied one-upmanship of London's beau monde. A signifier of wealth and status was employing Robert Adam to design your new house.

Delancey's head bobbed a few times, then he sipped his tea and gave a nervous laugh. "Quite so. Anyway, if I might intrude upon your valued time, regarding to Archibald McGovern…"

"Do you have the blueprints at hand?" Black asked. "I can perhaps show them to Archie when he stops by."

"Um…" Delancey coughed. "Unfortunately, I don't have them on my person today. I can show them to the gentleman if he is interested, though…"

Black continued the conversation, blandly promising he would raise the matter with his friend, but making no guarantees. This left Elizabeth space to ponder his reaction to Adam's name.

Black might know more about Delancey's alleged clients, or what the relationship between architect and trainee might be. It was possible Mr Adam didn't know Delancey was seeking patrons in Edinburgh, and would react badly to the news. Or the master architect had information on his trainee's abilities or conduct that would halt his fledgling career.

Unfortunately, she suspected getting information out of Delancey would be like wrestling a fish: he was too slippery to pin down. If pressed, he would probably lie...then continue to lie, spinning himself in contradictions and knots rather than admit a truth that reflected poorly on him.

"What do you think Delancey was lying about?" Elizabeth asked once they were back on George Street. "Most of what he said, or just some of it?"

Black shrugged, a sly smile on his face. "I would have estimated two-thirds of what came out of his mouth was a lie of some hue."

"His unwillingness to furnish his proposals is a little suspicious."

Black tapped his umbrella against the cobblestones. "I suppose acquiring genuine architectural renderings or forging his own would not be too difficult." He settled into contemplative silence for a moment. "Initially, I resolved not to subject Archie to that gentleman...but their meeting may be a useful test. I'm sure my friend would perform the service in exchange for my letting him get away with what he's charging me for the latest batch of conical flasks."

A shadow caught Elizabeth's eye as they turned onto Princes Street: a figure in a heavy greatcoat walking on the other side of the street. As she watched, he turned back on himself at the corner, hesitated, then crossed the street and walked away in the opposite direction.

Black caught her staring.

"Is everything alright, madam?"

"Hmm..." Had she imagined the man change his mind about where he was going as soon as he realised Elizabeth had noticed him? "I suppose so." The figure was already turning back onto George Street, heading toward the Assembly Rooms.

If he'd turned right instead of left on George Street, she might have wondered if he would continue to follow them towards the North Bridge, one street parallel to them. However, he'd just departed in the opposite direction.

Black shot her a questioning look, but she shook her head and resumed walking. There was no reason not to be mindful of her surroundings, but the odd behaviour of a stranger when she looked his way didn't mean he was following her.

"Do you think Mr McGovern knows enough about architecture to tell if Delancey is lying about his qualifications?" she asked, returning to the matter at hand.

Like many of the men Black befriended in Edinburgh, McGovern came from humble origins and worked to a position of commercial success. Knowing men who completed that trajectory, Elizabeth imagined there would be some residual hostility to pampered, privileged upstarts. Even if Delancey didn't start much further down the social ladder than him.

"I know Archie was very involved in developing the North Berwick blueprints," Black said. "And I think he will find it an enjoyable charade, trying to catch a puffed-up youth in a trap."

19

Before returning to Nicholson Street, Black and Elizabeth called in at Cullen's house. A few minutes later, Thomas slipped out of whatever spot near South Gray's Close he'd been hiding and joined them.

When she caught his eye he shook his head. No luck catching Berry.

They appraised Cullen of the day so far. He nodded along until Elizabeth described her conversation with Molly.

"I heard Clarence Young's name crop up in my morning's enquiries. His illegitimacy is the subject of widespread gossip."

That Young would be engaged in duplicitous dealings did not surprise her.

"What is nagging me," Elizabeth said. "Is for all Weston's talk about the popularity of her grapefruit, she didn't bring them to the dinner party to impress Godfrey's other guests. Did she, Thomas?"

Her husband shook his head. "No, there was apple and potato pie, and candied pears for dessert, from what I recall."

It was a lot to expect her husband to remember every dish served at a dinner party before he even knew it was important he recall these details. But Thomas Fulhame spent a decent amount of time thinking about food, even given his diminutive stature. Elizabeth joked her husband was more likely to eye other people's food than their wives.

"None of the dinner guests ever mentioned the grapefruit," she continued. "I certainly wouldn't have shut up about them." Most of the guests seemed like the last people to be in line to sample exotic fruits when they reached Edinburgh.

"Perhaps the gathering held little significance for Mrs Weston after all," Black suggested, speaking over the silent, yet loud, intensified frown of Cullen. "Or she actively wished to snub her fellow guests."

"If she wasn't hosting, why would she bring anything?" Cullen asked, skeptical. "The host didn't strike me as a man who cared about the status conferred by fruit dishes."

She supposed it did sound fanciful and womanish, to assume the dinner arrangements held deep significance.

But then a thought jolted into her mind. "Thomas, love? Did you say one of the dishes was candied pears?"

"Yes." Thomas swung his arms. "All floating in a massive silver bowl. Ye couldn't miss them." His eyes glazed over at the memory.

Elizabeth smacked her forehead. "That's why!" No wonder she'd felt a truth was staring her in the face, and she was failing to note its contours.

"Madam?" Even Cullen looked confused.

"We took it for granted that Mr Young remained cut off from his legitimate family, despite little evidence supporting hostile relations. What if, in fact, there had been a reconciliation?"

The light of understanding glowed in the physician's eyes.

"Between Mr Young and the Nicholsons?" Black asked.

"Yes!" Elizabeth almost jumped up and down on the spot. "The Nicholsons being the owners of The Pear Tree."

* * *

The old West Nicholson mansion stood at what was once the end of Nicholson Park, a leafy swathe of parkland stretching south beyond the former Flodden Wall. Most of the Nicholson's land had been sold to developers, and a wide road cut through the middle of what was once the park.

After discussion with the physicians, it was agreed Elizabeth and Thomas should handle this search. Black and Cullen were too recognisable, and their presence would raise the alarm if spotted.

"I hope ye're sure, Elizabeth," Thomas said. "Else we're freezing our hands off for nothing."

"It's not that cold," Elizabeth protested. Thomas was also refusing to wear gloves.

While the house was once the abode of the Nicholson family, like most nobles, they'd relocated to the New Town, and the grand three-storey building was broken into smaller apartments for rent. That said, the pear tree that lent the house its name still stood tall and proud at the corner of the walled garden.

"It must produce a sizeable crop," Thomas muttered as they approached the front entrance. "There were quite a lot of candied pears."

"Maybe they didn't all come from this particular tree," Elizabeth conceded. "But their presence was certainly symbolic."

"How are we going to navigate this? Ask the owner if Clarence Young came by last summer and took large quantities of pears? Oh, and do ye happen to recall why?"

"Young's left for Leith," interrupted a willowy girl hauling a sack of grain. "Said he had business down the Customs House."

"Oh." Elizabeth hadn't realised they'd spoken loud enough to be overheard. But the girl's weary face and swiftness to interrupt probably meant this wasn't the first time she handled questions concerning his whereabouts.

"You can wait in my ma's tavern room." She pointed behind her. "He lodges upstairs."

"Well, thank ye kindly..." Thomas began, but the girl had already wandered off, adjusting her grip on the oversized sack.

The lodgings house across the road had seen better days— as did the bits of West Nicholson House Elizabeth saw peeking above its walls—but upon stepping inside they found the floors swept and the surfaces dust-free.

The narrow entryway led to a front room on the left, which was actually an open tavern, albeit a subdued one. Its atmosphere was closer to a parlour, with men nursing glasses in calloused hands. Given the nearby crowded lodgings, Elizabeth supposed a parlour is what it was. No one noticed the pair hesitating in the hallway.

"She didn't say which floor Young has his rooms?" Thomas asked.

She hadn't.

"Was he the man with the strong camphor perfume?"

She had vague memories of being dragged past a well-groomed man by the Town Guards and catching a lungful of musk so concentrated she almost choked.

Thomas wrinkled his nose at the memory. "He did apply it rather liberally, yes."

Well, that was a starting point.

"I can look upstairs." Thomas' voice dropped to a whisper, and he pointed with his toe. "See if his room is obvious. Everybody seems to be out at work."

"Be careful, won't you?" Elizabeth peered into the front

room. None of the men seemed ready to stand, but there would be at least four lodging rooms for Thomas to check, and he could only move so fast.

Thomas followed her gaze. "Think ye can distract them for a bit? Nothing too overdone, just to keep them in place?"

Elizabeth nodded, then looked around for inspiration. All she had in her purse—aside from paltry grubby coins—was a book she planned to give to Phoebe when they stopped by the Stephens' later that day.

She patted the outline of the book.

Hmmm.

"Yes?" Thomas asked, a note of worry in his voice.

There were quite a few books strewn around the room, as well as mangled broad sheets. The men in the room seemed no more affluent than the Fulhames, but to be lounging around in taverns mid-morning...

"Do these people strike you as artists, sweetheart?"

"Some look like musicians—think I might have seen that fellow on the left playing in an oyster bar," Thomas conceded.

"Creative intellectuals. Then yes." Elizabeth traced the spine of her book. "I have a plan."

Her husband looked relieved.

"Good, I'll try to be quick."

"If you'll allow me five minutes to get the act underway," Elizabeth began. Then she paused.

Her woolly plan depended on the men in the tavern deciding to interrupt a woman they'd never met before, while she was engrossed in a book.

"Give me two and a half minutes," she clarified, before swooping in.

Since no one paid any attention to her arrival, Elizabeth sat on the central table and propped her book open, hastily flicking to a point two-thirds of the way through.

Then she sniffed. She blew her nose and rubbed her eyes.

She wouldn't call herself an expert at crying on command, but after summoning as many horrible thoughts about her loved ones, a few tears began flowing. This time, she let out a tiny sob.

"A handkerchief, madam?"

A man in his early thirties appeared at her elbow. He was dressed in rough clothes, but his lack of a cravat or neck scarf, and unbuttoned undershirt, suggested a certain artistic inclination.

"Oh, I apologise. How embarrassing—I'm making such a fool of myself." Elizabeth took the proffered handkerchief and dabbed her eyes. "My companion will laugh at me when he gets here."

At the mention of a 'companion', she sensed several ears in the room prick. Had she specified she was waiting for her husband or fiancé, the bachelors would have returned to their drinks or papers. But the term 'companion' suggested a certain degree of...availability.

"Ah, the power of a good book." The man leaned on the table, relaxing into his posture. "It truly transports us into other worlds and lives. What are you reading...?"

"Nothing, well...it's silly of me..." Elizabeth flipped the book to show the spine. "I'm getting all sentimental over the tale of Moll Flanders."

"Nonsense! It's quite refreshing to see a woman connecting so deeply with a novel. Plenty of the fairer sex only engage with what they read on a superficial level, without forming lasting opinions or feelings on the subject." The musician tapped the table edge. "You're different, I can tell."

"It's quite a tale, is it not?" Another man puffing on a pipe in the corner commented. "Such horrors and depravities—rendered with exquisite sensitivity by the author."

Elizabeth did her best to force a few more droplets of tears out of her eyes.

"It's so unfortunate," Elizabeth whispered, choking on her words. "That poor woman."

"Moll Flanders?" the musician asked. "It all turned out alright for her, luv, if you've not reached the end. She repented and lived a virtuous old age."

"Why did she repent?" Elizabeth asked, making a show of wiping her eyes and snorting back mucus. "Moll Flanders did nothing wrong."

The musician threw back his head and laughed. "You're quite a witty little woman."

"I'm serious." Elizabeth closed the book. "The poor woman isn't to blame for any of the calamities that befell her."

The musician gaped, still unsure if he was dealing with a jokester, but unable to control himself.

"Madam! Moll Flanders was a thief, whore, transported convict, and a bigamist. She committed incest with her brother."

"A very unfortunate misunderstanding. I don't see how she can be blamed for that." Elizabeth felt a tug of relief that she didn't have to fake tears any more.

"What about the scores of children she abandoned? What kind of mother would do such a thing? She stole from widows, orphans and hard-working shopkeepers." The musician was spluttering now. "She never showed remorse for her actions until the end."

"She could only do as circumstances forced her," Elizabeth replied, sticking her chin up.

At this, the pipe-smoking man in the corner lurched to his feet.

"I worry, madam, that you have failed to grasp the subtle yet compelling points the author was trying to make about the nature of poverty and criminality, and its effect on the feminine mind..."

"No, Brian!"

The exclamation from the other side of the room suggested Brian was known for this course of action, which appeared to be berating other people into submission. The rest of the room was trying to decide whether Elizabeth—despite her woefully misguided opinions—deserved what was coming to her.

Brian ignored his warning. "As a matter of fact, the author's decision to..."

It was hard to determine which parts of the argument she was meant to respond to, because the musician was trying to interrupt Brian and disagree with some of his points, and other men were rising from their chairs to break up the argument. From the way the musician's face turned scarlet, Elizabeth deduced there was residual animosity at play between the two men.

"Sorry for the delay." Thomas bumped against her. "Since it's nice outside, how about we take a walk instead?"

"Gladly." Elizabeth rose quickly, but her presence in the room seemed forgotten as Brian and the musician started gesticulating and the other men attempted to prise them apart.

"What happened here?" Thomas asked as they jogged onto the street. "It seems the entire room is in uproar."

"I stated an opinion they felt compelled to correct," Elizabeth said. They slowed to a brisk walk. "Success, I gather?"

"Let's hope so." Thomas patted his pocket. "It seems a little slim for all the secrecy, but I couldn't find any other papers in the packet and was running out of time to look, so I hope this is a helpful starting point, at least."

20

By the time Cullen ushered them into an empty ward at the Infirmary, Elizabeth still didn't know what they'd stolen. She wanted to investigate the package, but feared being spotted examining it in the street.

"I hope we aren't disturbing your rounds, Dr Cullen," Thomas said.

Cullen laughed. "Nonsense. I need an excuse to get away from Gregory. He's being pernicious today, for some reason."

During the winter, professors stoked collegiate grudges for the same reason Elizabeth stoked her hearth: to keep warm. Cullen's grievances with Dr John Gregory lay dormant in the balmy summer months, but flared up when the temperature plunged.

Still, if it gave them an opportunity to examine their findings, she'd take it. I felt like they'd chased this document halfway across Edinburgh.

The wad of paper, tightly folded and compressed, took some time for Elizabeth to ease open. Surprisingly, the wad started barely the size of a letter, but unfolded to almost the length of her arm.

"A blueprint?" Cullen leaned over and frowned. "No, that can't be right."

"It looks to be a copy of an architectural design," Black said, appearing at Elizabeth's other shoulder.

The cause of confusion was obvious. While the buildings were rendered in crisp detail, in a style Elizabeth found vexingly familiar, no additional notation was provided. Whoever had copied the plans used just enough paper to get every detail down, with no explanatory text.

"Is this the Adephi Terrace in London?" Cullen asked, confusion still humming through his voice. "No, surely not…"

"But it is Robert Adam's drawing, is it not?" Elizabeth asked, now piecing together the source of its familiarity. She couldn't recall ever seeing a sketch of the neoclassical terrace with its oversized arches on the banks of the River Thames, but she'd seen enough of the Adams brothers' other creations to recognise the similarities.

"It certainly bears his hallmark style," Black conceded, wariness creeping into his voice. Elizabeth immediately understood his guarded reaction. Mr Adam was responsible for the design of several university buildings, as well as half the fashionable developments in Edinburgh. Implicating him in Kitty's murder and underlying dirty business wasn't something a respectable gentleman would do lightly.

The Adam architectural style was grandiose: sweeping colonnades, wide arches and buildings constructed on a monumental scale. They were designed to awe onlookers; giants of grace.

Yet what they were looking at seemed to exist on a scale beyond that. This went beyond the sweeping townhouses of the famous Adelphi Terrace.

"It's like the Parthenon, or the Forum in Rome," Cullen muttered.

The blueprint showed a long street of neoclassical buildings, some rising four or five storeys high, interspersed with bridges, walkways and arches. The design seemed to show more than a single street: it was an edifice of granite or marble unto itself.

"There's nothing on the back, Mrs Fulhame?" Black asked.

She flipped it. "I'm afraid not." Not even the faintest graphite smudge.

"Is this wholly a flight of fancy?" Cullen pulled back to study the image from a distance. "Yet it's intricately thought out. Copying the original alone would take a day."

The truth snapped through Elizabeth like a lightning bolt.

"It's the South Bridge."

The professors stared.

"It is. See, those supporting arches and bridges are all on the same plane behind the buildings in the foreground." Her sense of nagging familiarity finally had an outlet. "It's from the perspective of a viewer on the Cowgate looking towards the Grassmarket. That's Adam Square in the left-hand corner."

"Of course it is!" Cullen smacked the table. "We went through that whole drama with Mr Adam a few years back. The Lord Provost and friends invited him in as a consultant for the South Bridge back in 1785, or whenever the first round of proposals and fundraising began. But Robert misunderstood their invitation. The Lord Provost only meant his inclusion as a flattery, or a way to add prestige to the undertaking; Robert seemed to think he'd been appointed chief architect, so began submitting these ridiculous design proposals. He came to visit Edinburgh several times, and apparently no one was brave enough to point out we'd found our own local architects to complete the project. This could be one of the original blueprints he handed over—it was well outside the town's budget, and everyone else preferred a more pared-down style. You can see how much space his proposed buildings would take up, as if the current works aren't disruptive enough!"

A certain energy came back over the professor. Cullen hated being behind the curve, and his relief at grasping the situation was palpable.

"But why would someone be smuggling these old architectural plans around Edinburgh?" Elizabeth asked. "They're nearly three years old."

"Mr Adam's proposals were widely discussed at the time," Black said, sounding a note of agreement. "His fit of pique..."

"Tantrum, Joe."

"You can call it that, yes—his displeasure once his designs were rejected was very public. I can't recall if William or I ever saw the originals, but the gist of his proposal was no secret."

"So why does Kitty Holm, sorry, Grenville, have anything to do with this secret blueprint?" Thomas asked. "Or is it a coincidence and her murder was motivated by something else entirely?"

It was Black's turn to look thoughtful. "It occurred to me Kitty was in Edinburgh with Malcolm Holm around the time Robert Adam was sketching those blueprints. At one point, I wondered he would turn up for the reading of James' geological paper. Holm's goal—the reason for his return—was to hijack the Town Council to serve his own ends, setting the university and wider city back on a path he considered more moral and Christian. Which meant he was targeting the class of Edinburgh citizens involved with planning and funding the new bridge."

"That's a maybe, then." The Holms could have stumbled into a conspiracy they thought they could leverage to their own benefit, or set a plot in motion back in 1785 that was now only coming to fruition.

"Or this whole thing could be a futile pop-gun of a plot,"

Thomas said. He looked tired. Elizabeth couldn't blame him: what he believed a onetime favour to his former professors was sprouting legs and wings, and forced him to hiding as an accomplice to a murderess. "We have a conspiracy of grocers, wine merchants and slimy ex-militiamen. They may have a strong conviction, they may even have decided upon a romantic plan. But I don't see how they have the influence or power to enact anything that would give us cause for concern."

"Well, the rich and powerful of Edinburgh would know better than to get too involved," Elizabeth said. "They have their proxies and messengers. We wouldn't see their influence at first glance."

"The freemasons!" exclaimed Thomas. "I know Jeremiah isn't a high-ranking brother..."

"...But he doesn't need to be," Elizabeth finished. "He'll have access to the most powerful men in Edinburgh, and them to him."

Black nodded. "If there's a wider conspiracy a-foot, the lodges are an obvious pre-existing framework to bring the players together."

Useful up to a point. Now Elizabeth had to devise a way to test this hypothesis.

"Is this the original?" Elizabeth didn't understand what was missing in this chain of events, but something must be. Someone had taken care to remove all identifying markers from this copy. "Why conceal ownership of a rejected blueprint?"

"I suppose if its exactitude told us something about how it came to be in the hands of Kitty and her associates."

"Only the Lord Provost or his closest associates could tell us that," Black said. "Assuming they still have the originals, or remember enough of it."

Elizabeth sighed. This looked like another dead end.

"That said, madam..." In the corner of the room, Cullen's eyes took on a shimmering glint. "We can waste several days poking around making enquiries of people in Edinburgh who *might* know something. Or..."

A spark fluttered through Elizabeth's stomach as Cullen's smile cracked wider. "We can take this straight to the top."

21

NIGHT OF THE MURDER

He knew more now than he did then. Black cast his mind back to the night of Kitty's murder, when he walked into the room containing the killer.

Mr and Mrs Berry trailed him into the dining room. The central table filled half the space, with a narrow sideboard covered in dishes and bottles at the back, and bay windows overlooking James Court, with shutters drawn. In the furthest corner, a narrow spiral staircase disappeared into the darkness.

"What is going on?" demanded a short blond man, his face flushed. "What is all this talk of murder? Where is Mrs Grenville?"

Black stepped aside to avoid getting splashed with the man's glass of port, which swung wildly under his nose.

"Thomas, leave as quietly as you can," Black instructed. Thomas was just inside the door, engaging Berry in conversation. *"Find George and stay with him."*

"Will someone pray tell me what is going on?" Delancey continued, raising his voice. "What did Godfrey mean when he said the Town Guards are on their way?" He stared at Black, ready to click his fingers if Black's attention didn't snap away from Thomas' retreating back. "You! Who did you say you were?"

Black held the young coxcomb's gaze. "Dr Joseph Black, at your service." He inclined his head slowly. His movements had to be slow, or else the nausea would return.

Delancey gaped as if Black had punched him in the stomach. Something Black was sorely tempted to do.

"You're Joseph Black?" Delancey appeared too awed to feel embarrassment at his rudeness. "Can this be true?"

"Quite so. And you are...?"

"Oh, gosh, yes. Ralph Delancey, is my name." He prattled on about visiting his father in Edinburgh. Part of Black's brain stopped listening, because his immediate question was why, if Delancey was a son of Edinburgh like he claimed, he couldn't recognise Black on sight.

"Is it true that poor Kitty has been murdered?" Two gentlemen peeled away from the wall and approached Black. That would be Clarence Young and Silas Lowell. Both held empty wine glasses.

Black cast around for the host. Godfrey had slipped out, presumably dealing with Elizabeth, the body of his cousin, and the cook, whose hiccuping sobs carried down the stairwell. Black couldn't hear anything else beyond that din.

"She was murdered in her bedchamber? While we sat around talking?" Lowell leaned closer and peered and Black. He had a dark silkiness to his movements, like cooling tar. Out of all the individuals here, he appeared the most self-assured. His partner Young didn't stop moving: tiny rearrangements of his posture and expression, as if never satisfied with how he looked.

Black adopted a grave expression. "I fear so."

"So what was Moll yammering about an Irish gal?" Young asked. He spoke with an exaggerated crispness, as if he were mocking a proper English accent rather than mimicking one.

He had unusually bright blue eyes, which made his gaze piercing. "She starts screaming about murder, then Godfrey rushes upstairs, leaving us all in the dark."

They were turning towards Black for answers, because it would be incomprehensible for a natural philosopher as distinguished as him to not know what was going on.

"Did anyone venture upstairs between us bringing Godfrey's manservant inside, and the cook discovering Kitty?" Black hoped Cullen was calming the situation. If someone ran to summon the Town Guards—and the Town Guards sprinted over—they would arrive within minutes. If he got a useful answer out of someone in this room right now, he could head upstairs and extricate Elizabeth from this mess.

"No, Dr Black." Delancey spoke first. "I can't recall anyone leaving the dinner table."

"We hadn't really settled back down to our plates after that manservant was carted past us," Young interrupted. "Most of us were standing about, then your companion— wherever has he got to?—came in demanding to speak to Hugh about the chap's general constitution and recent health."

Black could sometimes detect when a person he knew was lying. They had a tendency to throw in too many details into what would otherwise be a banal response. For that reason, he didn't think Delancey was lying, but Young might be.

Lowell said nothing. He merely looked at Black with what could have been faint mirth, as if he recognised Black's attempt at lie detection.

"Did you see anything?" Black asked calmly.

Lowell shrugged. "I was battling with a wine cork in the corner for most of that time. I couldn't tell you anything about who was going back-and-forth." There was a note of challenge in his voice, daring Black to press him further.

In the doorway, Mrs Weston was gathering her belongings.

She was taking her time knotting her shawl and glancing at the stairs, no doubt hoping her host would re-appear so she could exchange words. Then she shrugged to herself and slipped away. Black saw a flash of red through the open door. Town Guardsmen were rushing to fill James Court.

"That's what's called an Irish exit," Lowell observed, also watching Weston depart. Neither of his companions broke into a smile.

"Are all of you acquainted?" Black asked, motioning to the room at large. "Did you meet through Mr Godfrey?"

Delancey, Lowell and Young all glanced at each other, then shook their heads.

"I can't say that we are," Young replied after a pause. "We all know Hugh, of course, but to each other we are strangers."

22

Cullen's plan had to wait a day, because the Lord Provost's business—and threatening snowstorm—kept him in Leith overnight.

Having assured Black they'd keep their wits about them, Elizabeth set off with Thomas and George in the direction of the now-frozen Duddingston Loch. In the summer, this was a leisurely mile and a half stroll around the base of Arthur's Seat; this morning, tramping over frost-packed earth and navigating frozen puddles slowed them all down.

Despite the biting wind stinging her cheeks, Elizabeth's chest unclenched the further they got from Edinburgh.

The sky was an airy, marbled grey—promising gentle snow flurries before sunset.

"How are Phoebe and the twins doing?"

George smiled, in spite of himself. "Phoebe remains concerned for my wellbeing. Emma and Abby seem more concerned with the promise of their next meals."

"I envy the short-term concerns of babes," Elizabeth said wryly.

Duddingston Loch was proving a popular site today,

with at least twenty individuals taking to the ice. Elizabeth had begged a pair of skates off her former tenement acquaintances still in Edinburgh. Since the ice appeared likely to remain into next week, Morag and her family hadn't objected to the loan.

Neither she nor Thomas were the most adept skaters, but they could manage a careful circuit of the frozen lake.

"I think I was eight when I last skated," Thomas admitted. "Don't suppose ye forget it. Dr Stephens looks like he's been practising, though."

For someone who often appeared uncertain on his feet, as if the entire world was ice he risked slipped on, George moved smoothly around the lake with crossed arms and long sweeps of his legs.

"Did you skate a lot as a child?" Elizabeth called out when their friend next overtook them.

As usual, George looked sheepish. "We had a horrendously cold winter camped near New York. Skating was a reliable way to keep warm."

Phoebe Stephens promised to bring the twins along later, and her arrival would no doubt herald the end of the activity. Elizabeth let the other skaters whizz past her and Thomas, and set to thinking.

"I presume you had no luck tracing Maybelle this morning?"

Thomas sighed. "I've found a few places she's *not*. She's not staying with her family, and none of the places I've been told she's lodged at before have yielded any clues. Apparently, her husband is in Lyon right now, conducting some sort of trade negotiations."

"Would Maybelle have fled to join him?"

"I gather—from casual chitter chatter, mind—that she's not one for travel. A poor stomach for the seas and long-distance carriage rides."

That was a comfort. "I imagine, given the tragedy in her life, she might be reluctant to travel alone."

Thomas agreed. "At any rate, the corporal can't be checking in on her often. But I'm getting a good idea of his habits, so hopefully it will become apparent when he deviates from said routine to visit her."

Further rumination on that topic was halted by a sudden, loud crack bouncing off the frozen lake and reverberating back from Arthur's Seat.

Elizabeth's initial reaction was to assume the ice had fractured. But a heartbeat later she released the sound came from a flintlock.

Then a second shot was fired.

Now the lake was filled with screams and panicked skaters tripping over themselves to flee. Thomas tugged Elizabeth against him as they cast around for the source of noise. It seemed to come from everywhere at once.

"Thomas! Elizabeth!" George swooped in and tried to grab both their arms. "I think they're after you."

"Pardon?"

There was always that moment of paranoia in the wake of street disturbances: *they must be after me*. It was an automatic, conceited reflex that Elizabeth always tried to reason against. But this time, the sneaking fear about the pistol shots being intended for them had glided alongside her. Given everything that happened with Mrs Grenville, and the worrying implications of subsequent discoveries, she calmly accepted this fact.

"I saw two ruffians eyeing you from the opposite bank," George continued, urging the couple along. "Then you disappeared into the crowd back there and I think they lost you."

Elizabeth glanced around. A woman about her age had fallen and was clutching her ankle, wailing. She had dragged down two boys attempting to help her.

"They're clearing the lake," George hissed, seeing her look.

"We must head to the west bank and back through the trees. God help us, I hope Phoebe gets turned back."

George's complexion was pale, and his darting eyes exposing the core of fear under his otherwise composed demeanour. Elizabeth could understand his dilemma. But Phoebe wasn't expected to arrive with the twins for another half hour—she thought she'd heard St Giles chime shortly before the attack.

The lake was emptying of skaters fast, still fleeing in all directions. The armed ruffians still weren't visible. But they had minutes to slip away before they were spotted.

"Right." Elizabeth took a deep breath and fought to remain calm. "We'll...no!"

"Elizabeth!" Thomas gasped in horror as she stumbled.

"My skate..." She couldn't believe it.

"Move!" Thomas and George lunged for her.

"The left skate bindings are coming loose!"

She stumbled, and as she did, the whole skate wobbled. She could feel the bindings come undone around the blade and ankle.

Curse Morag for not checking her skates before giving them to her. Curse Elizabeth for not stopping to check the bindings earlier.

"Keep moving, Elizabeth." Thomas fought to keep his voice level.

"I..." She raised her foot and felt the whole skate collapse underneath. Both Thomas and George tried to prop her up, but Elizabeth was struck by the futility. In another moment, the blade and bindings would part from her foot, leaving her with one functioning skate.

"Fuck, fuck, fuck..."

"Put yer arm over my shoulder..." Thomas could support her weight, but it nearly brought him to a complete stop. Maybe she could glide along on one leg, but that...

"There they are!"

It was too late. The last stragglers, including the downed woman and her compatriots, had diffused across the loch. Twenty metres away stood two men, a faint cloud of smoke hanging around them. They were covered almost head to toe by dark scarves, long greatcoats, gloves, and caps. Even from a distance she saw the pewter glint of pistols and blades. Between them, they'd discharged two shots: they'd have at least two more.

Thomas hissed beside her. That was when she saw a thick trail of blood smeared across the ice between them and the ruffians. It followed the largest group of skaters to the nearest bank, where a few dark figures lay wounded in the rushes.

The ruffians began skating in a circular arc towards them, blocking their route to the nearest bank.

"I'll distract them." George pushed away from the Fulhames. His pale face was set.

"They're after us, George," pleaded Elizabeth. "That won't work."

"It will if I charge toward them." George gave Thomas a threatening shove backwards. Elizabeth yelped as her balance wobbled. "Go!"

Without looking back, he took off towards the men.

Elizabeth felt her heart leave her body. Too horrified to scream his name or demand he come back. What would she tell Phoebe if he died? How could she bear to see his wife's reaction? How could she bear the guilt? From the way Thomas froze, she suspected he was wrestling with the same horror.

George exploded across the ice, massive kicks of his legs propelling him towards the assailants. The men refocussed, recognising him as a threat, but unsure if they should waste another ball on him.

Then the one on the right—wearing a green scarf—cocked his pistol.

"Get down!"

Elizabeth smacked into the ice with bone-jarring force. Pain shot through her palms, and she felt her knees crack on impact. George was between them and the shooters.

A third pistol shot rang out. George dropped into a half crouch, momentum still propelling him forward. He swung his leg through and rose back to full height.

The other ruffian raised his pistol, but George showed no sign of slowing down. At this rate, he was going to fly past the attackers...

Then George jumped. The knee of his free leg swung forward, and as it kicked back, his skating leg rose and corkscrewed behind him. As he flew through the air, George spun in a complete circle between the two ruffians. One of his legs lashed out in front, the other kicked back like a donkey.

"Jesus Christ have mercy!" Elizabeth saw the spray of blood. Both men crumpled forward as George landed, half-tripping and flying at terrifying speed.

Getting lacerated by ice skate blades in the abdomen and thigh—which was where their friend appeared to have aimed —was too horrendous to contemplate. She wondered in a daze if George struck to kill, or if he lacked that degree of control.

"He's alright." Thomas was almost on his feet. Elizabeth hadn't doubted for a minute that George was alright: she was simply too shocked to move. Thomas tried to tug her up, but then he froze again. "There's more."

The prone attackers on the ice weren't moving, but Elizabeth saw three more burst from the trees on the opposite bank.

They'd probably concealed themselves there to intercept the Fulhames if they tried to sneak away that side. Which was exactly what George had wanted them to do.

Except George was now almost on the other side of the loch from this new threat, and these three men—also disguised under thick coats and scarves—were sticking further apart as they stepped onto the ice.

"They have skates too."

Elizabeth didn't have the energy for further terror. Her sense of mental exhaustion and resignation were already at their peak. George wouldn't be able to get between them in time, and these fresh attackers probably had six pistol shots between them.

Thomas didn't tug her back. He too seemed paralysed by the threat.

"Let them come closer."

An idea formed. Basic theories leaping from disparate corners of her mind, knotting into a plan.

"Elizabeth?"

She tugged off her gloves. "And when I say jump...you jump.."

"Ahh..."

Elizabeth focussed on rearranging as much of her skirt and coat fabric under her screaming knees as possible. She kicked away her remaining skate.

The new attackers were brandishing their pistols, but believing their quarry to be cowed by fear, they weren't ready to fire.

She looked at the trees and blemishes on the ice, trying to figure out distances. This was pure guesswork—what her strength could manage, the speed she might strike, how quick her attackers could react if they saw what she was doing.

Thirty more metres. She heard Thomas swallow.

She'd no idea where George was. Hopefully, too far away to get hurt.

She pressed her palms into the ice.

"Jump!"

Elizabeth forced a wave of aether-electricity into the ice, wiling it away from her body. For a moment it seemed to crackle and circulate within her, as if it decided not to leave, then it fanned across the ice, like a white glittering wave.

Thomas thudded back down, and she heard the ice groan around her.

The assailants only had time to slow in confusion before the electrical wave crashed against them, erupting through their skate blades.

23

Phoebe took the news of what transpired better than they'd feared.

"That was *extraordinarily* foolish, boy. I can't tell if you're trying to make me a widow through such behaviour, or trying to make yourself a widower by sending me into an apoplectic fit in response."

George sat rocking one twin by the hearth. Elizabeth suspected this was more about putting a shield between husband and irate wife than comforting his sleepy child.

"They would have caused a lot more anguish if I hadn't tried to stop them," George said, some of his fierce moral conviction peeking through. Then it retreated. "I think I pulled my hamstring, though."

In the corner of the room, Thomas snorted. "Well, who else would have pulled yer hamstring?"

George opened his mouth, then closed it.

"I'll help you scrub those pots," Elizabeth said to the other woman, hoping to calm the situation. Phoebe nodded.

"What an awful thing to experience," she said to Elizabeth, with a little more sympathy.

Elizabeth fought the urge to glance out the Stephens' window. She told herself no one had followed them back here, and it was safe to remain here until the streets got darker and they could move about with less attention.

"Who do you recall telling about our plans for today?" she asked Phoebe. "I'm not blaming you…"

"I know that, Elizabeth."

"Right, because none of us thought anyone might pursue us, so we didn't think to withhold the information."

"I don't think I told anyone. Between George telling me yesterday and now, I was mostly at home baking." A halibut pie on the table was proof of Phoebe's endeavours.

"I told Morag, because I borrowed skates from her." Elizabeth wasn't in the mood to return to her friend and explain why they were returning half of the skates they'd borrowed, and she felt a certain bracing anger at the condition Morag kept them in. Perhaps that was irrational anger.

"I picked up mine from Dr Cullen's son, Robert," George said. "But I also didn't have a good way to carry them, so slung them over my shoulder on the way home."

"I really hope it wasn't the Cullens who spilled the secret," Thomas muttered from the corner of the room. He'd been in an unsettled mood ever since the attack.

"Or perhaps they watched us head towards Duddingston with our skates this morning," Elizabeth said quickly. "And decided to set their trap there." The implication that someone they trusted exposed their location was an unpleasant one to contemplate.

"I wish we'd got a better look at the attackers." Thomas had been tapping his mug against the table for the better part of an hour. "But if they're able to hire five ruffians at short notice…"

By the fire, George shuddered.

"We're in a mighty deep hole now," Elizabeth commented.

. . .

Thomas insisted on walking Elizabeth back to Nicholson Street.

"Maybe I should stay with Phoebe and George..." Elizabeth offered.

Thomas shook his head. "I think the professors will be less anxious if they can keep ye in sight. It's safer for us to not be seen together."

Her husband walking her home put them in no small danger of discovery, though she supposed he was more fearful of his wife being recognised without him there to protect her.

She swallowed. "Have you heard any gossip...about us? When you were hunting for Maybelle?"

Thomas' pace sped up. "Mmm, not a lot." That sounded like a lie. "More talk about ye than me, though." Unfortunately, that sounded true.

They were rounding College Wynd. Not much further to go. The promised snow was morphing into sleet.

"I assumed those men today were after us because of our implication in Kitty's murder," Elizabeth said, dropping her voice. "But what if they weren't?"

"Why else would they be searching for us?" Thomas sounded baffled.

"Because we're making enquiries into Kitty's murder and bothering Godfrey's guests. No one claims to have seen me— the escaped murderess—in Edinburgh?"

"None of the rumours matched where I knew ye to be," Thomas said, ushering her across Nicholson Street.

They were playing with fire by venturing out into Edinburgh. Her new hair colour would only avert so many suspicious looks. Eventually, someone would recognise her as the woman who escaped the Tolbooth. Every day, every trip outside, increased the odds of that.

"I don't understand why every gentleman and his lady assume the worst of ye," Thomas said, monitoring a passing carriage until it rounded the corner. "No one doubts yer guilt, and there's only so much I can argue with 'em until they get suspicious of my intentions."

"It's the Pamela-Shamela dichotomy," Elizabeth sighed. "Men will either view us as Pamela—virtuous saints, untouchable purity—or conniving Shamela, seducing men to feed their insatiable sexual hungers. There is surprisingly little middle ground."

Thomas had the decency to look shocked by this observation.

"Why would ye wish to occupy the middle ground, Elizabeth? I'd have thought it better to be a Pamela?"

He *would* think that.

"Having read both novels, I pity the fate of Pamela more than Shamela. Her virtue was rewarded with what? Marriage to a lecherous rake. Shamela can at least be said to have got exactly what she wanted."

"I don't think of ye as a Shamela," Thomas said, no doubt sure he was giving his wife a compliment.

It wasn't Elizabeth's intention to get into an argument; she'd only meant her remark as a wry observation. So she cleared her throat.

"Dr Black would surely accept you in for tea, sweetheart."

"Errr..." Thomas' hesitation was refusal enough. "Seems courting too much danger, me coming out of his house. Will cross the street at the haberdasher and then double back."

That was fair enough. She gave him a peck on the cheek before he could hurry away.

"Take care, sweetheart."

"And ye." Thomas nodded briskly, then was gone.

· · ·

After passing through Black's front door—feeling no small amount of relief when Morris closed the door behind her—Elizabeth saw the parlour was occupied.

"Good, I think she's returned…" Black said to the occupant. That sounded like an invitation for her to enter.

Well, at least today would yield some insights into the machinations of Ralph Delancey.

Archibald McGovern had a broad Scots accent and ruddy complexion, making him look a youthful five-score years. He sprawled across Black's settee; A man who equated taking up physical space with projected confidence. Elizabeth wondered briefly if he rouged his cheeks to make them look appropriately red for mercantile clients. She suspected his accent was a point of pride.

McGovern looked pleased when Elizabeth entered the parlour. His wink in her direction suggested he enjoyed an audience when spinning tales. "Well, that was enough entertainment for the month, Joseph. Won't need to visit the playhouse or opera. In fact, I would find the performances dull compared to what you put me through with that Delancey pup."

"He's not an architect?" Elizabeth blurted out.

McGovern frowned. "Nah, love. Quite the opposite: I couldn't trip him up. Asked all sorts of tricky questions about joisting, masonry, tried to catch him in any trap I could think of…nowt. The bairn knows what he's talking about, alright."

"But he didn't train under Robert Adam?" She'd been sure Delancey was deceiving them about something. But if it wasn't his architectural credentials, then what else it could be?

Again, McGovern disagreed. "I suspect he did. But even if his rants against the man came from another point of contention…he trained under a top master. The blueprints were in his hand, and he has genuine talent. Shame it's wasted on a strutting cock like that."

Black, perched on his armchair in the shadow of McIntyre, looked as puzzled as her. "What did he rant about then, Archie?"

"Well, since Joseph told me there was something afoot between him and Robert Adam, I tried to bait him. Nothing too needling—just gushed a bit about ol' Rob and how I might consult him for future projects. Didn't need much bait, it turns out: barely enough to catch a minnow. Delancey told me his former master was a lazy charlatan, who exploited his trainee's talent and hadn't had an original thought in decades. I lend scant credence to that opinion, since the same gentleman tried to convince him of his own pedigree by dropping the name 'Robert Adam' to impress me as often as he dropped it to disparage him."

Delancey sounded exhausting to deal with. She wondered how long McIntyre tolerated his presence. "Did you uncover what happened between the two?"

"It was impossible, love. Mr Delancey was still half-pretending he was the championed protégé of his former master, and that he had his full support. Wouldn't admit to a rift. That said..." McGovern chuckled. "I would bet a hundred guineas the enmity, however it formed, is mutual."

It was too much to hope Delancey would spill the nature of his disagreement with his former master. He was foolish but not stupid, and McGovern wasn't able to furnish much insight into what caused the souring.

There wasn't much else McGovern could provide, and he disappeared into Black's study to discuss the professor's latest laboratory requirements. She could hear his booming laugh from behind closed doors.

Elizabeth sat leafing through last year's almanack until Black escorted his friend to the door, returning with a tired expression.

"You really have no acquaintance with Mr Adam?" Elizabeth asked, probably not for the last time.

"I'm afraid not, Mrs Fulhame." Black looked pained. "Any letter of mine going to him would come across as an unsolicited attempt at gossip. Perhaps Archibald can write under the pretence of seeking a reference."

If the architect was still in London, it could take weeks for them to receive a reply. Nor was Mr Adam likely to spell out the whole truth about his quarrel with an apprentice.

"We can ask around to locate people better acquainted with Mr Adam," Black added. "They might have more information. Although if Mr Delancey feels he's free to seek business in Edinburgh, it suggests negative rumours concerning his reputation have not taken root here."

Once the chemistry professor departed to take care of his personal affairs, Elizabeth intended to lock herself in his guest bedchamber, shove a pillow in her mouth and scream. On the surface it appeared they were making progress, but none of the new pieces of insight fit together, or brought them closer to answering why Mrs Grenville was killed, and what the survivors of that party were planning.

"We might not need to know more than this," Black said, recognising her mounting frustration. "Perhaps Kitty threatened to expose the rift between Delancey and Robert Adam, so he silenced her?"

"Because he feared the loss of his patronage?" Being someone who never had that kind of income to lose, Elizabeth couldn't understand murdering someone over that. But Delancey seemed a fragile individual under his projection of success, over-compensating and making an annoyance of himself. "Can a man be that insecure, that fear of character defamations made public is enough to drive him to rash violence?"

24

Cullen insisted on bringing Elizabeth along for this part of the investigation.

"I know the Lord Provost," he explained. "We're well acquainted."

"Indeed," Black retorted. "Such is the state of your acquaintance, the Lord Provost Sir Hunter Blair is known to fake headaches and family crises to get out of a room containing you."

This wasn't a helpful development.

"Since you have to report to the Board of Trades in half an hour, Joe," Cullen sounded equally sarcastic. "It makes sense for me to take care of this. I know how to wrangle the truth out of the man."

Elizabeth didn't doubt Cullen's skill...provided the Lord Provost didn't flee upon sight of him.

This was unfortunately where she suspected her presence came into play.

"This will be a charm offensive," Elizabeth commented. "Like Dr Franklin sent to negotiate in France, who promptly had the women at Versailles all showing him their beaver pelts."

"I've met Dr Franklin, actually," Cullen said, pretending she hadn't said the last part. "When he visited Edinburgh two-score years ago. Very erudite gentleman."

"Is that how you learned electricity was an aetherial component?" Elizabeth asked.

Cullen rewarded her with a tiny nod. "Indeed, madam. That was something we discussed. It's more accurate—and expedient—to think of *everything* as an aetherial component of some flavour. Light, energy, heat, force, electricity."

She'd heard his aether theory before, and wasn't in the mood for a lecture. Elizabeth tugged the list of names from her purse and eyed it as they walked. Cullen's handwriting was now smudged by carrying it about for several days, and the edges of the paper torn.

"We're dealing with falsehoods upon falsehoods," she said. "None of Mr Godfrey's guests claimed at first to be acquainted with Mrs Grenville before the night she was murdered, but we found out several were lying. Clarence Young, for starters."

"We might have to trace Kitty's routine from the week before she died," Cullen said. "Though in our initial enquiries, it seemed she kept to herself and rarely ventured from her cousin's house."

"However, that is a different proposition from *never* venturing outside." Elizabeth pointed out. "And she was writing plenty of letters, we suspect."

Cullen nodded. "Aside from visiting the church on Sunday and an occasional stroll, it seems she did nothing of note. But people aren't telling us the full story."

As if this whole situation wasn't alarmingly complicated before being dragged into a rendezvous with a man who'd do anything in his power to avoid William Cullen.

"Let me guess," Elizabeth sighed. "Your plan, Dr Cullen, involves springing a multi-facet trap for the Lord Provost: pretending a local inn is his friend's country manor and the innkeeper is his friend pretending to be an innkeeper, or something equally convoluted."

"Such machinations did cross my mind," Cullen admitted. "However, I recalled the Lord Provost's mistress is reputed to be Miss Evelyn Binns, the famous *blonde* soprano." He glanced meaningfully at Elizabeth's hair. "So I posited, if you'll excuse me, madam, that the trap would be a simple case of us presenting a windmill, and letting our adventurer tilt at it."

"Expedient and economical," muttered Elizabeth, begrudgingly untying her bonnet and tugging free hair pins.

Through the semi-helpful reflections of Cullen, Elizabeth decided the *Dulcinea* in question probably attracted the Lord Provost's attention through blonde hair and a helpless tone, which she assumed was affected.

Thus, when she entered the second floor shop, with Cullen loitering out of view in the turnpike, she adopted a breathless air approaching the solitary shopkeeper.

"If you wouldn't mind helping me select a wine for our dinner tonight, I would be so grateful," she entreated him, wide-eyed. "I get so overcome when faced with all these options and end up choosing something silly."

"That's quite understandable, madam," the shopkeeper said. From Elizabeth's childhood experience selling cloth, the shopkeeper would be assessing what level of overpricing he could get away with. "Our Flemish wines are quite popular at this time of year. What dishes are you serving tonight?"

"Seabass and parsley," Elizabeth replied, letting him guide her to a row of bottles near the back of the shop.

They'd watched the Lord Provost enter his shop a few minutes ago, and he was presumably conducting account-work in the back room.

It grated to play a giggling fool, and she was sure her performance was too exaggerated to be believed. However, a certain class of men couldn't tell the difference between real and fake flirtatiousness, and believed the patently fake kind was sincerer. The Lord Provost would certainly hear her in the back.

That said, he was probably busy. Or his lecherousness was overstated. Because there was only so long Elizabeth could drag out the transaction before the shopkeeper, Wilfred, tired of the interaction.

Was there a better way to lure their target out?

"Mmmm, this wine reminds me of the claret my physician prescribed," Elizabeth said, tapping the bottle with her nail. A muted ringing noise filled the shop. She smiled at the shopkeeper. "Back when I was suffering low mood and anxious spirits..."

She heard a floorboard creak.

"Its effect was quite rejuvenating," she continued, raising her voice. "Though I think my physician would recommend I return to a regular half-pint, as I often return to such moods in the winter months..."

"Good day, madam. You are finding a wine to your satisfaction?" In the backroom doorway, clad in a velvet blue coat with a fashionable high collar, was the Lord Provost himself.

"Very well, your lord. Mr Wilfred has been most kind." Elizabeth smiled sweetly. Unfortunately, some men were drawn to women of a fragile disposition, and talking about their ailments incited their curiosity.

It was at that moment Cullen made his entrance, while the Lord Provost's attention was on her, giving him no time to spot the threat.

"Good day to you, sir!"

The Lord Provost fixed Cullen with a look implying the quantity of goodness in his day had decreased rapidly by the sight of a beaming Dr William Cullen striding into his shop.

"I'm so glad we caught you..." Cullen smacked the blueprint on the table between two wine bottles and took a step sideways, getting between the Lord Provost and the door to the back room. "The following confidential architectural blueprint came into our possession, and we wanted to alert you to its migration through Edinburgh."

"Fortuitous, indeed..." The Lord Provost suddenly appeared five or more hours short on sleep, but couldn't help lean forwards to look at the sketches. It was likely his office and the Town Council dealt with a lot of sensitive architectural plans that he wouldn't want exposed to the public. "Hmmm..."

"It appears to be a copy of Robert Adam's 1785 South Bridge proposal, do you recall it? It's quite alarming that this is circulating amongst some unsavoury characters. You're lucky we intercepted it."

"I doubt that's what it is," said the Provost, stepping back and straightening his lapels.

"But you can see..." Elizabeth began, pointing to the recognisable features.

"What I mean, madam, I beg your pardon..." Unlike most of the other men she'd dealt with him pursuit of this folly, the Lord Provost fixed all his attention on her, as the alternative was dealing with William Cullen. "Is that firstly this plan is far more detailed and expansive than anything Mr Adam showed us two years ago. The blueprints he furnished us with were half the size of these, and much rougher in their composition, because they were meant only as a starting point in the discussion."

"You remember their likeness?" If he did, that would make his memory unusually sharp.

"One could not forget the extraordinary meetings that took place in the city chambers. In all my years of city politics, madam, I don't think I've seen the like." The Lord Provost tapped the leftmost end of the bridge structure. "We spent four hours with Mr Adam arguing over his placement of the north-most arch, because its inclusion would warrant the complete demolition of the Tron Kirk; with him insisting it was integral to the *aesthetics* of the piece."

"With the agreed-upon plan, you only had to tear down the east wing to accommodate the end of South Bridge."

"Quite so." Any Edinburgh citizen with functioning eyes or ears would have noticed the Tron Kirk losing a wing, but Lord Provost's tone implied Elizabeth made a clever observation. She ignored the patronising edge of his remarks. "This drawing seems to have repositioned the final bridge arches to avoid cutting into the foundations of the Tron Kirk. How curious."

"So this here is a more recent rendering?" Cullen asked. "Updated to reflect Town Council pushback against flaws in the original?"

Though he claimed otherwise, the Lord Provost's flat tone showed little curiosity in this irksome interruption.

"Given how unequivocal a rejection the Town Council rendered, I consider that unlikely. Mr Adam is a proud man—a genius, but not without the prickly ego such men are wont to carry—but even he knew not to push the matter." The Lord Provost set his purse on the table and pushed the wine bottles out of his way. "Let me tell you: Mr Adam's call to demolish the Tron Kirk in its entirety was the *least* contentious part of his proposal. Also, the least objectionable."

"What issue did the august councillors have with his

design? I think it looks very pretty." If Elizabeth had an opinion, it was that the design they were arguing over looked gauche and hideous, but she sensed the Lord Provost was expecting feminine stupidity from her, and she needed to understand what actually happened in this architectural spat.

"You have a discerning eye, madam," the Lord Provost said, with no feeling whatsoever. "But Mr Adam's proposal was projected to cost upwards of ten times what we paid for the current South Bridge construction. His footprint was more than double the other proposals, and would cost a country's ransom to tear down all the Cowgate dwellings, not to mention destroying the Kirk."

"Oh."

"I'm sorry to disappoint you, madam. Had we an infinite budget, Mr Adam's South Bridge would have been an architectural marvel. Edinburgh would have surpassed London as the architectural light of Britain, possibly Europe. But we couldn't justify the cost."

"So why would a second, amended version of Mr Adam's rejected blueprint be floating around under high secrecy?" Cullen sounded impatient, perhaps because he was being ignored, or perhaps because he found Elizabeth's theatrics ridiculous.

The Lord Provost shrugged. He nudged the paper back to Cullen and cleared his throat in a clear signal of dismissal.

"There are plenty of benign reasons, even with the moribund state of the project. Mr Adam may be indulged himself in harmless fancy revisiting the idea. Or perhaps someone copied it as an exercise in draftsmanship. It really isn't a concern of mine."

They'd taken all of two steps onto the West Bow when Cullen's hand gripped her forearm.

He was thinking the same as her.

"It's Delancey's blueprint!"

Behind them, a woman Cullen's age swore. "Dinnae jist stop in the middle of the feckin' street! Lord save me..."

Cullen gave her a dirty look as she hobbled around them.

"He finds, or is given, Robert Adam's old South Bridge design while he's still on speaking terms with his master, then takes a copy up to Edinburgh..."

"Where he circulates it."

She'd initially believed Delancey's stated profession a convenient fabrication, to conceal his true purpose in Edinburgh. But architecture was his calling, after all.

"It's a strange crowd he circulates it amongst, is it not?"

If the Lord Provost was to be believed, no one of the Town Councillor sect was even aware of the design's re-emergence.

"Not when you think about it," Cullen said, thoughtful. "He has the Nicholson's bastard child doing business on behalf of the family, a well-connected freemason, and the Westons, who are active in the association of Cowgate merchants."

"Wouldn't the Westons be opposed to a larger South Bridge?" Elizabeth asked. "The Cowgate merchants have complained nonstop about the effect the construction has had on their businesses."

"Well, see..." Cullen steered Elizabeth by the elbow into his local tavern, a few doors down the street. At the first free table, he pulled the blueprint back out of his pocket. "My usual John, thanks. Now...Weston's association raised an ungodly fuss about the loss of hardworking proprietor's livelihoods, damage to businesses city-wide, et cetera, and eventually the Council caved and agreed to construct a second street off Infirmary Street, getting better access to the Cowgate from the High Street and College sides. But this plan..."

"...Calls for a wider promenade, with shopfronts built into the colonnades."

The tavern keeper set a glass of claret next to Cullen's elbow. He frowned, then moved into onto the blueprint, to guard against breezes for the doorway.

"Yes, I could see this proposal damaging a lot *more* Cowgate businesses, but you could imagine, shall we say, 'early adopters' finding their support of the scheme advantageous."

If Marion Weston played her cards right, her grocer's shop could enjoy pride of place in one of the most fashionable, elegant new builds in Britain. And there was enough space to house the businesses of most of her friends.

"Is this really what this is all about?" Elizabeth wondered. "It seems odd that Mrs Grenville would involve herself in this venture. It doesn't appear to align with her strongly held values."

Why would Kitty care about civic projects? She viewed the Town Council and the ilk who surrounded them as a blight upon Christendom. The knowledge of her impending mortality could motivate a soul to any number of last acts. So why focus on this one?

"Nor is it clear why the parties are choosing to act now, nearly three years after Mr Adam's plans were first rejected." It seemed presumptuous of Delancey that he would attempt to convince the Town Council to take up a proposal the great Robert Adam himself failed to secure backing for. Here was a young fop possessing a fraction of his master's talent and none of his reputation. Including Berry, Weston and Young made sense—Delancey was securing buy-in from the influential of Edinburgh—she couldn't see what role Kitty or Silas Lowell played in this venture.

Fortunately, Cullen didn't seem to know either.

"Why would they care about a new bridge design when

the current one is nearly complete? Are they trying to argue for a second phase of construction?"

"Given the time and money wasted so far on the first phase, I'd be surprised if anyone has the stomach for late amendments," Cullen agreed.

"But you agree that something nefarious is afoot?"

Kitty Grenville was dead. That was a lot of blood to spill over an outdated architectural design.

"I'd suggest returning to the bowling green, madam," he said. As he put his claret glass down, a drop flicked onto the blueprint. A small red circle blossomed under the bridge arch. "This Lowell fellow seems like an unsavoury character, and I suspect his inclusion in the plan heralds bad tidings."

25

The Town Guard was changing shifts around now, which meant Corporal Daniels might return to his cousin Maybelle. That meant watching the guardhouse from a safe distance.

Given what happened, Elizabeth didn't want Thomas completing his vigil alone, even on a busy street. She was quickly regretting they'd pursued this venture at all.

"Sweetheart, we need to leave."

Thomas frowned, cutting short his instinct to remove her grasping hand. "But he's just..."

"People are recognising us." She hissed the words out proculopathically, hoping her oblivious husband won't make the situation worse by looking uneasy.

What she first thought were Town Guards dealing with complaining citizens was in fact a clump of on-duty and off-duty guardsman loitering in a patch of warm sunlight. The expression of their collective face when they glanced her way was confused recognition—they had not yet decided she was the escaped Irish prisoner, but that felt like only a matter of time.

"We're losing Daniels. Once we're round the corner, they won't bother following us."

"I'm not..." Was she paranoid in thinking the men were now conferring, glancing her way as they did so?

"If they stop us, we'll deny everything. Put on a Midlands accent." Thomas tore away from the receding figure ahead. "Sweetheart, they can't *prove* anything about us."

"I don't like this," Elizabeth repeated. Thomas wasn't the target of their attention; they probably didn't even recall his presence at Godfrey's.

A man in uniform broke away from the gathering at a brisk pace in their direction. He could just be heading back to the Guardhouse...

"Fine." Thomas heard her silent plea. "Let's go this way instead." At the last second he swerved them into a wynd. This one took them to the Cowgate, where they could either head up and towards the college, or try to vanish into the Grassmarket crowds.

The Fulhames trotted along in silence, moving as hastily as they could over puddles and clotted refuse without appearing to flee.

"I don't think anyone's following," Elizabeth whispered. Thomas merely grunted.

As they emerged onto the Cowgate, Elizabeth stole a glance back and didn't see any flashes of red.

Her husband continued to the Lawnmarket. Once they were safely navigating the market stalls, Thomas drew to a stop near the herring seller, on the basis that no one wanted to linger nearby.

"I'm sorry," Elizabeth said. "Perhaps I overreacted."

Thomas shook his head, his curls bouncing. "They were looking at us awfully queer, love. I just wanted to catch Daniels. We can head up West Bow and see if we can spot him again."

"I should probably head back to Dr Blacks," Elizabeth said, hanging her head. "They're less likely to recognise you than me."

Thomas studied her, trying to decide if his wife had thrown him a trick question. "I suspect I'll be out of luck, at least for today."

"Well, give it half an hour. We can meet at George's tomorrow to discuss what's next."

Her husband slipped off, leaving her to trudge up College Wynd, tugging her bonnet down.

She hated feeling like an enemy in Edinburgh, to be driven out when caught. She hated looking over her shoulder in a city she felt more at home in than Navan. Part of her was furious at Thomas and blamed him, even as she recognised there wasn't much he could have done to protect her.

She refused to stay cooped up indoors, though. Maybe sticking with Black and Cullen could keep her safe, since even the most belligerent Town Guard would hesitate to accost the august physicians.

Black's manservant let her in with a courteous nod. She realised—with an odd pang—that his manner would be a lot warmer if she were Black's actual niece.

It didn't matter that Black would never claim her presence an intrusion. She herself felt that way, and couldn't shake it. Right now he was probably calling on Hutton.

"I wish the bastard who killed Mrs Grenville would make themselves known," she muttered, closing her bedroom door. "I want my Edinburgh back."

* * *

It was with a heavy heart Elizabeth knocked on Morag's door. That her friend opened the door and regarded her with a beaming smile, baby balanced on hip, made her feel even more guilty about the purpose of this visit.

"Ah, Beth! Come on, let's get ye in before you let out all the heat. Can ye manage a cup of tea?"

"I drank a pot before I came over," Elizabeth lied.

The single room Morag's family occupied in the attic caught most of the warm air from the floors below. Thick curtains, rugs and sheets were all pressed into service, covering cracks in the walls. Morag's young sons lay sprawled in front of the hearth, manoeuvring toy soldiers along the uneven floorboards.

"Duddingston Loch wisnae too crowded yesterday?" Morag asked.

This was probably an indirect way of asking why Elizabeth hadn't returned her borrowed skates yet.

"Ah, I snapped on the bindings on your left skate, Morag." Elizabeth tackled the unanswered question first. "That was my fault—Thomas is picking up a replacement this afternoon."

Morag grunted. It was hard for Elizabeth to convey this information without giving offence, implying it was Morag's fault for not taking better care of her skates. The promise she wouldn't bear the cost of replacements seemed mollification enough.

"I had to ask..." Elizabeth wished she'd accepted the tea now because it might have put Morag in a less defensive mood. "Did you tell anyone Thomas and I were going to skate at the loch?"

"Naw. It wisnae like there was a queue of folk asking tae borrow my skates," Morag replied ruefully.

She decided not to push further. At least, not yet. Morag's bairn—named Stewart, after his father—had finally fallen asleep thanks to his mother's jiggling. The look on Morag's face told her this sleep was a long time coming. Better to steer the conversation into calmer waters for now, then revisit when Morag was no longer on edge.

The Fulhames had known Morag's family for years. They lived close to each other in High School Yards when Thomas was a student. The thought of her close friend betraying her was painful, even if accidental.

"Ye sure ye'd no' like tea?" Morag asked after an uncomfortable pause. "Ye seem a bit flighty this morning, Beth."

"If it's not an inconvenience..." Elizabeth offered the ritualistic second refusal.

"Of course it's no'. The pot is still fresh." Morag rose from the sagging rocking chair. "Get oot from under my feet, boys."

Her sons giggled and rolled away.

"The ice skating was a little disappointing, I'm afraid. A few things happened that spoiled the day."

"Aye, I heard there was a stramash on the loch yesterday. Didnae ken if ye saw it." Morag brandished a cracked teacup, thick curls of steam wobbling above it.

"It was quite scary." Elizabeth admitted.

"Ye dinnae think they louts were after ye, Beth?" Morag laughed. "That cannae be why ye were asking who kenned ye'd be there?"

"No, of course not," Elizabeth replied quickly. She thought for a more plausible excuse. "Some of my friends have been dealing with the mystery of a woman slain in cold blood, and Thomas is getting pestered about it."

Morag nodded forcefully enough for wee Stewart to whimper in his sleep. It didn't matter that Elizabeth's answer made no sense whatsoever: Morag had the helpful habit of stating her assumptions outright, so Elizabeth didn't need to explain the link as much as confirm whatever sweeping assumption came out of her friend's mouth.

"Ah, they were pestering yer man about it at the loch?"

When Elizabeth mumbled a vague affirmation, Morag leaned back with satisfaction.

"That's no' Kitty Grenville yer talking about? God rest her soul."

"It is, as it happens." Elizabeth could tell from the way Morag's tired eyes lit up that her friend hoped this was the case. "How did you hear about her?"

She asked out of partial curiosity about the state of rumours surrounding 'the Irish woman,' and also because she never felt comfortable calling Dr Black her friend in front of Morag. Morag and her husband couldn't boast of 'physician friends.' The sophisticated physician-philosophers at the university were a universe away from Morag's world.

"My water caddie told me the other day. She kens my interest in auld Kitty—we've talked about her before." Morag spoke matter-of-factly, as if this was something Elizabeth was already aware of.

For a moment, Elizabeth was too stunned to speak. Not at the water caddie part: Morag was the type to hold up her water caddie with gossip until the contents of the caddie's water barrel evaporated. But rather...

"Is that true? You knew Kitty before she married Malcolm Holm?"

"Aye," Morag nodded. "Lived in the same lands—no' quite the same floor, though."

That was not a revelation. Morag's family was probably crammed in either the cellars or the attic with other lowly servants. Kitty was unlikely to have dwelled on the prime middle floors, but probably was only a floor above or below.

"You wouldn't be well-acquainted, then?"

Morag shook her head. "Well, we played a lot as weans. Racing up and down the turnpikes, what have ye. Her mother was a widow, worked as a dressmaker until she remarried.

She'd no' keep her girls out of mischief making enough to feed them."

"Was she particularly pious?"

Morag laughed. "That's the funniest thing! Naw, she wisnae. Had tae be dragged into kirk by the ear most weeks."

Elizabeth thought for a moment. There were scores of girls she played with as a child whose names she'd lost over the years. They'd vanished into the recesses of memory. This process was more involved when you factored in the trajectories of different social classes. It was interesting Morag remembered Kitty Holm.

When she said this aloud, Morag smiled sadly.

"She wis always a shy, strange one. Very melancholic, even aged seven. I remember being confused—because even at that age I pitied her, then got confused because shouldn't it be the other way around? Her father—God rest his soul—left enough for his widow to survive on until she remarried, and they never struggled, that I saw. Poor girl. She missed her father, and I dinnae think her new father wis a kind man."

This was odd to hear, because from what she'd heard, Kitty Grenville was a woman of unwavering conviction, gliding along on faith with her place in the world.

Morag continued, seeing Elizabeth's curiosity growing. "We were a few floors apart, but I swear I heard her crying to sleep some nights. Said nobody loved her, wis frightened of new people."

"Did you...keep in touch with Kitty?"

Another laugh. "Call it no more than idle curiosity. No' like she wasted a moment's thought on me—I wis the one minding her goings-on. Got the shock of ma life to hear someone was courting her—I assumed she'd die an old maid. It pains me to say it, but I thought she *wanted* to die an old maid."

"How did they meet?" Elizabeth asked.

"No' in Edinburgh. She travelled to Paris one summer with an uncle—word came back she'd married someone she met there and was staying."

"When she returned to Edinburgh a few years ago, did you see her?"

"Hard to miss. Didnae give it much thought at the time. I'd no' thought about her in years by then. She seemed so hoity-toity walking down the High Street, I barely recognised her. My man had to point her out. 'That's Kitty MacBride just walked past.' Fright of my life when he said that."

"Malcolm Holm must have changed her a lot," Elizabeth said.

"Naw, I suspect she wis still the same girl underneath. She used to hide behind her books. Now, she's hiding behind a Bible." Morag hesitated, then shook her head. "God rest her soul. Maybe the woman she became deserved what happened to her...but no' the wee lass I once kenned."

"So you saw her when she was staying with her sister in the Lawnmarket a few years ago." Elizabeth took a sip of tea. "How did you learn of her latest reappearance?"

"Think I spotted her coming out the Tron Kirk with her cousin last Sunday. I ken the man vaguely—but no' enough to wave and start a conversation in the street." Morag glanced in the direction of her sons to make sure they remained out of mischief. "At the time I couldnae be sure it wis Kitty with him —scarce recognised her, truth be told. Next thing I hear, she's dead."

Elizabeth didn't want to dive into the specifics of what Kitty Grenville had done, and to whom. Maybe Morag would mulishly defend her, even after learning of her crimes. Maybe she and the professors were too harsh on Kitty: a woman whose insecurities were exploited by Holm, and who covered her flaws with many layers of Bible-thin paper.

She didn't need to forgive or pity the woman who was once Kitty Macbride. But she needed to understand her, to understand why she died.

26

Peering out the parlour window, Elizabeth watched a woman dallying on the other side of Nicholson Street. Even in the foggy weather, guilt poured off this woman in the way she carried herself.

She looked familiar...

Five minutes later, Elizabeth was stomping into the haar and tugging a shawl over her gown.

"You'll catch your death out here, Mrs Berry. Please come inside."

The woman gulped, looking for a minute like she would prefer to bolt. Then she nodded and followed Elizabeth back into the house.

"Is your business with me?" Elizabeth asked, trying not to sound accusative as she guided the woman into the parlour.

Again, hesitation followed by guarded affirmation. Berry stole a longing glance towards the hearth, which had been stoked a few minutes ago.

"I saw ye on Princes Street a few days ago and recognised ye from Mr Godfrey's party." Berry had a high-pitched voice, which sounded like it belonged to someone twenty years younger. "Ye were with Dr Black."

Elizabeth recalled the person following them from the Assembly Rooms. She thought it was a man, but maybe it was Berry all along.

It occurred to Elizabeth she'd never seen a situation where the metaphor 'wringing their hands' applied. But Mrs Berry was doing exactly that: twisting her palms through each other, squeezing her fists, as if attempting to remove every drop of sweat from them.

"Can I get you a cup of tea, Susan?"

Despite the gentle tone, Mrs Berry flinched at her name as if she'd been struck.

"I dinnae want tae bother ye," she mumbled.

"Not at all. I was about to prepare a cup for myself," Elizabeth lied.

She'd yet to find a single chip or hairline crack in any of Black's chinaware, and Elizabeth was resigned to Susan Berry breaking one of his cups through shaky, slippery hands. But after Elizabeth set the cup on the table, her guest promptly forgot it was there.

"That's a handsome lace fichu you're wearing," Elizabeth said, trying to nudge her guest into conversation.

"Mmm...it was a gift. Yer very kind tae say that."

Elizabeth took a sip of tea, trying to observe Berry without staring.

"My husband...disnae ken I'm calling upon ye," Susan Berry eventually stammered.

Elizabeth had already concluded that, but she nodded as if her jumpy visitor had confided a great truth.

"Whatever you wish, we'll do what we can to assist you."

Her husband would sarcastically interrupt via proculopathy and claim a lunatic asylum was what this poor wretch needed, if he were here. Her conjured voice of her husband was almost as loud as the real thing, but she felt more comfortable ignoring it.

"I ken ye wondering wha' happened tae Kitty. But ye must swear…"

"You have my word that if I'm asked, I did not hear this from you." Elizabeth wished Mrs Berry would take some of the tea, not only because of the effort she took to brew it, but because the woman's mouth sounded bone dry. It dried Elizabeth's tongue just listening to it.

"Jeremiah's been working with a Town Councillor, they've been meeting in taverns after the Masonic gatherings. He comes home after midnight smelling of tobacco, whisky and the midden heaps. Has been for months now."

"So you suspect this Town Councillor wanted Kitty dead?"

"She was disrupting his plans," Susan continued, practically whimpering with relief when Elizabeth stated this out loud. "Asking too many questions, Jeremiah says. The Town Councillor was getting worried she'd tattle."

"What were their plans?" Elizabeth stopped herself a second before she mentioned the blueprints. It wouldn't do to admit how much she already knew.

Susan paused, gulping like a fish. "I dinnae ken," she said after a moment. "Jeremiah didnae want me mixed up in it."

"And the other dinner guests? At Mr Godfrey's? Were they all involved in the conspiracy?"

"Some, mebbe." It was hard to imagine Mrs Berry asking anyone a direct question. She looked like a woman with a knack for keeping herself out of awkward situations, fearful of conflict. She'd not made eye contact with Elizabeth once since she'd come inside. "The Town Councillor was pulling strings."

"Do you know who this Town Councillor is?" Elizabeth asked. The conversation made her uneasy. It was partially that Mrs Berry's nervous energy could displace anyone within her vicinity from calm, but also a deeper undertow tugged at her conscience. Something wasn't right here.

Susan Berry nodded. "Lord Kildare."

Elizabeth swore inside the confines of her head. For once, couldn't they be gifted with a revelation that made the situation *easier* to navigate?

"Tell me, Susan…" Elizabeth spoke gently, as one might coax a spooked horse forward. "Do you know who murdered Kitty that night? Did you see anyone leave Mr Godfrey's dining room between our arrival and when Kitty's body was found?"

Berry squeezed her hands tighter.

"I dinnae recall. My husband never left my side."

"You were conversing with him the whole time? Even after Dr Black and myself brought the unconscious manservant inside?" Elizabeth asked, feeling a flash of annoyance. She was sure Mrs Berry's confession was leading up to the revelation that her husband committed the deed on behalf of his shadowy patron. But Berry was stumbling through her account in full defence of Jeremiah.

"My husband wouldnae let me be alone with Mr Lowell," she explained apologetically. "The man wasne a friend of the fairer sex."

"I see what you mean." Elizabeth didn't need *that* spelled out. Her own instincts told her the same. "He didn't just target unmarried girls?"

Berry shook her head. "He always stood a little too close, held your hand a little too long. He knew better than to try his luck with Mrs Weston—she'd have knocked him out cold— but he seemed interested in the late Mrs Grenville."

"Yes, I suspect her widowhood was an obvious attraction. Is Mr Lowell a bachelor?"

"His wife passed away several years ago, I believe." Emboldened by Elizabeth's agreement, she leaned closer. "Mrs Grenville had *snug prospects*, he said. Was sure he could charm her."

Could it be as simple as that? Silas Lowell took advantage of the confusion to sneak upstairs and speak to Kitty: either to suggest marriage or make a sexual advance upon her? Spurning a man could be enough to make him grab a knife. Would a man that monstrous feel even a sliver of guilt after the fact? He'd claim it was the woman's fault for provoking him.

She shuddered.

"Did Mr Lowell speak of his intentions towards Kitty to others? Did she know he wished to marry her?"

Come to think of it, where would Kitty's 'snug prospects' come from? Was that a reference to an inheritance left to her by Professor Grenville, or connected to her actions in Edinburgh?

"The impression I got was that Mr Young also kenned something of the matter," Berry said. "I recall the two standing together when Mr Lowell confessed his plan, and he didnae look surprised at the news."

More confounding complications. Some suspects knew Kitty had come into money, but the way Berry described it, the inheritance was news to her.

She took a calming breath. "Is it your belief, Mrs Berry, that someone in Lord Kildare's employ carried out the murder of Kitty Grenville?"

Berry hesitated, staring at the fire as if transfixed.

Elizabeth knew she was heaping distress upon an already fragile woman, but she doubted she'd have a second opportunity to question her. "Do you believe another guest of Mr Godfrey's committed the murder?"

"Many of them kenned Lord Kildare," Berry mumbled. "I dinnae ken who else my man was meeting with those times."

* * *

"Mrs Berry called upon me less than an hour ago," Elizabeth said. "In a state of apparent distress."

She was getting good at communicating in the language of academics, because Black and Cullen, still fussing over the removal of their coats, instantly looked suspicious.

"You believe her distress was affected, madam?"

"I'm not sure. Quite frankly, the woman is naturally of a nervous disposition, and I'm sure much of her nerves were unfeigned. It is the underlying cause of her distress I'm uncertain of."

She filled the professors in on the implication of Lord Kildare in the conspiracy.

"...All of which she told me in strictest confidence," she added, in as straight a tone as she could.

"We will be careful how we disseminate this information, then," Cullen said, setting himself by Black's hearth. He then coughed. It was the kind of cough older men usually relied upon to dislodge phlegm from their gullet, but the ferocity of Cullen's repeated hacks made it seem he was achieving little more than rotating the placement of phlegm around his airways.

"Does Kildare's involvement seem plausible?" Elizabeth asked once the coughing abated.

"He was around Edinburgh at the time of Hutton's kidnapping," Black said, hand on chin. "And I don't recall him *not* being involved in the South Bridge development meetings, if that makes sense."

"It would be odd if he recused himself. Kildare's been on the Town Council since when, Joe? 1780?"

Every Town Councillor worth their salt would have wanted their fingerprints on the South Bridge development.

"Would he have a motive for getting involved with such a dark plan?" Elizabeth asked. Directly or indirectly, it had led to murder.

"I wouldn't call him a particularly...conscientious man," Black said slowly. "His family avoided active collusion with the dark chymists, but a lot of merchants in Edinburgh have sworn off working with him a second time."

Hmm, so that suggested a lack of scruples or consideration for business partners. The trouble was, Elizabeth had to separate her disdain for obnoxious men like Kildare and the likelihood of them orchestrating murder.

"I don't know if I fully trust Mrs Berry's word," Elizabeth said. Nothing about the woman struck her as reliable. If she'd been a bird, she'd have spent all her time in Black's parlour crashing into the windows. Ad infinitum.

"Well..." Cullen scraped to his feet. "We can question the lordship on your behalf."

"Would it not make more sense for Thomas and I to come with you?" The words were out before Elizabeth had a chance to couch herself.

"To guard the perimeter and such?"

Elizabeth started to speak, took a breath, then tried again. "Lord Kildare has a few female relations and companions, does he not? Perhaps I can be better-placed to speak with them and see what they know?"

A spark of annoyance fluttered in her stomach. Berry's information was her prize, and she didn't want to hand it over whole-cloth to the professors. Especially if it led to the culprit.

Cullen sighed.

Women had a reputation for guilting their husbands and deploying emotional wiles to get their way, but Cullen's sigh was the classic reverse gambit: a weary sigh from a put-upon husband or father, designed to indicate the woman he was speaking to caused him great inconvenience, that he was nonetheless honour-bound to comply with. It wasn't a sigh designed to stop this specific round of argument; rather, he deployed it now to raise guilt in the offending party for the next time.

"If it pleases you, madam."

27

If there was any confusion in Elizabeth's mind about the identity of Lord Kildare, the person-sized portrait in his entrance foyer, depicting a heavy-set man in full military colours brandishing a flintlock, cleared that up.

"His lordship is occupied with business, but if you would be so kind as to wait in the dining room?" His valet greeted the three with impeccable courtesy, as if three uninvited guests on a busy day were no hassle at all.

"Yes, much obliged," Cullen said. "We wish to cause as minimal a disturbance as possible."

The lushly dark dining-room, with thick red velvet curtains and lacquered chinoiserie, was arranged to seat twelve. A door at the other side of the room probably connected to the master bedroom or parlour, because Elizabeth could hear male voices conferring softly behind it.

"It's a shame Dr Fulhame couldn't join us," Cullen noted, seating himself at the head of the table.

"I agree," Elizabeth said. "He told me he spotted Corporal Daniels enter one of the lands at the far end of Grassmarket and wanted to head back this afternoon to look for Maybelle."

Black frowned. "He hasn't much luck finding her. I take it there have been no rumours as to her whereabouts?"

"Thomas said he asked five different people and received ten different stories." Elizabeth shook her head. "The corporal is keeping her well out of sight."

"Good for him, I suppose..." Cullen began.

But at that point the connecting door was opened, and in strode Lord Kildare, looking for all the world as if this unsolicited interruption was of equal importance to everything else in his diary.

"Drs Black and Cullen! A pleasure, gentlemen. And this?"

"My niece, Isabel Burnett," Black said, shaking Kildare's hand. "I can only apologise for our abrupt entrance."

"Not at all." Kildare perched on the table, his ample behind nudged aside a silver bread plate. "I told my companions I would return to them in a few minutes, but I wished to learn of your business briefly."

"I'm sorry to interrupt your friends, your lordship..."

"Think nothing of it!" Kildare laughed easily. "We were getting distracted—I started telling them about several rare duets in D minor I'd received last week. Composed by Joseph Haydn, no less. Lovely pieces...but nothing to do with herring exports, which is what we were supposed to be discussing!"

"We learned of a concerning plot involving members of the Canongate Lodge and wished to bring it to your attention." Black spoke quickly, mirroring Kildare in his casually clasped hands.

Kildare nodded gravely. "I see."

Elizabeth couldn't tell if he was concerned or annoyed at this development.

"While we believe our source is sincere, your lordship," Cullen added. "We hoped to bring the matter to your attention first, rather than risk the situation spiralling out of control."

"Yes, you are right to approach me." Kildare slid off the table. "I will wrap up my business as promptly as possible, and be back within a quarter hour. Make yourself at home, gentlemen and madam."

With that, he returned to the study, closing the door with a muted click. The low patter of voices resumed.

"I worry about the wisdom in warning him about these allegations," Elizabeth admitted, adjusting the bread plate back into its original place. "He now has enough time to devise excuses while we wait here."

"*Conceiving* excuses, yes, madam." Cullen rose to his feet. "But he's still in the back room, which means he won't have time to hide any incriminating evidence."

"Surely you...?" Elizabeth groaned.

But Black was already on his feet. "Let's make this quick, Elizabeth. Three sets of eyes will get the job done faster."

Kildare's house was one of the largest in the New Town. A long corridor stretched the width of the first floor, styled with rococo moulding and oversized Grecian vases.

The first doors on either side of the corridor led to bedchambers, which both professors dismissed.

"Not his lordship's, and not where he'd keep secret papers," grumbled Cullen.

"But surely the least obvious locations would be the most sensible place to hide valuables..."

"Not if he wanted to consult them, madam." Cullen was already moving towards the next door on his right.

Sighing, Elizabeth opted for the door on the left. She'd not heard any signs of life up here, and was expecting a servant to demand they explain themselves any minute now. But arguing with the professors would delay the exercise too long, so she may as well cooperate.

It didn't look like Cullen was satisfied with what he saw behind his door, so that left her to check...

"No!" Elizabeth almost fell over in shock. A hand—either Cullen's or Black's—grabbed her shoulder to steady her. "Not again!"

This time the blood was streaked across the floorboards, suggesting the victim had crawled some distance. A wound wasn't immediately obvious, but because they'd curled into a ball, it was likely another stab wound to the stomach.

Unlike Kitty, this victim was still grasping on to life with faint moans and spasms.

Also, unlike the murder of Kitty, both Cullen and Black were now restraining Elizabeth from going any closer.

Oh, heavens.

"It's Young! We have to ask if he..." Elizabeth began.

Out of the corner of her eye, Cullen shook his head. Young's ragged breaths were fading into wisps, and his twitches slowed.

What was he doing here?

This whole tableau was surreal, and she wondered if her mind was playing a cruel trick on her, because its component pieces made no sense when put together.

She took in the scene as best she could, aware the professors were doing the same thing.

The windows were closed. No sign of a violent struggle: all the demure parlour furniture appeared in place. Doors led off on either side to adjoining rooms. Both doors were closed, they'd need to check if they were locked. From the blood trail, Young must have been stabbed while he sat on the largest settee, or just having risen from it. He was crawling towards the door to seek help, no doubt. He might be wearing the same crimson jacket she'd glimpsed him in at Godfrey's.

Which came too late. Or could never have helped.

"What is the meaning of this?" A booming voice caused all three to jump.

The professors moved to block Kildare's line of sight into the room, but they were just a little too late. Besides, blood was spread half across the room.

"Good grief!" Kildare's horror seemed unfeigned, but Elizabeth wasn't going to assume anything. The man might be a talented actor. "Is he...?"

"I suspect so." The body lay still, no longer groaning.

"If you'll permit me?" Cullen took a hesitant step forward.

But Kildare differed from Godfrey. He had military experience behind him, and the sight of a recently deceased body—even of a friend—wasn't enough to rattle him. He crossed his arms. "Why is that woman in here?"

Elizabeth opened her mouth, only for a jab of energy from Cullen's fingertips—the arthritic ones restraining her left side—to cause her to start. He'd not shocked her hard enough to hurt, but as a warning signal, it rang loud and clear.

"She is with us," Cullen said firmly. "We all entered the room at the same time, witnessing this awful tableau barely five seconds before you showed."

Kildare might have just shifted his weight innocently, but it had the effect of moving him a couple of inches to the side, blocking the doorway.

"The woman is Irish, is she not? I heard her speak."

Elizabeth clamped her mouth shut, not wanting a second jab from Cullen, who didn't seem shy about electrocuting her.

"She's my niece Isabel Burnett," Black said, an unmistakable warning in his voice. "Visiting me from Ulster."

Kildare matched Black's tone with a scowl of his own. He wasn't going to utter the words 'escaped murderess', but the silent accusation was clear.

"With your permission, your lordship. I would like to

inspect the body, to properly determine the cause of death," Cullen said before Kildare could argue.

"You'll do no such thing!" Kildare's attention snapped from Elizabeth to Cullen as footfalls in the corridor grew louder. "My personal physician will inspect him."

From his reaction, Kildare evidently knew Young was in his house, though an explanation for why the host left him alone upstairs wasn't forthcoming.

"The longer we hesitate here, the longer the murderer will have to escape and conceal his tracks," Cullen said. He sounded irate. He'd also not let go of Elizabeth's shoulder. "Unless, your lordship, you are aware of something we are not?"

Kildare folded his arms. The footfalls in the corridor fell silent. Whoever had gathered was standing just out of sight.

"It seems you've weaselled your way into my house under false pretences." The threat in his voice was unmistakable. "You presented me with a salacious but flimsy rumour..."

"Do you know a man called Jeremiah Berry?" Elizabeth asked, not bothering to hide her incriminating accent.

"Yes, he sits ten pews behind me in the Tron Kirk, and is a fellow Masonic Brother." Kildare swatted the question away. "The man is an impertinent nuisance. "

"But you conduct business with him?"

Kildare's disinterest couldn't be more apparent. "Our respective roles within the lodge make that tragically unavoidable."

It seemed incriminating by itself that two associates of Lord Kildare—Jeremiah Berry and Clarence Young—were involved in Kitty's plot. But that made their host's rising suspicion and fury ever more terrifying.

Cullen was thinking along the same lines as her.

"A man is dead on your floor, Lord Kildare. You seem almost excited at the prospect of implicating us in his demise."

"That is a scurrilous accusation to make, Dr Cullen. And I find it mighty circumstantial..." Kildare's voice rose, now speaking to a wider audience. "That Drs Black, Cullen, and an Irish woman you claim is your niece are found standing over another dead body, less than a week after the first. One instance might be a tragic coincidence. Two times...is a little less tragic, and a lot less coincidental."

"Are *you* making an accusation, Lord Kildare?" Cullen finally let go of Elizabeth to hobble forwards. "You know who we are."

Kildare snorted. "Your honourable reputations won't protect you, Dr Cullen. Not with the friends I have."

Elizabeth didn't know if the man was bluffing. Both Cullen and Black enjoyed widespread popularity among the Scottish nobility, and had powerful friends at their disposal. But by the way Cullen's mouth hardened, she suspected he was taking the threat seriously. The professors weren't invincible.

"Unless you can give us a very compelling reason why you are on the first floor of my house, wandering into rooms with closed doors?"

She saw Cullen's eyes flick at Black. Elizabeth's heart sank a fraction of an inch. Cullen wasn't the best at lying on the spot, and he'd just appealed to his friend, which meant he lacked an excuse of his own. Nor could Elizabeth help, because her mind had gone perfectly blank. She hadn't considered anything drastic occurring.

Unfortunately, Cullen's silent glance at his colleague hadn't gone unnoticed.

"Dr Black?" Kildare prompted with exaggerated courtesy.

Elizabeth tried to think. They were standing in the drawing room. She could see a slim bookcase filled with romantic novels, a pianoforte, and a series of very dull landscape paintings.

"You mentioned your recent acquisition of sheet-music for several of Haydn's rarer duets in D minor," Black said with perfect confidence. "I was curious about the compositions."

Oh yes, he had bragged about the duets and trios. She remembered once prompted, but Elizabeth had immediately disregarded that information because...

"My violin and viola duets? I didn't know you played the violin, Dr Black."

But he didn't! Black was an elegant flutist, she'd heard him play at dinner parties, but he'd also admitted his childhood musical training didn't go beyond flute and song.

"I do, as a matter of fact. It's something I've taken up in recent years."

She was amazed Black sounded so assured in his lies. Well, he'd have to be, with their reputations on the line. But how had he not noticed...

"Well, we have a violin here. My *niece*..." The way Kildare smirked that statement made her believe the woman in question was his mistress and he believed the same relationship held true for Black and her. "Likes to accompany me on the pianoforte. Perhaps you wish to sample the duet, Dr Black?"

By all rights, Elizabeth should be leaping to his defence. She was tolerable on the harmonica and pianoforte, but her family's bankruptcy put an end to her musical training before she got to stringed instruments. Cullen was proudly unmusical.

"Your lordship, this seems a little in poor taste..."

Kildare seemed annoyed Black would draw his attention back to the still-warm body on the floor. "Well, if leads to the Town Guards dragging murderers away in chains, perhaps the exercise won't be for naught. Unless there is something you wish to unburden yourself of, Dr Black...?"

"I will make my demonstration brief, in that case." Black strode over to the pianoforte and picked up the violin.

Kildare didn't move. His expression was close to triumphant. While Elizabeth suspected his musical mastery was not as overwhelming as he projected, he'd know enough to see through Black's lies of proficiency.

Black held up the violin, studied it for a moment, then tucked it under his chin.

Beside her, Cullen held his breath.

Then Black slid the bow across the strings and worked through a series of chords.

"Hmm." He paused. "It's a little sharp." He adjusted a peg.

She heard Kildare's nostrils flare.

Turning his attention to the sheet music already laid out, Black frowned, then brought his bow down.

The notes began hesitant and a little choppy but, slowly, a pleasant tune emerged, cautiously expanding into the sweat-stained air and twirling round the furnishings.

Cullen released his breath.

"Fine!" Kildare all but stamped his foot. "You've made your point. Now get the Hell out of my home."

Cullen made to grab her elbow, but Elizabeth was already ducking past the irate lord through the door.

"Oh, and Dr Black?" Having taken the time to put the violin back in its case, Black was last out. Kildare must have held out an arm to bar his exit. "Two times may be a tragic, cruel coincidence. But a third time you're found standing over a dead body? No performance will get you out of *that*."

28

"What in God's name prompted you to learn the violin, Joe?" Cullen waited until they were halfway down the street, and not obviously being tailed. Then he yelled.

"I told you I bought one last year, did I not?" Black asked mildly.

Elizabeth tried not to laugh. It would be unseemly, and an admission of how terrified she'd been, but it was a relief to know Cullen seemed as surprised at the developments as she did.

"Yes, and some music for beginners. But I didn't think you'd actually *practiced*, Joe."

"I admit I'm at somewhat of a late age to learn to play the violin," Black admitted. "But I'm a great believer in doing things people say are implausible."

"But why?" Cullen seemed more agitated about Black concealing violin lessons from him than stumbling upon another body and being accused of murder.

"It's an exquisite instrument, when played well," Black insisted.

"Thank you," Elizabeth interrupted, before the argument

got too far out of hand. "For not immediately abandoning me." Again.

Cullen waved a hand. "We couldn't have done a sweep with only two points of triangulation, anyway. And I'm not sure how much good it did the first time."

Maybe it was just selfish pragmatism. But Elizabeth smiled to herself. If anything, the fact Cullen tried to dismiss it as such made it more likely that wasn't the only reason.

"I'm not convinced we're in as much danger as Lord Kildare claims we are," Black added hastily. "I'm unclear which powerful friends he alludes to."

"But we could be in a lot of danger..." Elizabeth spoke slowly. "If Young's murder was the trap that I think it was."

She thought the lack of comment from the professors on this being a set-up was due to the self-evident nature of the fact. Instead, two minutes later, it was apparent the self-evident part...wasn't.

"I suppose the timing seems a little suspicious..." Cullen thoughtfully conceded.

Elizabeth was ready to tear her hair out.

"But why on Earth would you stab someone to death minutes before we walked along the corridor, opening doors? It could be reasonably said that Kitty Grenville's murderer had no idea we would wander upstairs looking for her. But this time? We admitted we were looking for something—everyone heard us. Again, the murderer committed the deed minutes before we stumbled upon them, at no great risk to themselves."

She sensed she was getting through to Black, so appealed more directly to his common sense.

"Kildare said it: two murders we've stumbled upon within days go beyond coincidence, does it not?"

"Yet, I don't think Kildare killed Young," Black spoke carefully, no doubt attuned to her displeasure. "He was downstairs, engaged with his colleagues while the murder occurred, surely? There was no possibility for him to sneak upstairs ahead of us."

"The speed at which he jumped to accusing us *is* a little suspicious." Cullen spoke as if he were still mulling over the situation.

"Call me a fanciful woman, Dr Cullen, but it does not surprise *me* we'd get accused of murder under the circumstances, despite the eminence of my company." She thought of the fierce-faced ruffians prowling Duddington Loch—someone was trying to harm them.

Cullen shrugged—a partial concession to the point.

"No one has had any reason to doubt my word before, madam. Nor Joe's."

Those black physician garments must be so nice to wear, Elizabeth thought bitterly. They protect the wearer from so much in this world.

"None of us are invincible," Black said, looking at Cullen. "But I'm unclear what benefit accusing us of Young's murder serves, I admit."

"Because we're asking questions? Because we're digging into something we shouldn't?"

"Bribery would be simpler," Cullen responded, with absolute sincerity. "Or sending thugs to menace us in the street. I'm not sure stabbing someone to death in another person's drawing room as we're walking past is the most efficacious way to deliver a threat."

"Well, if someone wanted Young dead, then maybe the energy balance of the system readjusted." She thought back to Kitty's 'serving two masters' warning.

'Disappointed' seemed like a wilfully churlish reaction to news of a second murder. But part of her remained annoyed at Young for dying. The threatened exposure of his duplicity possibly ended Kitty's life, and now that duplicity had caught up with Young before Elizabeth and the professors had time to question him.

Another part of her wondered if his death was her fault. Thomas had stolen the architectural blueprint from his lodgings, and maybe Young's carelessness angered the wrong people.

Elizabeth saw the contours of her entire future change. It was only through Black and Cullen's intervention this time that she wasn't carted back to the Tolbooth. The presence of Edinburgh's most famous physicians was still a protective barrier. But anyone with sense would see she was the weakest link in the group and try to isolate her. Could she make the physicians see that? To understand how her situation differed from theirs?

They traversed the North Bridge in stony silence. The wind kept everyone's head bowed.

"I apologise," Elizabeth said, her words shaky. She hated doing this. "I took Mrs Susan Berry at her word and assumed she approached with good intentions."

"That still might be the case," Cullen said. "I daresay feeding a woman that erratic incorrect information was not a labourious task."

Elizabeth shook her head. That well of kindness had dried up. "With hindsight, I consider her deception obvious." She sighed. "My weakness was the charitable belief in my fellow women."

Cullen seemed to disagree, but held his tongue. He glanced at Black a few times. "If that was the case, her reasons for such deception might be complex. She felt threatened by her husband, for instance."

On an intellectual level, Elizabeth knew all this. But her heart didn't want to know. It wanted to burn and rage a little longer. So she snorted and looked away.

"The exercise was a helpful one," Cullen said, thoughtfully. "I imagine Mr Young's time on earth was limited, even if we hadn't been pointed in his direction. The slaying seemed more vindictive than Kitty's."

"Or by a less competent hand," Elizabeth pointed out, hoping to push the conversation as far from the banks of her discomfort and guilt as possible.

"I'm not sure about that," Black said. "The murderer waited until the last possible second to kill his target, knowing we would stumble upon the scene. There was no small risk the dying man would name his killer with his last gasps."

"Making the killer vindictive, but also *precise*?" A shudder rose from the base of Elizabeth's spine. Was he hiding behind one of Kildare's doors the whole time, listening to them argue? "I would prefer him to be reckless."

29

Returning to Parliament Close was almost as terrifying as being trapped in a fire balloon drifting west above Edinburgh. But Elizabeth forced herself to walk as if she was in no hurry.

"The last thing the guards would expect is for you to walk past the Tolbooth you escaped from," she told herself. "So give them no reason to be suspicious. Breathe normally."

Plenty of Edinburgh citizens were going about their daily business as she passed St Giles, keeping to the edges in the shades of shop awnings. These days, Parliament Close looked more like a square than a close thanks to the new buildings crowding its edges, and some people were calling it that.

Her circuitous route eventually brought her to a second storey shop, up a precipitously narrow turnpike stairs. The reassuring aroma of warm ink greeted her as she edged inside. She paused on the threshold, because the smell contained a confusing undertow of shaving soap.

"Greetings, madam!" The handsome man approaching her, raising his voice to be heard over the groans of the floorboards, was somewhere between his fortieth and fiftieth year, with pewter hair loosely rolled and braided. He rubbed his hands on his ink-stained apron, smiled sheepishly, then bowed.

"Good day," she responded. "Am I speaking with John Kay, engraver and proprietor?"

She was fairly confident of the man's identity, since Kay had a distinct mole on his jaw that people often mistook for an ink smudge, even before he took up his infamous quill.

"Alas, it is true." Kay spoke with cheerful, disarming ease. It was probably a holdover from his previous vocation as a blade-wielding barber, which required calming many an anxious client. "You look familiar, madam. Can you remind me of your name?"

"I'm no one of importance," Elizabeth replied brusquely. Before Kay could digest her change in tone or words, she shot her hand towards him. Kay had only time to notice a flash of metal before she placed a guinea in his unresisting palm.

The two stared at each other for a minute. Kay frantically trying to make sense of this mad interaction, and Elizabeth praying he would play along.

Then the guinea slid into his apron pocket.

"Understood. Forgive me, madam, you seek assistance?"

Kay's posture betrayed residual curiosity, but he was doing a good job acting as if strange women bribing him upon introduction were a normal part of his day. Maybe it was.

"I'm trying to understand Mr Clarence Young of West Nicholson St." Elizabeth caught a flicker of recognition. "You might be the man who knows the most about what is going on in Edinburgh, from her cellar taverns to the upper floor apartments."

"Call it a professional necessity, madam." Kay gestured for her to follow him into the back office. Here, the walls were crammed with sketches and cameos of Edinburgh's most illustrious figures. A great artist he was not: Kay's distinct spindly figures, always in profile, all looked the same to her. But they possessed a magnetic quality in their composition, capturing the spirit of his targets, if not their likeness.

His desk was piled with sketchbooks, busts, and inkpots. As they approached, a tabby cat rolled off the central pile, stretching luxuriantly and regarding Elizabeth with sly pride.

Kay motioned for her to sit, then he continued. "I started out in Edinburgh as a barber, doing what barbers do best. We talk to our clients, and because we see each other so often, our conversations range far and deep. Parliament Close is the hub of this city, and many influential men came through my doors. I also see them walking back and forth below my window." Here Kay gestured to the window, propped open with the mouldering remnants of a book. "I started doodling sketches of the most amusing anecdotes I'd heard that day. Just to pass the time or calm my mind before bed. Then before I knew it, people were coming into my shop for my caricatures, not my shears."

"Your caricatures have always brought me great amusement," Elizabeth said. "You provided a more concise summary of the South Bridge development saga—Lord Provost Hunter Blair in a hole outside the Tron Kirk shovelling soil out, while the Right Honourable Sir Hay stood shovelling the soil back in—than a year's worth of meeting minutes ever could."

Kay frowned at that example. She'd hoped her hints about Young and the South Bridge would have prompted more recognition, but it appeared he missed the allusion. Then he stretched to his left, other hand resting on the cat's shoulders, and tapped a picture on the wall.

"I'm letting this one sit for a while. Sometimes I think up an improvement to the composition a day or two after the fact."

Elizabeth swallowed, because Kay had pointed to a sketch of Black. The professor stood in his chemistry classroom. He appeared mid-lecture: notes and equipment were piled on the demonstration table, and his academic robes billowed around him. As an anatomical study, it left a lot to be desired. Black's arms appeared half their normal size. But Kay had captured the way Black twirled his glasses when extemporising, and a sly smile played about his lips.

"You've attended Dr Black's chemistry lectures?" Elizabeth asked, hoping her voice didn't betray her nerves.

"Back in December, yes. I drew this from memory a few weeks ago." Kay turned back to regard Elizabeth, his face impassive once more, as if he hadn't delivered a warning he knew exactly who she was. "But you asked me about Clarence Young. As you can see, I tend to get distracted, but those distractions often yield the most intriguing tales."

"I'm concerned Mr Young is getting mixed up in dangerous dealings." That was true enough.

"Mr Young has never been a client of mine," Kay focussed on the cat, currently stretching a paw towards his chin. "But I always adhere to principles of client confidence. It's perhaps egotistical of me to consider myself on the same vocational ladder as august physicians and surgeons. But a barber isn't that many rungs below them."

"No," agreed Elizabeth. "I suppose they are not."

Satisfied Elizabeth agreed to his unspoken terms of discretion, Kay continued.

"Clarence is an unfortunate soul. I don't think I'm revealing any secrets by saying that. He was ostracised by his influential father, and watched his natural family torment his poor mother. The Nicholsons hold enough sway in Edinburgh that many followed Lady Nicholson's lead in their dealings with the boy, despite him having done them no harm."

"Some of this hostility has cooled in recent years, though?" Elizabeth asked.

Kay exhaled quietly. "A good deal of malice was unleashed

on the boy in his formative years: I fear not all of it can be undone."

He was probably right about that.

"What prompted the reconciliation?"

Kay looked out of his window. He was probably conjuring up the memory of Clarence walking across the close. "The merits of Mr Young became more apparent with maturity. He always handled himself with grace, even in the face of stinging insults, and as he came into his own in the tyre-making business, his originality and clarity of thought shone through. Soon, not even the Nicholsons could ignore this fact, especially when he did nothing to warrant their continued hostility."

"So he didn't spurn the Nicholson's overtures?" Elizabeth could understand the pragmatism on the Nicholson's side, but it was hard to imagine Young embracing them wholeheartedly.

"Edinburgh noticed the reconciliation when it was publicly acted upon." Kay looked pensive. "I cannot tell you, madam, how long the Nicholson's wooing went on before it reached that stage."

Maybe that was at the heart of Young's duplicity—serving the Nicholsons while colluding with another party to enact his eventual revenge?

"What did this public reconciliation look like?" she asked.

"Young became a kind of secretary-amanuensis for the surviving Nicholsons. He conducted a lot of business negotiating with tradespeople on their behalf. I wouldn't consider it particularly noble work, just useful acts." Kay tapped a sketchpad in front of him. "When Lady Nicholson's middle son—Mr Young's half-brother—got in trouble with his military superiors for misplacing a shipment of gunpowder, Mr Young acted as a go-between for the family and the captain's superiors. He smoothed a considerable quantity of ruffled feathers, and the captain avoided court martial."

"That seems like quite a scandal," Elizabeth admitted. "Losing an entire shipment of gunpowder? How is that possible?"

"Oh, it was only temporarily misplaced," Kay laughed. "It turned out the ship received instructions to dock in Portsmouth when it was supposed to go to Yarmouth. The Nicholson's boy was guilty of messing up communication lines and delivering vague instructions, not a grander conspiracy. But it came at a politically sensitive time in the war with the Colonists, when it was clear Britain had bungled their response to the uprising. Captain Nicholson would have made a convenient sacrifice to cover the ineptness of those just above him."

British military incompetence didn't shock Elizabeth, so she nodded. Then a thought occurred to her.

"Is that how Mr Young became acquainted with Lord Kildare?"

Kay started in surprise at her questions. Then he nodded.

"I'm not sure you need my insights, madam, given you possess many of your own. Yes, I believe Lord Kildare took to Mr Young during that business. I saw them a few times in the street. I would characterise Lord Kildare's interest as close to fatherly."

She scrutinised her memories of Lord Kildare reacting to the sight of Young's blood seeping onto his carpet. She wouldn't call his muted reaction as 'fatherly.'

"Did they remain on good terms?"

Kay studied her for a long minute. "You'll forgive my observation, madam, but it seems your questions are leading a trail towards a particular answer."

"I can only see one step in front of me on this particular

trail," Elizabeth admitted frankly. "And I confess I lack an appreciation of the significance of the destination."

Her answer seemed to satisfy Kay, at least for the moment.

"Well, I heard they'd quarrelled a few times in recent months. The first rumour I dismissed, because it didn't appear to be a public argument. Then I heard a second report of raised voices in a tavern and Young storming out. Kildare was becoming exasperated with Young, it seemed."

But exasperation, arguments and recrimination could be 'fatherly,' Elizabeth reflected. It would be a drastic step for Lord Kildare to arrange the murder of Young, just because of a few heated words.

She took so long musing on this that the pair sat in silence for several minutes.

Kay nudged his cat off the table. It hopped onto the floor as if it desired a change of scenery, anyway.

"I'm going to ask this question bluntly, I'm afraid, madam..." Kay began.

She heard the tiniest shake in his voice.

"He's dead," Elizabeth replied, not wanting to hear the question she knew was coming. "His body was found at Lord Kildare's home yesterday." She paused. "I'm sorry."

She didn't know if she had the right to offer condolences. Kay's breathing sounded shaky. She wasn't sure how he would react to the news of the death of a man he vaguely knew, and it was probable he didn't know either. She rose. "I should take my leave. I've impressed too long on your time."

"Kildare wouldn't have killed Young, madam." Kay stared at the chair where she'd sat, not watching her open the door and squeeze out. He swallowed hard. "I'm not going to claim a deep level of affection where one did not exist...but his lordship has four sons close to Young's age, all of whom sorely tested their father's patience at one time or another. My opinions may have led you towards one conclusion…but his lordship was used to obtuse young men trying his patience. It would take a special callousness to murder someone for the crime of being youthful and obtuse."

30

The discussion with Kay left her with a lot to ponder. Elizabeth was trying to decide if any of the revelations were pertinent to either murder, when a blur of movement exploded out of Borthwick's Close towards her.

She didn't have time to step out of the way before the barrel of a pistol was shoved into her cheek.

"Dinnae think so, lass." The voice hit her ears a second before the smell of rotten teeth doused in back-alley gin hit her nostrils.

She tried to step back, but another hand had already grabbed her sleeve, hard.

"Men usually make even a pretence at conversation before shoving their weapon in my face," Elizabeth said, turning to face her assailant.

The ruffian—a man thirty years her senior, disguised by an ill-fitting brown wig—merely shrugged.

"I already ken ye, Elizabeth Fulhame. And I'll *politely* direct ye to where ye need to go, as long as ye extend me the same courtesy."

The second man, the one who'd almost barged into her,

had ambled back to his colleague, twisting his blade back and forth in his hand until he was certain Elizabeth had seen it.

The bruiser holding her sleeve looked more than willing to knock her teeth out, gender be damned.

The question of resistance was made mood at that moment, because someone dropped a tarpaulin bag over her head and grabbed both her wrists.

* * *

The sound of a door unlocking behind her paused Elizabeth's attempts to free her hands. Her captors had bound her with rope that she could try incinerating, but Elizabeth feared her long sleeves would catch fire first. So, while left in this cramped room, she tried to extricate her hands. However, all it left her with so far was burning pains in her shoulder.

"Ah, Mrs Fulhame. No pleasure at all to see ye."

If the voice hadn't given the game away, the wave of brandy fumes rushing ahead of its owner certainly did.

Elizabeth fought the urge to spit on the floor. Until that moment, she believed herself at the mercy of Mrs Grenville's killer. This development was, in many ways, worse.

"Father Patrick Fay," she said flatly.

"It's *Reverend* Fay, and I think ye know it," the presence replied testily.

"You're a man of many cloths, Reverend Fay. You can forgive a simple woman her confusion."

"Popery is a blight upon Ireland, Mrs Fulhame." Patrick Fay stamped into view, scowling. "I disavowed myself of its heretical clutches a long time ago."

Elizabeth, who considered herself pious to an appropriate degree, did not wish to be dragged into a theological debate with Fay, or linger too long on his infamous conversion. Not when other more pressing issues were at stake.

222

"You'll forgive my state of shock, Reverend Fay, because I was under the impression you'd been transported to Newfoundland."

Fay looked scrawnier and greyer than when she'd last seen him, which suggested a transatlantic voyage or two played in his recent history. But that could also be because he'd not bothered to shave today.

"Storms caused a diversion in the North Atlantic. I decided nearly running aground in Nova Scotia was my sign from Providence to turn around."

"Yet the transportation was in lieu of execution, which I'm also under the impression still holds true."

Fay took another step forward. It might have been arthritis making his joints stiff, or it could be an effect of the brandy. "Here I see Mrs Fulhame expressing concern for my life, after her scheming led to my trial. Ye'd never believe what an unholy, wicked viper this woman was."

He took a swig from the brown bottle, then regarded it thoughtfully. Before she said anything, Fay threw the bottle at the wall above her head.

She flinched at the explosion of glass raining down on her back, getting caught in her hair and neckline. The ferocity of Fay's throw left her momentarily stunned.

Perhaps Elizabeth should have feigned outrage, demanding to know why Fay had kidnapped and was threatening a woman. Unfortunately, now Fay had revealed himself, nothing about the chain of events surprised her. He was a vindictive man, whose morality flowed as easily as the brandy he drank. If Fay did something, he considered it moral. Or necessary.

At least the killer of Mrs Grenville would stab her in the stomach and leave her to die. There was no telling what a scorned Fay would do now he'd caught her.

She shook her head, trying to dislodge the shards of wet glass. Fay watched her grimly, as if his outburst never occurred.

Sounds of carousing filtered from the floorboards. She'd either been taken to a tavern or a brothel. Not that it mattered: neither clientele would care to investigate a screaming woman.

Fay was still regarding her, perhaps undecided what he'd do to the women he blamed for his misery. It didn't matter that he'd smashed his bottle; he could easily find more.

"If it's pecuniary compensation you seek, I might be able to help you." Elizabeth kept her voice measured. "I know you're a practical man, Reverend Fay. There's a mark I need taking care of, and I think he has more money than sense, and more pride than both."

"This daughter of Eve twists herself in knots. Ye cross as many dolts as it pleases ye." Her captor's eyes flicked left then right, surveying the room.

"Inflicting violence upon me will only provide temporary gratification, probably for all of a heartbeat." She forced herself to look Fay in the face and not fiddle with her bindings. "It certainly won't turn a profit."

"Coins aren't the only thing I care about." Fay folded his arms. "Do you think any sum of money can make up for the indignities of transportation—months at sea on galley reeking of shit? Or the terror of wrongful imprisonment as you await execution?"

"No." Elizabeth wouldn't insult Fay's intelligence. He possessed an animal sort of cunning that was hard to deceive. "But the benefits will certainly last longer than your bruised fists."

A hand slid into Fay's pocket. She tried to ignore it.

"At this moment, Mrs Fulhame, I'm inclined to knock your teeth out anyway, break at least one arm...then *hear* your idea of fair compensation for destroying my life and reputation, in exchange for me not wringing your neck."

There was nothing for it. She told him the sum of money.

Fay barked with laughter. "Now I *know* ye're lying out of desperation. Where's a lowly wench like yerself find that princely sum?"

So Elizabeth told him. She kept the details brief, but specific enough to sound accurate.

"...But to lay your hands upon that mark, you need my *full* cooperation. And I need all my teeth and limbs."

Fay slid into the chair opposite her. He picked up an empty bottle that must have rolled into the corner, twirling it between his hands.

"I'm not convinced upon that point, Mrs Fulhame. It behooves ye to keep talking..."

31

It took a moment to orient herself once Fay released her. She emerged into the shade of Holyrood Abbey, darkened black with rain, rubbing her wrists and calming her heart. Her captor would be watching her leave from the upper rooms of the Queen's Arms, so she focussed on slow steps with straightened back, not glancing back.

She dreaded returning home, because it would mean telling Thomas what happened—forcing them into a long-overdue conversation about what transpired in Dublin. Elizabeth flipped through all possible counters in her mind: lying, distraction, pretending it had clean slipped her mind that she'd just been abducted. Instead, she got home to find Thomas sitting at the table with folded arms. On some level, he knew this conversation was coming.

"Patrick Fay found me," Elizabeth said bluntly, before she'd even sat down. "Heavens knows how, but he snuck back from transportation."

Thomas grunted. That was not his actual reaction, more of a placeholder reaction.

Elizabeth struck out her chin. "I believe I dealt with the

reverend by directing him to a more lucrative target. He needs to remain in Edinburgh for a few days to complete that lure, however."

There was a long exhalation from her husband, who sat with folded arms, refusing to meet her eye. That was no longer his placeholder reaction; more like a warning that his genuine response was seconds from bursting out.

"I *told* ye I didn't need help with him." Thomas continued to glare into the middle distance, his brows warping. "I told ye I'd just give Fay the money, quick and easy, to make the damned business go away."

Elizabeth said nothing. Every fibre of her being wanted to snap back a retort, to point out the obvious, but she could tell by the way Thomas's knuckles turned yellow then white in the crook of his elbows that the dam was bursting.

"All I cared about was getting Ma her farmhouse back. I told ye that." Her husband seemed to exist in the molten state between rage and grief. His eyes looked glassy. "Yet ye *had* to turn it into a game."

"For not one heartbeat did anyone think the false promissory note came from you." Elizabeth knew better than to comfort Thomas now. She kept her words taunt. "Or even if the sheriffs did, they didn't care. They would have slipped him a forged note themselves if I hadn't."

"That's not the point!" Thomas' fingers twitched. "We nearly lost our home thanks to my brother's demons and then your trickery. Fay wasn't even our problem."

"But he would have been, don't you see? He extorted plenty of marks in Dublin who made the mistake of borrowing money from him. Why do you think he would change for family? Distant cousins, no less."

Elizabeth didn't want to rehash those fraught arguments: her pleading with Thomas not to seek help from Fay, Thomas angrily demanding to know what choice he had when the Fulham farm was to be auctioned off within days.

"Well, at least take a day to think," she'd tried telling him. Thomas had scoffed that the longer they thought, the worse their eventual options would be.

By the time the bailiffs came for Fay, the Fulhames were on a ship to Glasgow.

Elizabeth warned Thomas that Fay had passed on a forged note to the auctioneers and would be arrested within days. Maybe her husband first assumed only Fay's greed was at fault. But a dull sea crossing was all it took to ferment his suspicions. As they stepped off the gangplank, Elizabeth glanced at her husband and knew that he knew. Dark clouds passed over Thomas' face, but they walked along the pier saying nothing.

There wasn't anything to say.

And she was damned if she'd apologise.

"Do ye know how much Ma has suffered?" Thomas was now shouting. "What the threat of losing her home did to her? How she could barely eat for days after seeing Patrick, because of what he did to the family? Then this...Elizabeth, then ye do *this*. If she knew what I let happen..."

"What you 'let happen?'" The outrage in Elizabeth's voice was unfeigned. "I'm your wife, Thomas. Not a dog you need to tether to the back door to avoid eating chickens."

"A dog knows no better: they do whatever instinct commands. Yer my *wife*, Elizabeth." The hurt in Thomas' voice was raw, brutal. "We're supposed to be on the same side. I told ye, no, I *begged* ye not to do this one thing...and ye did it anyway. Is that how little I mean to ye?"

"I'm not sorry..."

To her surprise, Thomas laughed. It was a bitter, twisted bark of a laugh. "I know yer not. I married ye knowing ye were a woman who would never feel bad about doing what she believed to be right. Ye don't think so little of me to assume I'd forget that, I wager."

"So you understand why I did it?"

"Yes, that's why I didn't shove ye overboard into the Irish sea, though God help me, I was tempted." She sensed Thomas' rage cooling, though only fractionally. He sounded a bit more like her husband.

"He would have made life worse for your mother," Elizabeth said, trying to sound more sincere than abrasive. "Men like Fay have a nose for the vulnerable. It draws them like a scent. Even if he bought back your mother's house and made not a murmur of fuss...he would have pounced upon her next whiff of vulnerability, especially with us no longer in Navan."

She wasn't trying to change his mind. Thomas was too proud, too caught in his un-bottled emotions to change the flow of them. She just needed to say her piece.

Thomas ran a hand through his hair. "I'd also by lying if I didn't wish Fay terrified ye with his threats today...but knowing ye, Elizabeth, I doubt a single bead of sweat formed on that brow the whole time."

"I was petrified, actually," Elizabeth said. Whatever composure she projected had not matched the jelly her innards turned to. "I knew Fay was not a man to be crossed lightly. And he isn't."

"Well, let's hope he takes yer bait." Thomas pushed his chair back an inch.

"You aren't going to ask what I proposed?"

"Why ask? I'm pretty sure I already know..."

* * *

A rattling shutter might have woken Elizabeth up later that night. She stared into the darkness, trying to guess what time it was. She guessed it was an awkward hour like four or five o'clock: still too early to rise, but with no time to get back to sleep.

Beside her, Thomas rolled over and sighed.

She'd probably woken him.

Elizabeth scrutinised the faint edges of the ceiling beam above their bed, tracing the lines in the darkness.

Instead of soothing her mind back towards sleep, it brought her thoughts into sharp clarity.

She tapped her husband lightly on the shoulder. He grunted an acknowledgment of temporary wakefulness.

"Maybelle once earned money as a lace-maker, is that what Dr Cullen said?"

"He might have done." Thomas' shrug told her he lacked any memory of that conversation part.

Elizabeth was sure she remembered Cullen saying that, so ploughed on. "Because when Mrs Berry stopped by Dr Black's to speak to me, she had a sparkling white lace fichu and hand-kerchief. I think they were a matching set, in fact."

Thomas' back straightened. "Did ye ask her about them?"

"She said they were a gift," Elizabeth said slowly.

Her husband snorted with laughter. "Is it that simple?"

"The earrys might not be housing Maybelle," Elizabeth cautioned. "But I wager they will be less discrete in their daily goings-on than Corporal Daniels, and some of those goings-on could bring us to the woman we're looking for."

32

George's hopes of a quiet end to his time in Edinburgh was cruelly dashed by his wife.

"Of course you'll help Elizabeth," Phoebe stated matter-of-factly. "She's a good woman who doesn't deserve to be hounded or accused of murder."

"What I'm being asked to do is not without risk," George tried again, his protestation weaker this time.

Still perched by the hearth darning his shirt, Phoebe snorted.

"All the more reason not to abandon her, don't you think? Besides..." She paused, snapping a thread off. "Elizabeth's a canny woman. She wouldn't throw you into danger without good reason or considering her options."

So that was that.

On Thursday nights, Lord Kildare shook off the staid New Town for a few hours of cards, dice and tobacco smoke in a dingy Canongate tavern. His companions were men of similar social standing, who felt psychologically free from their society wives when they returned to Edinburgh's old town.

"Why would he be expected to talk about Clarence

Young's murder tonight?" George asked Elizabeth, once Phoebe summarily dispatched him.

"These are some of his freemason brothers he's meeting with," Elizabeth said. "I asked around concerning Lord Kildare's habits, and this is what I heard from street caddies and the like. There have been no rumours circulating about Mr Young's unfortunate demise," she added.

"Therefore, it's your supposition he's keeping the tragedy secret from all but his closest confidants?" George asked, still wary.

"If eavesdropping yields nothing, you're welcome to interrogate him yourself, George." Elizabeth watched him from across the dining table. "Whatever you decide is the best course of action."

Mrs Stephens and Mrs Fulhame probably *conferred* on the subject long before he was informed, George belatedly realised. He had no idea when such a conference could have occurred, but the women in life exchanged information in mystifying locations, in ways both opportunistic and premeditated.

George's fate was thus sealed. He wouldn't argue with Phoebe. Elizabeth rubbed her eyes as she spoke with him. Faint shadows under her eyes suggested the past few days had taken their toll on her, though she took everything in stride. The thought nudged his conscience hard enough that he resolved to confront this Lord Kildare if he wasn't forthright.

"Does he rent a particular room in the White Horse Inn?" George asked.

"They have a second-floor gaming room set aside on Thursdays," Elizabeth said.

George thought he knew the room in question. His experience of the White Horse Inn was that every floorboard announced one's presence more effectively than any valet. The landing and corridor on that floor were narrow, with nowhere to hide.

"Knowing the location in question, I will either have to scale the outside of the building to eavesdrop, or kick my way in and single-handedly threaten Lord Kildare's military freemason comrades," George muttered.

Elizabeth fixed him with a long look. George decided apologising for the sarcasm would make the outcome worse for him.

"Whatever you think is most appropriate, Dr Stephens," she finally said, her expression impossible to read.

So George bundled himself up in a scarf Phoebe knitted, and trudged down the High Street.

Kildare sounded deep in his cups. There was a barely perceptible slur to his words, and an exaggerated modulation to his tone. It would take a lot of claret for a heavyset man like Kildare—presumably no stranger to drinking—to show signs of drunkenness.

The White Horse Inn was crowded by the time George arrived. Men spilled onto the narrow staircase, pinching bottles between their knees and yelling with the men above and below them, since there wasn't room for two people to sit side-by-side. George had to stretch his legs over several uncooperative drinkers to get to the second floor.

The nearby lanterns had gone out, plunging the landing area into darkness. Since nobody was nearby—the men spilling out of the main tavern room were interested in loud, public conversations, not private ones, George decided to kneel at the door to Kildare's card room and listen.

Unlike the Fulhames and the professors, George had nominal familiarity with the lord, as with the other military officers who resided in Edinburgh. The lord wouldn't recognise George—why would he—but would probably identify him as a former solider just from how he carried himself.

To George's relief, Kildare had reached the stage of drunkenness where his feelings about Young's death were making themselves known.

"I warned that dolt," he was ranting. "Stay away from those men. Don't talk to them. He knew if I'd shoot that bastard on sight if he came into my house."

"And he came in anyway?" a companion asked. Annoyance flickered through George. The identity of the 'bastard' sounded established within the group, so they might not restate his name for George's hidden benefit.

"Or he sent the physicians to do his dirty work. Anyway, the rat's gone to ground," Kildare continued. "I'll nail that fuckster to a tree myself if I catch him."

His colleagues murmured in support.

"Stupid boy." Back to Clarence Young, George supposed. "Not a lick of common sense."

"You didn't uncover what that viper was plotting?"

"I confess I'm not in the mind to ask many questions when I get ahold of him," Kildare paused, probably gulping down more claret. "I know his type: they'd steal anything not nailed down, and bludgeon a man to death because they coveted his jacket buttons. Flogging them achieves nothing. Soon as they can move their fingers, they're pinching again."

A suspicion took hold of George. Elizabeth had asked about Silas Lowell, a man claiming to have served as an artilleryman. She also said Lowell and Young were seen associating with each other. He shouldn't let an assumption blind him to other possibilities, but the way Kildare spoke about this 'bastard viper' implied he was also a soldier.

Though Lowell was a lobster-back like himself, wasn't he? It seemed strange that Kildare thought Lowell capable of ordering around Drs Black and Cullen. But Kildare's drunkenness was taking the edge off his coherence. He might be referring to multiple men as 'he' in this rant.

"Short of locking the fool up, what could I do?" Kildare was saying. "I tried every trick, every threat I could think of to get him to confess what he was involved in. Nothing worked. Now it's too late."

George wished one of Kildare's friends would ask one of *his* most burning questions: why was Young murdered? Perhaps that had already been discussed before he arrived. However, it was more likely that no one but him considered it a question worth asking. If they knew of Kildare's woes, and his frustration with Young, they might consider the boy's murder an unsurprising consequence of whatever dark business they suspected him mixed up in. Kildare thought Lowell the type to murder someone over a petty grievance—what more of a motivation did they need? These weren't the type of men to obsess over details. Details were for subordinates.

George pulled away as lingering longer became riskier, and he doubted the rewards were worth it. Kildare and his colleagues were talking about other things now—scornful words about wives and serving girls. Just then, Kildare's voice rose, carrying into the corridor.

"I told him too much about those cursed dock-masters. Ranted when I should have held my tongue. Of course, that came back to haunt me."

A scrap and a thud from inside the room sent George scurrying back to the main tavern area. He kept his back turned as one of Kildare's friends stumbled downstairs, loudly demanding the wenches bring up more claret.

Another cryptic fragment, which may mean everything or nothing. Why couldn't any part of this bloody mess be straightforward?

33

It was shaping into another chilly, bright morning. Elizabeth envied the ladies bundled up in furs, their breath misting up the windows of their sedan chairs as they were carried across North Bridge.

Thomas had spent the first part of the morning following the Berrys. It was a risky pursuit: Susan Berry knew Elizabeth now, and it was reasonable to assume they'd recognise Thomas on sight, too. She just hoped her husband would hang back far enough to avoid detection. The Berrys lived halfway down Peebles Wynd, close to the intersection of the North Bridge and High Street.

When her husband found her, Elizabeth was walking in tiny circles and rubbing her hands to keep warm.

"They disappeared into a tenement a few buildings down from theirs. They've been in there a good half hour."

"Do you know which floor?" Elizabeth broke into a trot.

"I think they're on the third. I snuck inside the turnpike, but couldn't hear much."

"Thank you, sweetheart."

Thomas glanced sideways. "Ye sure ye don't need me along, too?"

She was sure. "Based upon what happened with Maybelle, a male presence may be oil poured on the fire."

"That said…" She knew Thomas worried about Jeremiah Berry, or what would happen if multiple people set themselves on her.

"All will be well," she said firmly.

At this hour of the morning, Peebles Wynd was still submerged in freezing shadows. Elizabeth skidded several times on frozen puddles and icy cobbles. Her husband vanished into the clamour of the High Street, heading off to speak with Dr Cullen a few closes' down the hill.

The truth of what befell Kitty Grenville and the murky plot she was embroiled in lay within her grasp. But Elizabeth felt distanced from the answers, like they were trapped behind a sheet of ice.

She hoped this wasn't another useless thread, the kind that took an eternity to unspool, but led to naught at the end.

Yet Kitty must have been preoccupied by many things on the night she died. The dinner with her conspirators, the cancer eating away at her body, and perhaps already contending with the person who would kill her. Yet despite all these things, she'd taken the time to pen a letter to Maybelle and threaten her over…something.

A second shadow fell over her. She just had time to look away from the tenement door and register a figure barreling towards her, when…

"You!"

She was simultaneously slammed off balance, banging into a shutter, as a meaty hand closed around her throat.

Scarlet filled her vision. A Town Guardsman's uniform.

Elizabeth's hands tried to pry off her attacker. She was jerked twice, like a rag doll. The man continued to yell at her.

She tried to refocus long enough to marshal the phlogiston and aether within her for a strike.

"Get away from her, Eli!" A woman's voice rose. "Leave her alone." Her voice sounded halfway between agitation and rage.

The man loosened his grip on Elizabeth's throat. With her assailant still panting with anger, Elizabeth ventured a step backwards. The visage of rage didn't leave Corporal Daniels' face, but he didn't re-close the gap.

The young woman appeared on his arm and tugged the guardsman back.

"It's not her fault..."

Elizabeth assumed this was the man's beau, come to drag him from the altercation. But then she heard Corporal Daniels mutter a name.

"You are Maybelle?" Elizabeth controlled the trembling in her voice. "I wished to speak to you."

"You'll do nothing of the sort..." The guardsman lunged forward.

"About Kitty Grenville," Elizabeth blurted out, aware she had scant time to convince the woman to talk. Maybelle froze. "Or Kitty Holm, as she was previously known."

Daniels seemed ready to explode under a paroxysm of anger. But Maybelle nodded and took a step forward, half-blocking her cousin's approach.

"Maybelle..."

"I don't need your protecting, Eli," she snapped. "Please, stop acting as if you know what's best for me."

"I only..."

"Please!" Maybelle was slight and delicate in stature, but she looked ready to stamp her feet. Chastised, her cousin dropped his head. The cousins shared the same pale skin and wavy dark brown, almost black, hair.

"Eli sometimes gets over-protective of me." She stepped closer to Elizabeth. "Did he hurt you?"

"No," Elizabeth replied, rubbing her neck. She refused to look at Daniels. There'd be bruising later.

She hoped she didn't look too shaken.

"I made him tell me what Mrs Grenville's letter said. He really didn't want to, and claimed he forgot all the details, but it worried me a lot, thinking of what she might be planning."

"How did you come to be acquainted, Maybelle?" Elizabeth tried to keep any judgment from her voice.

"Back in early '85, I visited the Kirk a lot. A lot was weighing on my mind, and I found Greyfriars a place of solace."

Elizabeth nodded. She didn't need to pry further, but suspected Maybelle was dealing with the aftermath of her assault and the unwanted baby.

"I met Mrs Greville, or Mrs Holm at the time, during one of those visits. We prayed together, and she offered me some psalms she said helped her get through tough times. I was so appreciative of her care, I confessed more than I should have."

"You weren't to know of her unpleasant nature," Elizabeth gently said. "I'm sure she was very convincing in her concern."

Maybelle sighed. "I still believe Kitty's concern was genuine. Perhaps inappropriately manifest later, but I did not doubt her sorrow or empathy. She told me her husband was a minister, but was travelling."

No doubt Kitty Holm was comforting Maybelle while her husband arranged the kidnapping and ransom of James Hutton. That took place in April or May of that year, did it not?

Elizabeth tried not to let those calculations distract her. Maybelle spoke haltingly, swallowing half her words, but refusing to stop. Her cousin glowered a few paces away.

"We didn't just talk about my...I mean..." She trembled, looking on the verge of tears, then balling up her fists and pushing on. "I told her about my brother. I was afraid for him too, because his regiment was seeing action in Boston. It seems foolish to think I thought her a close friend, having known her for barely a few weeks, but I showed her some of his letters. He wasn't supposed to tell me, but I found out he was serving as an engineer. His team was testing new explosives, and their officers tasked them with devising better ways to destroy buildings."

"Siege warfare?" That sounded a little anachronistic to Elizabeth.

"No, more like destroying town buildings and homes. Places where the enemy might hide. They also practiced blowing up bridges, but Mrs Grenville never seemed interested in that."

Sweat beaded in the small of Elizabeth's back.

"Mrs Greville was interested in your brother's military duties?"

Maybelle looked at her toes. "I never understood why. It never occurred to me she'd be interested in such a thing, and I barely noticed her steering the conversation back to my brother and what he was doing. Until..."

"That's what her recent letter alluded to?" Elizabeth's heart rate picked up.

"My brother has been living in Falkirk these past few years. Eli said her letter demanded she introduce me to Simon, to assure his cooperation and discretion, unless..."

"You don't have to say." It was hard to tell who was more distressed, Elizabeth or Maybelle. "But you should know Mrs Grenville's late husband was involved in dark, violent business when you met her."

Maybelle's jaw slackened.

"Their plans were halted before they came to bloody

fruition," Elizabeth added. "Destroying buildings wasn't the means they settled on."

Holm had trapped the nobles, former dark chymists, in a room and tried to murder them with mechanically generated electricity. Perhaps it turned out cheaper or more reliable than using gunpowder to tear down the tenement with them in it. Or maybe Holm, in his twisted way, thought an explosion too impersonal.

Maybelle pressed a hand to her mouth. "But she wanted to try again?"

Elizabeth took a step back, away from Maybelle. She needed space to think. She felt hemmed in.

"What regiment did your brother serve in?"

"The eighty-second. Why...?"

Where did Silas Lowell claimed he'd served? He said he was artillery, not an engineer...but maybe he was lying. No, he could have been seconded to the engineers, or gleamed enough just from watching their tests—that's why Kitty needed Simon. But in a pinch, Lowell would do.

"I don't think you are in danger, Maybelle. The conspirators are going ahead without your brother. But..." Elizabeth took another step back. She had to warn the others. "For God's sake, stay away from the South Bridge."

"I found out why Kitty wanted to blackmail Maybelle. She needed his brother's explosives expertise. Or maybe not need all of it...Silas Lowell is providing some of that insight."

"Into effectively blowing up buildings?" Cullen had covered his head with his hands. She couldn't tell what his true feelings were.

"You heard the Lord Provost, Dr Cullen. His only objection to Delancey's—or Mr Adam's, I suppose—plan was the cost. But what if Delancey found a way to remove the accompanying demolition costs?"

"But the South Bridge is almost complete." In the corner, Black's face was shut down. "Why would the Town Council even contemplate switching to another design at this late stage? They love inertia almost as much as they hate expenses."

"Because they intend to blow up the entire South Bridge, Joe." Cullen's sigh could be heard from across the close. "That's what Mrs Fulhame is leading us towards, isn't it? They'd disguise it as a structural collapse, an unfortunate tragedy, but Delancey, Lowell and the like would be certain to take out the tenements obstructive to their blueprint. Why wouldn't the Lord Provost give his support to Delancey? The previous design was just proven too faulty to re-attempt."

Elizabeth shuddered. The plan sounded pure evil inside her head; hearing Cullen state it so baldly made it an atrocity beyond imaging.

Black sealed his mouth shut. Cullen hadn't moved. He looked ready to slither under the table in weary despair.

"Why would Mrs Holm involve herself in this? It seems to serve little outside of Delancey's ego. If we take her involvement at face value, she was selling knowledge of explosive expertise to the highest bidder."

"Could she have been the one to inform Delancey of the opportunity?" Elizabeth asked. "I wondered whether her presence in Edinburgh during Robert Adam's visit back in 1785 was a sign of her involvement in the blueprint side of the equation."

"Hmm." Black approached the table. "You're suggesting she might have gleaned some knowledge of those secret Town Council debates, then convinced Delancey he would have a chance where his master did not, if only they addressed the Councillors financial concerns?"

They hadn't painted a perfect picture, and Elizabeth

sensed their realisation missed some nuance, because the chain of events seemed too glib. But she nodded.

"Then Delancey killed Kitty to silence her?" Cullen's sharp eyes peeked between splayed fingers.

"I'm not sure," Elizabeth admitted.

"Me neither." Cullen heaved to his feet. "But I think the general outline, the damned blueprint of our hypothesis, is sturdy enough."

"We're two weeks away from the proposed opening of the bridge," Black said. "But that's merely the official ceremony date."

An icy silence settled on the room. Tradesmen were still hammering away on the bridge—she'd heard them this morning—but another portion of the workers were dismantling scaffolding and tidying the site. If the conspirators wished to destroy the South Bridge through covert means, they were about to lose the best source of cover.

"Would the Lord Provost really just...let Delancey destroy half of Edinburgh?" How many people would die in crushed tenements, or buried under the collapsing bridge? Elizabeth hated asking the question.

"Knowing the honourable Lord Provost..." Black spoke slowly. "He is unlikely to ask too many questions. Not if he suspects he won't like the answer."

"What can they do anyway, madam?" Cullen asked, a little more testy. "Refuse to re-build? Leave the South Bridge and Cowgate a barren mausoleum for all eternity? No, I wager Delancey's revised proposal will still save them money after accounting for the first bridge, plus they get the prestige of his sumptuous architecture."

"But does the Lord Provost know? Was he lying to us about not having recently seen those blueprints?"

She was looking at Cullen, but Black cleared his throat. "I can't speak to the character and inclination of the other conspirators, but I doubt Mrs Grenville would counsel exposing the plot ahead of its execution. While the Town Councillors may be...reticent...to raise moral concerns, I could imagine them fearing the reputation damage complicity in such an arrangement would bring."

That sounded like most men Elizabeth knew. Unwilling to incriminate themselves, but brazenly averse to interrogating the circumstances of such a boon.

Cullen seemed to agree with his colleague's assessment. "Delancey's development will rival the New Town, should it ever see the light of day."

"It won't." Elizabeth pressed her palms onto the table. "I swear it won't."

To her surprise, Cullen let out a throaty laugh. "Well, it will be your endeavours more than mine that stops them, madam. The infirmities of old age will see to that."

34

A potent gust of wind sent Elizabeth stumbling to the left as they approached the end of South Bridge.

Black motioned her into the shelter of the Old Library wall.

"I told George we'd wait here, so let's hope any proculopathic messages will reach us."

Elizabeth nodded. She drew her shawl around her shoulders and surveyed the bridge. In the grey pre-dusk, it looked desolate. Bags of sand, ropes, and pulleys littered the bridge, still covered by wooden planks. The northern end of the bridge seemed nearer to completion, with paving already laid.

Black studied the scene with a similar expression to hers. "When was the last time you saw the site?"

"Last night when I called upon you." Elizabeth studied the near-complete bridge, trying to recall what had changed overnight. It was dark, and she was too anxious about warning the professors she hadn't absorbed much. "I can't see anything different."

Yet the thought nagged at her: something *was* different.

Black must recognise it too, because he pursed his lips while his eyes flicked back and forth.

Elizabeth was glad the street remained near-deserted. In the past week she'd seen several men—plus one or two plucky women—brave the construction site and walk across the planks. She didn't want to be the one who tried to convince anyone to turn back today, without letting slip why.

"Do George and Thomas know where we're located?" she asked, rubbing her arms.

I explained we'd be observing from the edge of the college grounds," Black replied. He wore a slightly heavier wool coat in winter, and black gloves, which was the only concession to the temperature. He didn't appear bothered by the chill.

The other pair were going to ambush the saboteurs underneath the bridge, hopefully driving them off and breaking any fuse trails. Part of her shivering was because they'd almost certainly be out-manned. The professors didn't have time to bring in anyone else, so George and Thomas had to be aggressive if they had any hope of driving the saboteurs off. Neither of the men were naturally belligerent, though George occasionally surprised her.

Something about the stillness of the tableau made her uneasy: it was like looking at a puzzle, trying to determine the missing piece.

"Did you hear a shout?" Black asked.

She hadn't.

Black relaxed again. "It might have come from Adam Square."

Then it struck her.

"Dr Black...those winches weren't there last night." She pointed to two winches on their side, dropping rope into the remaining gap between the central pillars.

The chemistry professor tensed.

"How sure are you, Elizabeth?"

She thought a cry carried on the wind, but it was muffled when Black broke away from the wall and began striding towards the bridge.

"George reckoned they could drive anyone they found into the Cowgate and away; he assured me they wouldn't corner anyone unless it was absolutely necessary."

No, she'd not imagined it. The ropes were moving. It was a hesitating jerk at first, like a python dislodged from its rock, but then the coils of rope began running smoothly, picking up speed.

Black froze, as if struck in the head. He raised a finger to his temple. Elizabeth tried to focus to catch his message, but her attention was drawn to the shifting ropes.

She couldn't see all the winching mechanisms, but a counterweight probably dangled just below the bridge, which was now being dropped so something could rise.

"George says there were too many to ambush." Black spoke urgently. "He and your husband hid until they left, and they're going to cut the fuse once they've dispersed. But they're coming up instead of leaving by the Cowgate. Five men, he said. Including Silas Lowell. They're all armed."

"So we run?" Elizabeth asked. She could see Black biting his lip.

"A distraction might be best," Black said, a blotch of red appearing on his cheek. "We don't want them to return to the check their gunpowder or fuse."

A dark figure appeared, scrambling onto the bridge. Then came a second one on the other winch.

"But any man with an un-addled pate will know better than to chase us, because it's obvious we are drawing them away."

Lightning flashed in Black's eyes.

"I'd prefer we flee, madam. Because the alternative is trapping them in place and blocking the winches so they can't descend and attack your husband. And there's no feasible way I can achieve that alone."

In his careful way, Black was asking her a question.

"But you think we can...we can achieve it together?"

Black shot her a thin smile. "Well, we'll have to, won't we?"

The two men knelt by the winches, feeding rope into the bridge's maw. Neither looked like Lowell.

"We need to wait until they're all on the bridge." Black's eyes darted back and forth. "I'll go for the left-hand winch and destroy it immediately. Hopefully, that will create enough of a distraction for you to break the second. I only need to hold them until George and Thomas confirm they've diffused the explosives."

Or until they failed, and the whole bridge collapsed in a catastrophic explosion.

Black squeezed her hand. "Elizabeth, these men are armed, and they're probably trained soldiers. This is going to be vicious." His grip tightened. "Don't assume they'll be merciful because you're a woman. If you run, they are liable to shoot you in the back."

Elizabeth held his gaze. "You can consider me warned."

It was also an oblique warning from the chemistry professor that he might be the vicious one in this fight, and that she may not like what she saw.

She remembered a long-ago conversation with her husband: *The way Dr Black spoke...I think he may have killed someone...*

A third and fourth head popped above the boards. Then came a fifth. The men began dispersing, tossing the ropes aside.

Black took off, rushing onto the bridge. Elizabeth dropped behind a pile of sandbags, hoping to avoid detection.

If Black or the men yelled, it didn't carry over the wind. Instead, she saw the flare of a pistol discharge.

She didn't have time to inhale a scream, because Black kept moving. A blazing flash from his hand shot towards his feet.

Now she could hear bellows and shouts. He must have burned through the ropes.

She fought the temptation to burrow into the ground, covering her head and hiding from the conflict. She had at least marginal safety here. But cowardice would endanger Black, not to mention giving the men a clear route back towards her husband and Thomas.

Ducking low, she rushed onto the bridge.

Terror almost froze her. The first few yards of the bridge were easy enough since she crossed laid paving stone—but almost immediately the gaps appeared. South Bridge was still mostly compromised of beams and struts, with planks laid over the gaps.

Come to think of it, hadn't most of the impatient pedestrians crossed the bridge on the left-hand side?

Black wouldn't have knowingly sent her over the more dangerous side of the bridge.

She could inch to the far left and use the balustrade for support, but the planking appeared looser on that side.

She stepped onto the board in front of her. It wobbled.

Curses! This side of the South Bridge was also bathed in the long shadow cast by the college. The wooden planks were covered in frost.

Another pistol shot. She saw Black duck. A blast of white flashed out, but he missed the shooter.

Elizabeth clamped her jaw shut. She took the last few yards at a low run—partly to avoid detection, but partly because she felt reassured keeping her arms close to the ground.

Lowell stood in the middle of the pack, brandishing a pistol. Despite the cold, he wore neither a coat nor a hat.

One attacker, his plum-coloured greatcoat flapping behind him, hopped onto a plank and took a few shuffles to the side, raising his pistol. He was trying to get in a better position to shoot at Black.

He'd need to jump onto the board nearest to her for that.

Elizabeth nudged that board with her foot. It rocked, slightly.

She kicked it.

The end of the board slid off its supporting beam. It seesawed into the air as it fell, startling the attackers.

She tried not to listen out for the crash. For all Elizabeth knew, her husband and George stood below. She didn't want to know what it landed on. Or for how long it fell.

Two more aether blasts shot from Black. One caught the attacker in the chest.

The body fell silently. This time, even though Elizabeth screwed her eyes shut and tried to close off her ears, she heard the muffled impact below.

Lowell forgoing extra clothing made a certain sense in these windy conditions. There was no extra fabric to slow him down or unbalance him. He hopped confidently across a gap in the boards, taking refuge behind a pile of bricks.

She had to break the remaining winch. Any second now, it would dawn on the men that *someone* had knocked the board down.

The winch was a hefty wooden contraption, weighed down with sandbags and stone. She mentally checked her options off.

Fire, force, aether...

Black had sent a concentrated blast of heat to burn through the ropes—wrecking the winch in the process—but his platina wires gave him the power to do that without raising a sweat.

For her to achieve the same result she'd need to grab the rope with both hands, which meant...

Nothing for it.

Elizabeth reached under the winch and grabbed the dangling line. It was a sturdy rope, so she raised the heat in her palms slowly...

"There's a second one!"

She ducked back and sideways as a pistol shot rang out, scrambling behind the relative safety of the brick pile, even though it exposed her head. She hadn't time to completely burn through the rope, but it was too frayed to support weight.

Lowell's dark eyes bobbed back and forth, his lip curling in concentration. He stared at her in puzzlement for a moment, before recognition settled.

But Elizabeth's own contemptuous expression—which she made no attempt to hide—wouldn't incline anyone towards mercy, especially not someone as vicious as Lowell. As he stood deciding what to do, Elizabeth knew this man more than capable of murdering Kitty Grenville and Clarence Young.

She ducked as the first shot rang out. It might have been a fantasy that she felt the ball whizz past her shoulder, because there was a panicked scramble to right herself on the boards, and a treacherous moment where her foot met nothing but air. Then she found purchase and was pulling herself up and back.

"The rope, Elizabeth!"

She heard Black's voice almost as soon as she got her knees under her.

"Throw me the rope!"

He better be yelling about the loose rope dangling

between the boards to her left, because Elizabeth didn't have the space in her mind to look for any other ropes, or fiddle with the broken winch a foot from where Lowell was reloading his pistol.

Elizabeth doubted her ability to throw anything, but this rope wasn't one of the thick winch ropes. It was possibly used to secure wooden boards together.

She fumbled the frayed end dangling into the abyss, haphazardly tossing it in the direction of Black, who crouched and caught it.

Another pistol shot rang out. This time Elizabeth squeezed her muscles and stayed still, in case she rolled off the board. In the gap between those boards was a grey-brown expanse: she couldn't tell if she was looking at a tenement wall, or the muddied ground below.

"*Stay down,*" Black commanded. She saw him stand up, staggering slightly as another pistol shot rang out. Had the professor been hit? His coat was too dark to show obvious bloodstains.

Lowell and the remaining man watched their quarry. She saw Lowell adjusting a dagger in his grip. The way he held it tight to his body suggested practiced confidence with the weapon. Not that he needed much skill: if he hurled the blade at Elizabeth she'd either roll aside to her death or remain paralysed and have the knife embed in her.

Black took off at a pelt towards the Tron Kirk, still holding the rope. Lowell nodded to his companion, and they both moved right, circumnavigating the chasm in the bridge.

Elizabeth watched the pile of rope next to her rapidly unspool as Black ran. Except the other end of the rope was bound to the smouldering remnants of the winch ballast Black just destroyed. Lowell and his comrade were too intent on Black, aiming their pistols at the fleeing man's back, to notice the thin rope flying along the ground in a loose curve...

Did Black really think he could…?

The final two shots rang out and Black dived to the left. This time, Elizabeth shrieked.

The now-taunt rope whipped across the bridge at knee height. It wasn't a heavy rope, but it smacked into Lowell and his comrade with enough force to send them flying.

This time, Elizabeth closed her eyes and jammed her hands into her ears. It didn't quite block out the screams. But at least she didn't have to see their expressions before they disappeared from view.

If Black hadn't timed the move right, then it wouldn't matter that she curled on the ground shaking: she would be a dead woman. But she'd heard enough of the fading screams and crumpling abruptness of its end to know neither Silas nor the anonymous thug would get her.

"*Dr Black?*" She cast her voice out. The last thing she wanted to do was open her eyes and see a fallen body. Or worse yet, the absence of a body.

"*Are you injured, Elizabeth?*"

She almost sobbed with relief.

"*No.*"

"*They caught me in the arm,*" Black said, his proculopathic voice as calm and unhurried as ever. "*But it is only a graze.*"

It sounded so incongruous as to be comical: measured, academic tones from a man who'd just killed five men through a combination of aether strikes and knocking them to their deaths.

"*I've not heard from George or your husband, so move off the bridge as fast as you can. Just as a precaution.*"

A deeper terror settled in Elizabeth's stomach as she scrambled to her feet: she'd forgotten about Thomas in the last frenzied moments. It wasn't a good sign that Black hadn't heard from him.

But there was nothing she could do right now, so she bit

down her fear and turned towards the safety of Nicholson Street.

"Bitch!"

A blow on the side of the head sent Elizabeth sprawling. Before she even hit the boards, a force was pummelling her from every direction.

"Did you even stop to think about what you were doing?" her attacker howled.

Did you? Elizabeth muttered inside her head, because she now recognised her assailant as Weston, who must have crept up the bridge behind her. There wasn't time for more introspective thought, because Weston shoved her towards the yawning gap Black knocked Lowell through.

The blow only grazed her head, which was just as well because Elizabeth was no match on Weston's rage and strength. She was now clinging onto the board she'd fallen on, rocking under both their weights.

The board was also still coated in ice. Assuming she fought back, doing so might send one or both of them plunging to their deaths.

"I *hate* women like you," Weston spat. "Betraying their sex for the first man that crosses your path, even after bemoaning the unfair treatment in the world."

Elizabeth didn't know how to *begin* arguing with that. Did Weston not realise how many women were currently in the buildings she wished to blow up, still asleep or preparing to start their day?

She wriggled further along the slippery board, flinching as it pitched back and forth under her weight.

Weston didn't immediately pursue to continue the beating.

"Do you have any...*any* idea how hard I worked?" The woman continued. "Everything I endured. The insults. The sardonic smirks. 'Oh, pass on my regards to Mr Weston.'

How I had to drag that useless sack around to be taken seriously, because no one believed the wife knew more about the grocery business than her husband?" Weston's fists shook.

Pieces of the story began slipping into place for Elizabeth. "You're afraid that if your husband dies, you'll lose everything."

It was more than avarice motivating Weston: it was fear. That didn't excuse her involvement in the murderous conspiracy, but it explained why she'd constructed this nonsensical lie that she was, somehow, acting in the collective interest of Scottish women.

Weston took a halting step closer. She seemed uneasy on her feet, and the board rocked. She was inches away from kicking Elizabeth off.

Exposing Weston's core fear made the situation more dangerous. Elizabeth was at the mercy of a woman who believed her life over if this plot failed. What was stopping her from taking Elizabeth down with her?

"The Lord Provost has a weakness for stupid blonde women," Elizabeth said quickly. "It's an act his mistress and other women have exploited to get what they want from him. He's never realised he's the stupid one."

"Aye, just pretend to be an eejit doll? As if that's no' what everybody already expects from me?" Weston drew up, bunching her fists again.

"If it came to being a poor widow requesting his clemency, then yes, that's what I'd do." Elizabeth said. She could barely hold on to the boards, and couldn't find purchase with her feet. "If it's a choice between survival and wounded pride, I know what option I'd choose."

"Not all of us would make that choice," Weston sneered, but she didn't advance. "Why should I pretend to be stupid, letting others take the credit?"

She didn't have a good answer. Maybe Elizabeth would also baulk at receiving similar advice.

"I know some physicians who might attend to your husband, gratis," she said, trying not to sound like she was pleading for her life.

Weston sighed. "He's beyond saving, luv."

"Well…"

But Weston was already walking away, carefully backing onto more stable boards. "Men and their pricks, eh? Seen one man and you've seen them all—isn't that always the case?"

Elizabeth eased onto her elbows.

Of all the suspects in Godfrey's house, Weston was the most astute and forthright one.

"Why did Mrs Grenville think Clarence Young was serving two masters?"

"Dinnae ken." Weston didn't turn around. "They never met each other."

"Elizabeth?"

Black stood on the other side of the gap. She could see two dark figures rushing towards him from the Tron Kirk, probably George and Thomas.

"I'm still uninjured." She would need to crawl in an undignified manner to reach relative safety, because her legs ached from Weston's blows, and getting up was too wobbly a proposition. She hoped Black wouldn't stare as she did.

"That woman…?"

"I don't think she'll be a problem." Elizabeth watched Weston turn right and duck into Adam Square. "Mrs Weston was just a bit frustrated."

Elizabeth lacked the strength to chase after Weston, even if she wanted to. She doubted the grocer wanted to lay eyes on her again. It was a shame she hadn't thought up a question that prompted a more helpful answer than the one she received.

Black nodded. "I'll meet you back at my house. George just informed me they cut the fuse ropes."

More to the point, there wasn't anyone left to light the spark. And in a few hours, the rain would wash in.

"George, Thomas and I have to act quickly," she called. "But we'll reconvene as soon as the mastermind behind this plot is dealt with."

35

It was slow going back to his house, especially since Black tried to conceal his twisted ankle and torn-up flank from onlookers. The wires on his arm had snagged on something when he fell, making a game attempt at cleaving his forearm in two.

Nicholson Street was shaking itself to life. Black side-stepped shopkeepers scrubbing their storefront paving and unfurling awnings. He nodded and grunted good morning to many familiar faces. A few individuals saluted him from their sedan chairs, and Black just kept focussing on getting one foot in front of the other and making it home.

He was navigating the front steps in a sideways shuffle when James Hutton bounded out of a sedan chair and rushed over.

"There'll be no trouble, after all," Black told him, before he got the words out.

"Ah, you stopped the plot?" Hutton beamed.

"The worst of it, yes. Unless you heard an explosion that I didn't on your way over here." Black continued inside.

He wanted to retreat to his bedchamber, but turned left into the parlour instead. Not that he resented his friend's appearance, quite the opposite, in fact. If he'd failed to stop Delancey's plan, Hutton was one of the people Black needed close by to get him through the aftermath.

Speaking of which, Black saw the other individual he'd summoned marching along the street, his walking stick brandished like a rifle and a stern expression on his face. Cullen would be assisting the Fulhames and George with the final pieces of their preparations.

However, by the time Smith entered the parlour, he was no longer alone.

"I found this young miss in a state of some agitation outside," he explained. "I believe it's you she seeks, Joe."

Black had already sprung to his feet, wincing as his ankle threatened to give out.

Susan Berry cowered next to Smith. While the moral philosopher stood rigid, Mrs Berry appeared aflutter amid a one-woman hurricane. She trembled so hard Black doubted she could get any words out.

"Perhaps I can get you a cup of tea, Mrs Berry?" Black said, inching closer. Elizabeth told him this woman called upon her at his house when he was on business, and that she was of a nervous disposition. He doubted she'd understated her temperament, which meant Berry had deteriorated since the last visit, where she'd angled them all towards a trap.

Hutton leaned on his elbows, studying the woman with open fascination from the sofa. Black's heart pounded in his chest. His entire body hummed with a sense of foreboding, but it had no outlet while Berry stood there mute.

"...My h-h-husband..." she faltered.

Black couldn't fault Elizabeth Fulhame for believing this woman. Her nervous hysteria appeared unfeigned, though he knew not to what end.

Then Berry removed her arm from under her shawl.

"Oh, Christ!"

Hutton almost pitched forward onto the rug in shock. Berry held out a bloodied knife. It shook so violently in her hands Black suspected the blood and gore would splatter across his walls.

"Please..." Berry continued to hold her knife out. Did she mean for Black to take it?

"Err, madam?" Smith cleared his throat. "Is it reasonable to deduce the blood on this instrument belongs to your husband?"

He phrased the question more diplomatically than Black would have managed, were he thinking that far ahead.

"You have to come. I...I...I left him in the kitchen." Berry's eyes shone like marbles; slowly tinting red as the tears brimmed over.

Black took another look at the blade. All five inches of steel were gore-streaked.

"Where did...I mean, where was your husband stabbed?" Black asked as gently as he could. He caught her wrist, as delicate as a bird wing, and eased the knife from her unresisting fist. Berry stared blankly. "In the chest?" Black clarified, before she repeated the obvious answer of 'in the kitchen.'

"...Chest and throat," Mrs Berry whispered, voice quivering. "Mostly."

Black took another look at her dark green and brown gown. The dark splotches he'd first dismissed as rain or sleet, or dirt...probably weren't any of those things.

Black made eye contact with Smith and Hutton. "...I don't think this situation requires undue haste," he said. Standing still caused throbbing in his knees. "Tragically."

Mrs Berry—he doubted anyone else was involved—had not only stabbed her husband repeatedly, but twisted the knife as she hacked. If Jeremiah Berry hadn't perished before hitting the floor, he would have drawn his last breath by the time his wife departed their dwelling.

"Shall Joseph and I accompany you home? Where do you live?" Hutton had recovered enough to rise and lay a reassuring arm on Mrs Berry's shoulder.

"Right..." Smith cleared his throat again. "This is a task for physicians."

"As it happens..." Black glanced back at the near-catatonic Susan Berry. "We may yet require the service of a moral philosopher."

"I didn't know where else to go," Berry whispered, snorting back tears and mucous. Hutton thrust a handkerchief into her hand. Knowing Hutton, it was probably covered in rock dust, but that wasn't important right now. "I have no one else. I have nothing."

Smith raised his eyes to the heavens. He wasn't the best at dealing with feminine tears; it was clear he was out of his element.

"I'm, erm, sure we can assist you as best we can, madam."

"She said she could help me." The handkerchief hung limp in Berry's hand, forgotten. "I tried to get him to change his mind. I pleaded with him...nothing worked. I don't understand what made him so angry at me."

Black's mind cast back to the night at the Godfrey's. He remembered this tiny woman trembling at the news of Kitty's murder. Black had wondered if she was going to cry, but the tears never came. It was a dull, empty shock in her eyes. Her husband stood with folded arms a few paces away, looking at the limits of his patience. Jeremiah snarled at his wife to compose herself, to not make a scene. Every word from Jeremiah's mouth fell on Susan like a lash.

The same thought Black had that night came back to him today.

What kind of husband scares his wife more than the prospect of a knife-wielding murderer?

"We'll assist you, Mrs Berry," Black said, exchanging a

more pointed glance with his friends. Smith harrumphed, but otherwise remained silent. Hutton shrugged a shoulder. His geologist friend wasn't the most perceptive, but he'd follow along with Black. "None of this is your fault. Now, let's see where you left your husband."

36

Her heart sank as they slipped in to the Assembly Rooms. It was naïve to hope the Rooms would be as quiet as they were last time, but the cold weather had driven Edinburgh society indoors, and the rooms were crowded. She couldn't see an empty table, and many more had been added.

"That's him." Delancey was seated in the far corner, at a small table set for one. His murderous expression—before he'd even caught sight of the Fulhames—suggested he was already aware his plans had been foiled.

Who could have told him? Perhaps he simply assumed reports of the explosion would have reached him by now.

The Fulhames and George stood out among the genteel class in the central hall, draped in furs. Delancey watched the party approach with narrowed eyes.

"You." He spoke flatly.

Well, that made things slightly easier. They didn't have to explain who they were before the threats started.

"Mr Delancey." Thomas spoke coldly. "Quite the excitement ye've caused in town."

All three showed signs of being in a fight. George had

scratches on his face; Elizabeth's gown was muddied, and her palms were scraped from where she'd gripped the ropes and board edges. Thomas reeked of gunpowder.

Delancey leaned back in his chair with a smug grin. "Come to threaten me, you rogues?" He raised his voice, causing several heads to turn.

"Not in the slightest!" Thomas laughed as if he'd heard a great witticism. Then, with more conversational tones, "We're not armed."

"Hmm." Delancey leaned forward. "Not much of a promise, given then rumours circulating about the abilities of your eminent teachers. But you wouldn't want to cause a *disturbance* in so public a venue. I imagine that wouldn't reflect well on the parties involved."

He had a point. Some individuals in the room may have been taught phlogiston-wielding by the professors themselves, but there was no telling how the others would react.

If this threat phased Thomas, it didn't reflect in his comportment. He leaned on the table. It rocked under his weight, causing Delancey's tea to splash into the saucer.

"If word of *yer* secrets gets out, Mr Delancey, ye'd be in a world of trouble. Plotting the deaths of blameless citizens to feed yer vanity?"

"Oh, please. The denizens of this fair city are hardly innocent lambs. Certainly not in the Cowgate. We'd be clearing out a brothel and opium den. I've seen that stretch of the Cowgate. Wife-beaters, adulterers and drunkards, the lot of them. I'm doing Edinburgh a favour by getting rid of them—anyone with sense could see that."

No wonder Kitty had been so taken with the plan with her evangelical disdain for vice.

George hissed quietly in disgust. Delancey fixed him with a sardonic expression, daring him to voice his thoughts. George declined.

Elizabeth had begged both men to avoid arguing with Delancey on the way over, pointing out they'd never change his mind. For now, both held to that agreement.

"Your friend Silas Lowell is dead," Elizabeth said.

Delancey laughed. "I wouldn't call him a friend."

"But he killed Clarence Young at your behest, did he not?"

Elizabeth wasn't sure if she'd crossed her own line in asking this question. But Delancey merely shrugged.

"Clarence was getting increasingly uncooperative. He knew what he was getting in to when he agreed to help us, and that there was no room for negotiation. Then he started up on that second bridge nonsense."

"Another bridge?" Thomas did a double-take. "Where'd they even put that?"

"He seemed to think building one near Candlemaker Row was a better idea. A second South Bridge, if you will. Connecting to the High Street in parallel." Delancey looked annoyed. "He wouldn't listen to reason. Eventually, he started making threats about exposing us when it was clear he wouldn't get his way. He became like an out-of-control animal."

While Young might have confessed to Kildare what was going on, Elizabeth suspected the main thing threatened was Delancey's ego. He was clearly the kind of immature man who took all challenges to his supremacy badly.

A second South Bridge risked challenging his architectural brilliance. If Young got his rival proposal in front of the Town Council quick enough, they might even decide against rebuilding the South Bridge.

Delancey spoke in a matter-of-fact tone, no trace of guilt or doubt in his words. "Clarence was merely tolerated by his natural family. No one likes a bastard hanging around, polluting the family name. They didn't mourn his death."

"You wanted the blame to fall on Dr Black and Cullen."

George's eyes narrowed. His skin paled. People who didn't know him might assume that was a sign of fear. "Young had outlived his usefulness to you. He told you and Lowell how easy it was to steal large quantities of gunpowder from the army."

She'd not believed Delancey and his small crew of conspirators could enact the destruction of a bridge that large, but Young must have told them how easy it was for his half-brother to misplace a shipment of English gunpowder. Then, in the course of his negotiations with Kildare, the older man let slip too much about lax port security and military communication issues. That's what George overheard him lamenting: giving Young the tools to do a better job of stealing explosives without anyone noticing.

Delancey seemed unperturbed by the accusation. "Dr Black and that woman," he pointed to Elizabeth. "They think they're better than everyone else. Always meddling. I know you sent Mr McIntyre to trick me."

If he realised Black—and by extension Elizabeth—had induced Archibald to test him on their behalf, it would explain why he tried to implicate them in Young's murder. It was also most likely Delancey's impetus for attacking her on Duddingston loch.

"You're angry that we nearly stopped your murder of Kitty Grenville." Elizabeth spoke as calmly as she could, checking she had not raised her voice.

Delancey snorted. "That wasn't my doing, miss."

"I'm surprised that's where you draw the line. Killing a woman you know is worse than killing entire nameless households?"

Thomas' outrage was waved away. Delancey looked amused at the outburst.

"I didn't shed any tears over that shrew's demise, and if someone else had grievances with her, I'm sure they're well-justified. We could execute her plan without her oversight, and the money had already changed hands."

"Sweetheart…"

Thomas reluctantly heeded Elizabeth's silent plea. She was just as outraged as him, but their time was limited, and they couldn't allow him to distract them. They needed to keep him talking for just a little longer.

"I wouldn't take this any further, sirs and madam." Scorn dripped from Delancey's voice. He flicked his gaze meaningfully to the left.

Three men loitered behind a pillar several yards away. While not staring at the confrontation, they weren't ignoring it either.

The leanness of their faces reminded Elizabeth of the attackers they'd confronted on Duddingston loch. They were unlikely to be the same men—they'd be spitting venom in the Fulhames' direction, were that so—but she suspected Delancey hired them from the same pool of men.

"How can he afford so many mercenaries?" George wondered. Her friend's gaze had turned cool, assessing the men with care.

"That's the pertinent question…" Elizabeth glanced at the balcony running around the room. *"I'm not sure he can."*

"Do you have any further business you wish to discuss?" Delancey asked. Sensing the group's distraction, he smacked the table to draw their attention back to him. It was a light smack, but the table wobbled again.

"There's four or five men watching us from the balcony," Elizabeth told George and Thomas, in case they'd not spotted what she had. *"They're watching Delancey's men, too."*

"Creditors?" Behind her, George discreetly craned his neck.

"The sharp end of debt collection," Thomas mused.

"We only want your assurance, Mr Delancey, that you will cease pursuing this blood-soaked vanity project." Inwardly,

Elizabeth was cursing. She needed to stall for time so George could assess the new threat, and for them all to think up a new plan. She hadn't anticipated loan sharks would already circle the architect.

The debt collectors were positioned so they could drop coins on Delancey's head from the balcony, but Delancey would have to swivel in his seat and tip backwards to spot them. His confident behaviour implied he wasn't yet aware of their presence.

"Are you gentlemen quite alright?"

George drew his attention back to Delancey with a guilty start. Elizabeth's first reaction was irritation that George had got caught staring at the debt collectors, before she saw Delancey's men follow his gaze. Immediately, their posture changed.

Any doubt the two groups of men were working in concert was banished. Now spotted, the men on the balcony pulled back.

A small stairwell connected the balcony to the main floor in the corner. Delancey had positioned himself a safe distance away from it, but he currently sat between his hired men and the whoever came down those stairs.

"We ought to get him out." Urgency filled Thomas' voice. *"Those creditors can't get him first."*

"His men all have flintlocks," George added.

"You're in trouble, Mr Delancey," Elizabeth said aloud. The architect couldn't miss the alarm in his men, but hadn't realised what the cause was.

"You have no right to tell me what to do!" Delancey's outrage was blinding him to the rising danger. "Architecture is my business, and the Town Council would be imbeciles if they threw away my proposals."

"Elizabeth and Thomas—grab him and run." George took a few steps back. *"I'll cover your escape."*

"It's not going to come to a fire-fight," Thomas insisted.

Delancey's men shoved towards them. Perhaps they thought them operating with the debt collectors, or else the two physicians and Elizabeth were an annoyance in their way.

"Yes, it is," George replied.

He then stepped towards the approaching men.

"No..." Elizabeth lamented, mostly to herself.

The man in front of George was reaching for his waistband. George elbowed him in the face, delivered a blow to his stomach, then tugged his flintlock loose. Without pause, he raised it over his head and discharged it towards the ceiling.

It felt like all eyes in the Assembly Room were on them already, but the gunshot dispersed that attention like shattering glass. Suddenly everyone was in motion, a frenzy of kinetic energy. Screams layered over the acrid smell of gun smoke.

The debt collectors burst from the stairwell, flintlocks and rifles drawn.

One of Delancey's men bellowed. George seized advantage of the confusion to duck away. Elizabeth glimpsed a second flintlock in his hand, this one unfired.

As much as she hated what was unfolding, she had to help.

She placed her foot on the edge of Delancey's table and kicked.

As expected, the spindly table toppled easily, sending fine china, silverware, and scalding tea flying through the air.

Thomas grabbed the stunned Delancey by the elbow and dragged him from his chair. The spoiled brat might not even have realised who was helping him, he just fled.

With the upturned table blocking them from easily chasing after Delancey, his hired men stood their ground and focussed on the debt collectors. More gunshots filled the air.

With Thomas and Delancey running ahead, and George behind her blocking the escapees from the pursuer's line of sight, there wasn't much Elizabeth needed to do beyond survive.

She bumped into another table, nearly tripping over an upturned chair. There weren't so many people in the Assembly Rooms that flight was difficult.

A haze of gun smoke now covered the Assembly Room, making the battling parties at the other end difficult to make out. Another crack of a flintlock sent one figure crashing to the ground. She couldn't tell which side had the upper hand.

She grabbed an empty teacup from the table and hurled it at a swarthy man in a tattered redcoat jacket as he aimed his pistol at George. The blow skimmed his head, but he jerked to the side, giving George the opportunity to fire first. The shot struck him in the arm.

George threw aside his used pistol and reached into his pocket. Elizabeth caught a flash of brass in his hands before charging another man, one of Delancey's debt collectors, and delivering a nasty blow to his gut.

George always preferred fists and firearms over his phlogiston abilities, though both seemed well-developed to Elizabeth. She supposed his military skills were ingrained earlier in life, and so came more naturally.

The number of standing figures at the far end of the room had now halved, and with most of their firearms discharged they were setting on each other with fists and blades. By the time Elizabeth stumbled past the final abandoned table, they seemed to have forgotten Delancey and the others entirely.

George and Elizabeth emerged onto the street, elbowing through the thick crowd of people. Far from fleeing, the net effect was of onlookers rushing to see for themselves what was happening inside.

"There!"

Thomas and Delancey were a few steps ahead of them. Her husband still gripped Delancey's arm, but as they watched, Delancey shook himself loose and struck Thomas across the face.

To Elizabeth, it was an inexpert blow, but Thomas staggered as if punched by a prizefighter. Satisfied with the damage caused, Delancey hurried away.

"Sweetheart, are you hurt?"

"Barely." Upon close inspection, Thomas' cheek was faintly red. "I thought it better to let him escape, to continue the plan."

"I suppose so..." Elizabeth assumed in all the chaos, their plan for Delancey had been completely abandoned. He was supposed to stay in the Assembly Rooms, after all. But the pieces hadn't been knocked off the chessboard completely.

Then a movement across the street caught her eye.

She tugged the pair behind a stationary carriage.

"Wait..."

Delancey, glancing over his shoulder and not looking where he was going, crashed into Reverend Patrick Fay.

Except no one would recognise him as such. Fay's long grey hair had been combed, for starters, and left hanging unpowered to his shoulders. He was clean shaven and dressed in a bright green frock coat. While the outfit stood at the cutting edge of fashion circa 1772, the garments were clean and well-maintained. Since Delancey didn't immediately lurch away covering his nose, Elizabeth concluded Fay must have come into contact with soap in the past few days, too. While not a picture of affluence, and lacking much in the way of youthful vitality, the overall image was of a genteel burgher, a picture of simplicity and modesty.

"Begging your pardon...but am I regarding Ralph Delancey, esquire?"

Delancey's posture instantly became guarded. But Fay's countenance was of such tranquility he must have decided this older man couldn't be another creditor.

It helped that Fay concealed his Dublin accent and spoke like a London-born Englishman.

"Who is making the enquiry?" Delancey's eyes narrowed like a cat.

"Right, the introduction would be the helpful part. Patrick Doyle at your service, though I was ordered to retain you by another..."

Delancey relaxed a fraction. Fay would never pass as noble origin, but in his current guise, he could easily be a trusted aide conducting business on behalf of his master.

"Service, you say?"

"Quite so. My master learned of your architectural genius while residing in London, and sought to secure said genius for his planned estate just outside of Dublin. He passed through Edinburgh just a few days ago but could not be detained given his return to Ireland, so asked me to stay behind and seek your out."

"He has travelled through to Glasgow?" Delancey asked warily, trying to sort out the travel itinerary he was presented with.

"Just so. You seem in a hurry, sir, and I don't wish to intrude upon the time of a busy man as yourself, but..."

"No, no—it's quite alright." Delancey glanced back at the Assembly Rooms. A mob remained at the door, with people trying to escape being hemmed in by people trying to break in, presumably men intent on quelling the disruption. He didn't notice the Fulhames and George watching. "Do you wish to tell me more about this proposal?"

It was hard to believe any man could fall for a ruse so conveniently laid. But Fay possessed a crusty charm that he was deploying to full effect here. He laid a hand on Delancey, the conceited youth who believed he was destined for greatness, if only people finally recognised it, who *also* desperately wanted to be rescued from a looming crisis in Edinburgh.

"If it wouldn't be an intrusion…"

"I can spare some of my next hour," he allowed, trying to sound nonchalant. Even from several yards away, Elizabeth could hear the eagerness in his voice.

"Splendid! This calls for a measure of claret…" Hand still clapped over Delancey's shoulder, Fay steered his victim down George Street.

"Do you think Fay's act can survive contact with alcohol?" Thomas whispered.

"Hmm…" Elizabeth had wondered the same question. "I think the Reverend Fay can conceal his true nature for several days at a time, perhaps a week or more with concentrated effort." It depended how much he wanted Delancey's money, and how many coins he figured he could wrangle from the cull.

"Is he not afraid of getting hanged upon his return to Ireland?" George asked, equally concerned.

"As I understand it, he's at risk of hanging even on British soil." Elizabeth nudged a stone with her heel. "He doesn't care."

"You possess quite a cruel streak, Mrs Fulhame," George noted, watching the figures vanish into the crowd. "It's impressive to behold."

"I consider my actions quite practical," Elizabeth retorted. "I've thrown a cobra to a viper—with any luck, they'll vanquish themselves and save the rest of us."

37

While her husband snored, Elizabeth assembled the morning's attire. She settled on her lace bonnet and dark shawl. It took some time pinning up her hair, ensuring every braid was tucked in neatly.

She glanced once or twice back at the bed, but knew by now it would take yells or the smell of cooking to wake Thomas at this hour.

Once dressed, she extracted a curt note from her purse, folded it, and placed it under the vase on their kitchen table. They often exchanged notes in this manner; alerting the other to changes in plans or whereabouts. Hopefully, he'd remember the arrangement before rushing out the door.

It was shaping up to be a nice day: chilly, but with cloudless skies and no wind.

Satisfied, she left the lodgings and went to speak with Kitty Grenville's murderer.

* * *

"You are leaving, Mr Godfrey?"

Hugh Godfrey sprung to his feet, temporarily wild-eyed.

"You are packing up furniture," Elizabeth continued, speaking in a conversational tone as she looked around the dining room. "At least that's how it appears."

"Wh-I mean, why..." Godfrey's eyes bulged.

"I asked your servant, Molly, to let me in." The woman believed Elizabeth when she said she was a friend of Godfrey, not questioning her unannounced appearance. She thought the woman had slipped back into the kitchen. But it didn't matter if Elizabeth had a witness to their conversation or not. She tugged the platina wire tighter around her fist.

Godfrey deflated. "Yes, as it happens. I'm heading back to Dundee to be closer to my family. At least until it gets warmer." He licked his lips. "If this is about..."

"My wrongful imprisonment isn't important." Elizabeth knew Godfrey recognised her, and that he remembered their previous encounter. "I know you killed your cousin, and I wanted you to inform you of this fact."

Godfrey tried to laugh, but it was a strangled noise that came out of his throat. He looked greatly diminished, and guilty.

"If it's pecuniary compensation you wish, madam..."

"I wouldn't say so," Elizabeth replied. She set herself at the table. For a moment, she wondered if she was sitting in Kitty's seat in the centre of the room. But that wasn't important either. "I too will leave Edinburgh soon, and I wanted to settle my affairs."

"You had no right to walk through my house." Another man might have sounded outraged, but Godfrey sounded more tired than anything else. "You brought your misfortune upon yourself."

"I don't believe I am the guilty party here, Mr Godfrey," Elizabeth snapped. "And I wouldn't wish to deprive you of your money, given you murdered Kitty to acquire it."

Another splutter from Godfrey.

She held up a hand. "Please don't accuse me of womanly speculation or fanciful thoughts. You never hid your need for money, after all."

Godfrey's knuckles whitened.

For some reason, his cowardly guilt infuriated Elizabeth all the more.

"A few days before her murder, your servant Molly said she saw Kitty come down the stairs and mutter something to Clarence: 'no one can serve two masters'. The fact she failed to recognise me as the woman she'd found kneeling over the dead body upstairs the night before should have clued me in that she wasn't the most perceptive."

Godfrey folded his arms.

"Because she wasn't talking to Young at all. This wasn't even an accusation of duplicity and double-dealing. She'd not even noticed he was standing there. Other people pointed out that Kitty had never met him, and for a while I was convinced *they* must be mistaken. But then I realised...Kitty was talking to herself following her conversation with *you* that day. It's a line from the Bible, is it not? 'No one can serve two masters...*you cannot serve God and money*.' I'd wager she came from an argument with you about the reward she was making from facilitating this deal, where she realised you wanted to her to split the money with you."

"Even you, who seem to be a smart woman, must spot how many layers of conjecture you're standing upon," Godfrey noted. "Knowing Molly as I do, I'd be surprised if she even remembered the actual words that came out of Kitty's mouth. Assuming anything did."

Elizabeth let the casually bandied insults wash over her. Godfrey wanted to distract and undermine her. "It was Kitty's intention to accept Delancey's money," she said. "But give it all to Susan Berry, to allow her to escape her husband."

There was a flicker of hesitation in Godfrey's eyes before he scoffed.

"Susan Berry came to your house while Dr Black was there, begging for the money Kitty promised her. You refused to help her, turning her away after a brief argument." She didn't point out that Black couldn't identify the woman's voice, or that Godfrey lied about who he was speaking with. Susan's actions after that meeting spelled out the tragic reality of what transpired. "You and the Berrys are both Tron Kirk parishioners, aren't you? That's where Kitty met Mrs Berry and learned of her plight."

Lord Kildare mentioned attending church with the Berrys. Then Morag told her she'd seen Kitty and Godfrey emerge from the Tron Kirk after last week's Sunday service. Church was one of the only times Kitty left her cousin's house in the weeks leading up to her death.

"I don't blame Jeremiah for reprimanding her," Godfrey retorted. "I've known the couple for years, and know far more about their marriage than you could ever. To be blunt, Susie has always been over-sensitive and anxious. I've watched her ruin more situations than I could count, and I lost all sympathy for her antics a long time ago. She never listens to what you tell her to do, then breaks down in hysterics when she inevitably missteps through her own wilful carelessness. If anyone deserved pecuniary compensation, it was Jeremiah for putting up with her."

The vehemence in his voice took Elizabeth aback. Godfrey's fists shook and his voice rose.

What was the point of arguing with him? She saw his protective self-deception: that he hadn't murdered Kitty because he coveted her fortune, but because he wanted to stop his cousin from wasting her windfall on Susan Berry.

He might not know Jeremiah Berry was already dead: stabbed by his wife at the apex of her desperation. Well, Black and his friends had discreetly intervened to conceal Susan's involvement in the crime—Elizabeth didn't press too hard on what they'd done. Rumour had it Jeremiah Berry was killed in a robbery.

Hopefully Black, Hutton and Smith had also provided funds to help Berry quietly begin a new life. It was a profoundly dejecting thought: Susan turned up on the doorstep of the people she'd tried to implicate in a murder, because she had no one else.

Godfrey's outburst was an admittance of guilt. Or at least, the closest he'd bring himself to acknowledging the truth of Elizabeth's accusations.

"If it helps," Elizabeth said in a quieter tone. "I don't think you set out to kill Kitty. I think you used the confusion caused by our appearance to sneak upstairs and attempt to argue with her for the last time. Maybe Mrs Berry hinted she would seek out your cousin if you didn't get to her first?"

"She came at me with the letter opener." Godfrey's mouth formed a snarl. "What was I supposed to do? Let her stab me? Take away the blade and go back to pretending she'd not just tried to kill me?" He threw up his hands. "You don't have to believe me."

She sighed. "The crux is not about who or what I believe. There's only so much I can bring myself to care."

Kitty Grenville, formerly Kitty Holm, formerly Kitty MacBride, was dead. She wasn't a nice person—in fact, she was a cruel and vicious one—but that didn't mean she deserved to be stabbed by her cousin over a tawdry money dispute.

Perhaps her charity towards Susan was selfless—recognition of a grace no one extended to her when she was a trapped wife. Or maybe Kitty had her own manipulative reasons for helping Susan Berry, knowing it came at the expense of helping her cousin.

What would have happened if Drs Black, Cullen and she got to Kitty before Hugh Godfrey did? Would their carefully planned meeting have accomplished anything? Would Kitty still be alive today?

She rose. Godfrey did not move. "I certainly hope you find peace, Mr Godfrey. But that's up to you."

38

"Ah, right on time, madam."

Pulling her cloak across her shoulders, Elizabeth made her way towards the two black-clad physicians standing on the other side of the court.

A sleety rain was pouring out of the grey sky. Black already had his green umbrella up, shielding himself and Cullen from the worst of it.

Cullen slid his pocket-watch back into his coat. The three began walking towards the High Street.

"You gentlemen were content to passively observe my confrontation with a murderer?" Elizabeth rubbed her hands together. They'd be frozen within minutes.

"We received your note," Cullen said, not breaking stride. "But thought it discourteous to barge in to Godfrey's if you were adequately handling the situation."

"Could you see into his parlour from across the street?"

"No, madam. We therefore agreed to wait a set length of time before trying to rescue you." Cullen glanced at his friend, staring resolutely at the puddles in their way. Black's umbrella was now mostly shielding Elizabeth. Water dripped from his tricorne hat. "I think this is the first time Joe here was urging swift action, and myself recommending we hold off. He wanted to charge in after ten minutes; I said twenty. We compromised on seventeen, but he was getting so crabbit after twelve I was going to agree we blast through the windows immediately. Fortunately, you walked through the door at the fourteen minute mark."

"Your confidence in my abilities is heartening." The High Street was quiet this morning, with water carriers and street caddies the only souls braving the biting weather. Elizabeth was already thinking about what soup she would prepare for dinner. Thomas would crave a hearty beef stew; she'd prefer something with more vegetables. Perhaps a potato-based soup?

"Did Mr Godfrey turn violent?" Black asked, glancing at her. They had to slow their pace slightly, for Cullen was more cautious navigating the slippery downhill cobbles.

Elizabeth shook her head. "He wasn't subtle enough to disguise his intentions. I meant it when I told him I didn't care what he'd done. I just wanted him to know that someone else knew. It's on his conscience, not mine."

"As you wish, madam." Cullen watched her, studying her expression for a moment. When he confirmed her sincerity, he cleared his throat. "I imagine Mr Godfrey will make himself scarce, and depart Edinburgh. One hopes his guilt will be punishment enough for him."

"Speaking of departures...?"

"To the best of my knowledge, Fay and his talking money bag struck west this morning." Cullen nodded in the general direction of Glasgow.

"You did a good job of making the reverend look presentable," Elizabeth said as she flexed her fingers for warmth. "We can compensate you the clothing..."

"Don't bother. That green suit hasn't fit me for the best

part of ten years. The wise Mrs Cullen is inclined to pay *you* for the favour of getting rid of it."

They were approaching the Guardhouse. Sensing her tense, Black shifted to Elizabeth's right side, blocking her from view of any guards looking out its windows.

"She deserved better," Elizabeth said. They skirted the Tron Kirk and last vestiges of construction equipment, slicked dark with rain. "Call it fanciful, but I want to believe that people can change. Or rather, perhaps, that when change comes, they don't immediately recoil from it."

"Not all change is desirable," Black noted, nodding to the South Bridge. "But I agree, Elizabeth."

She wished there was a way to capture Edinburgh at this moment in time, before the town she knew—the college, the warren of wynds around Cowgate—were lost forever. If she could put the town in front of her silver nitrate soaked papers and let the sunlight capture its silhouette. If she had the means to capture images for more than a fleeting second, before sunlight burned it away. It seemed a wish beyond her capabilities: all the will in the world wouldn't coax such an achievement from her. But who knows? Maybe someone else would look at her problem and minutes later see an obvious solution that would take her lifetimes to uncover.

EPILOGUE

"Dr Cullen?" She edged into the professor's study, breathing its familiar aroma of old books and wine.

The professor sat in front of his fire, empty glass in hand, lost in a reverie. He didn't look up.

"Professor?" Elizabeth tried again. She held her breath as she stepped closer to the scorching hearth. Cullen remained motionless, bathed in the flickering amber light. She supposed he might be asleep—making her hesitant about rousing him—but there was always that fear with a man as elderly as Cullen that one day you would approach them...shake their shoulder...and they wouldn't wake up.

Cullen still didn't move. His chin was almost propped on his chest, but she spotted the rise and fall of his diaphragm, and relaxed slightly.

"I hope I'm not disturbing you too late," she said, deciding to push on with it. "But a question about aether was troubling me, and I wished to seek your advice before we departed for London tomorrow."

George, Phoebe and the twins had departed by coach from

the Pleasance first thing that morning. She hoped they'd be well on their way to Oxford now.

Thomas claimed he'd never told Black about their distant relatives in London, who they could stay with until memories of them in Edinburgh cooled and it might be safe to return, but the chemistry professor took the news with a thoughtful nod, as if he'd expected the Fulhames to tell him that.

They'd not told Cullen in person, but telling Black was the same as telling them both.

She stood in front of the hearth, looking at the elder physician. In profile to the light, the lines of his face seemed etched particularly deep.

Thomas retired to bed early that evening, claiming he needed his rest before the long journey. She suspected he'd be snoring on her shoulder half an hour after their coach set off. She told him she was heading out to stretch her legs, and he waved her out the door from their bed.

"Ye can take care of yerself, no doubt?"

She could.

She stifled a yawn, the intense blaze from the hearth sapping her energy. Was she about to bother one of the smartest physicians in Britain with pure foolishness?

"Dr Cullen...I recall your hypothesis that aether was the key substance underpinning the cosmos: light, energy, heat and force are all facets of the same interconnected fabric of reality, flavours of aether as you call them. All things that Man is able to harness, once he knows how. It made me wonder..." Elizabeth's mouth was dry. She swallowed, rubbed her damp palms together, then blurted it out before she lost her nerve. "It made me wonder if...perhaps...you believe *time* is an aetherial substance, too?"

The fire crackled and popped. Cullen continued to gaze into the fire, not a muscle in his body moving. Until then she saw that, with glacial slowness, his mouth was rearranging into a smile.

"Ah, madam..." Cullen finally tilted his head towards her. His eyes glowed orange in the dim light. "I've been waiting for you to ask me that..."

Historical Note

Some of this actually happened.

As I've said before, Elizabeth Fulhame was a real person, who discovered the principles of catalysis and photography. *An Essay On Combustion with a View to a New Art of Dying and Painting, wherein the Phlogistic and Antiphlogistic Hypotheses are Proved Erroneous* was published in 1794. The early photographer William Herschel was familiar with her experiments, and credits her work with light-sensitive nitrate salts as underpinning his own. While a plethora of historical information exists concerning Joseph Black and his male contemporaries, we know next to nothing about Elizabeth's life. We know that she received some acknowledgement for her discoveries during her lifetime—she was made an honorary member of the Philadelphia Chemical Society in 1810—but the scant records we have suggest a tragic, ignominious end for such a pioneer.

My hope in writing these stories is two-fold: that more people learn about Fulhame, and that through fiction I can give her a happier story. The timing of certain real events featured in this story have been massaged to fit the narrative.

That said, the incident with Patrick Fay is not made up. *The Case of the Reverend Patrick Fay, now Under Sentence of Death in the New Prison, Written by Himself (1787)* spells out Fay's account of what transpired in Dublin. Fay's other criminal activities can be found in the public record.

We also know that the Fulhames spent some time in Dublin and London during the period of 1786-89, interspersed with stints in Edinburgh, thanks to references in Black's correspondence, Fay's account and Thomas' name appearing on the Edinburgh tax rolls. We don't know what prompted the Fulhames to relocate, or where exactly they lived when not in Edinburgh.

Robert Adam's expansive South Bridge sketches still exist, and I'll leave it to the reader to decide if it was a mistake for the Town Council to pass them up.

ACKNOWLEDGMENTS

First of all: I need to thank my readers. I'm grateful to everyone who has read, recommended and enjoyed my novels. Thank you for going on this tour of eighteenth century Edinburgh with me.

Extra thanks goes to my recurring ARC readers, my favourite characters in this story. You know who you are! Thank you for coming back time and time again, and continuing to support my work.

The Edinburgh Doctrines series as a whole rests on the backs of research collections, national archives, academic papers, PhD dissertations, and the incalculable number of people who make such things possible. Thank you in particular to everyone at the National Library of Scotland in Edinburgh, where I've spent a lot of pleasant weekends reading musty books and geeking out over rare 18th century manuscripts.

ABOUT THE AUTHOR

CL Jarvis holds a PhD in chemistry and worked as a science journalist, healthcare copywriter, and medical writer before sitting down to write her first novel. She's held together by cat hair and double espressos, and lives in Philadelphia, USA.

You can learn more about her at: www.clairejarvis.com.

facebook.com/cljarvisauthor

instagram.com/cljarvisauthor